Poplar River

This book is a work of fiction. Names and characters are products of the author's imagination or are used fictitiously. Any resemblance to persons, living or dead, is entirely coincidental. Some sites and places are portrayed and/or described as closely as possible within the telling of this fictional story for realism.

First Printing, October 2009

ISBN-13: 978-0-9822189-7-6
ISBN-10: 0-9822189-7-4

Cover design by ThomasMax (Lee Clevenger & R. Preston Ward)

Published by:

ThomasMax Publishing
P.O. Box 250054
Atlanta, GA 30325
404-794-6588
www.thomasmax.com

Poplar River

by Judith Barban

ThomasMax

TM

Your Publisher
For The 21st Century

Author's Note and Acknowledgments

Poplar River, located in the lower northeastern quadrant of Manitoba, originates in a watershed near the Ontario border. It flows westward through pristine wilderness and empties into Lake Winnipeg about 400 kilometers (240 miles) north of the city of Winnipeg. Much of the area is Ojibwe First Nation (Native American) reserve land which aboriginals still use for hunting, trapping, fishing, and plant gathering. With no roads, no logging industry, nor any development in the eastern section, this boreal forestland is an important habitat for a wide variety of flora and fauna, including several endangered species. The water is clean and clear, with a healthy aquatic population. The region is being considered for a United Nations National Heritage Site designation. The impact of Poplar River on the life of anyone who spends time in its solitude can be profound, even magical. It was for me.

The outpost on Poplar River is real. At the present writing it is operated by Wayne Letkeman's Thunderbird Lodge and Outposts. When I first came to Poplar River, it was one of the outposts of the Cobham River Lodge. The cabin in the story is an amalgamation of the picturesque log cabin on Poplar River and the floor plan of the spacious A-frame on beautiful Nance Lake, an outpost operated by my friend Kevin Walsten out of Kenora, Ontario. My husband and I have stayed in numerous outpost cabins throughout Canada. These two are my personal favorites.

Most of the wilderness adventures recounted in the story actually occurred. The ones we did not experience ourselves were told to us by outfitters, guides, or other fishermen.

In acknowledging those individuals who made the book possible, first and foremost, I must express my gratitude to Lee Clevenger of Thomas Max Publishers who deemed the manuscript worthy of publication when he selected it for the "You are Published" Award at the Southeastern Writers Workshop 2009. I want to thank Richard Hebel of Cobham River Lodge for introducing me to the stunning scenery and spectacular fishing at Poplar River. We pulled in a 41-inch trophy northern pike our very first day. Thanks also to Kevin Walsten who recommended Nance Lake and skillfully piloted us there and back in his floatplane. Trevor and Jodi Dick are the amiable hosts at Bolton Lake Lodge, the model for Baldwin Lake Lodge in the final chapters of

Poplar River. I am deeply indebted to Cedrick Lessard, our guide at Bolton for the past few years, whose vast knowledge of the wilderness and its creatures and his expertise in the art of fishing were major resources.

At home in South Carolina, I would like to thank members of the Tega Cay and Rock Hill Writers Clubs and my long-time friend and duo-piano partner, Ann Herlong. Their enthusiasm and encouragement kept me writing.

To Gene — my husband, my fishing buddy, my "life-friend" — a loving thank-you for taking me to Canada, teaching me to fish, and inspiring me to write *Poplar River*.

A Word from the Publisher

You hold in your hands the 2009 winner of the ThomasMax "You Are Published" award given annually to one deserving author at the Southeastern Writers Association Workshop.

Previous winners of the award are:

2006 – *The Resemblance* by Randall Arnold
2007 – *Written on a Rock* by Martha Ruth Phillips
2008 – *Principal Murder* by Kathleen McKenzie

If you are a writer, chances are that you would enjoy SWA's annual conference and workshop, held in June of each year. Our venue for more than three decades has been beautiful St. Simons Island in coastal Georgia, located near Brunswick, roughly halfway between Savannah and Jacksonville. Those who attend the conference and meet eligibility requirements may enter the ThomasMax contest (along with a host of other contests, most of which offer cash prizes). The ThomasMax winner receives a book contract and 25 free copies of the book; the author pays nothing unless ordering additional copies.

We invite you to check out our website at www.thomasmax.com and the SWA website at www.southeasternwriters.com.

To the many outfitters, lodge owners, and bush pilots whose services make it possible for us to experience the marvels and mysteries of the Canadian wilderness

Chapter 1: The Year of the Bald Eagle

Karen

Hundreds of untouched lakes, miles of pristine forests. I was marveling over the expansiveness of the Canadian wilderness when the little Cessna 180 floatplane banked steeply to begin the descent to Poplar River. On my left I could see nothing but land and water. To the right, nothing but sky. Something dark in the air caught my eye. As Bobby skillfully maneuvered the landing patterns, I leaned closer to my little rear window. Then I saw it again flying alongside the plane, moving as though it were escorting us toward the river, leading us into new and unknown territory to encounter an inescapable destiny.

For a moment I lost sight of it. Bobby leveled off and was making his approach for landing, when there it was again, this time closer to the window, the massive wings of the dark body in stark contrast to the white head feathers. A flash of exhilaration tinged with fear charged through my body: the feral eye of the bald eagle was looking directly at me.

Bobby landed smoothly on the water and taxied toward the cabin. As we skimmed along the surface, the wake from the pontoons sprayed up into the morning sunlight forming a thin silver veil on each side. I thought of the veil I had worn only two days ago when Steve and I faced each other in the sight of God and witnesses: "Do you, Karen, take Steve . . . ."

Not counting the usual last-minute glitches, it was the perfect wedding and the whole town regarded us as the ideal couple. The First Presbyterian Church of Spring Hill, South Carolina, was gloriously decorated with flowers and ribbons in my chosen colors, pale green and white. The three bridesmaids and the matron of honor, my sister Katherine, preceded me down the aisle dressed in identical willow green dresses and carrying bouquets of white roses with a spray of greenery. I wore the traditional long white gown. The next day, two commercial flights and a minivan brought Steve and me to Bobby's airbase on the Red River in a village north of Winnipeg, Canada, in the province of Manitoba — places I had never heard of before I met Steve. Once I settled into the back seat of the floatplane, I glanced at the ring on my left hand and tried to visualize it on the keyboard. A new life, a new world was opening. I closed my eyes and shuddered. Bobby started the engine.

The honeymoon had been a hot topic in Spring Hill. It gave Mama cause to wonder about my choice of husband when I announced that Steve was taking me for a week of fishing in the wilderness of northern Manitoba. Daddy loved the idea, but my friends were in shock.

"Couldn't he take you somewhere *romantic*? Paris, Acapulco, or at least Myrtle Beach?" my best friend Ellen asked.

"I think total isolation from all civilization on a lake in the wilderness *is* romantic!" I told her. "Besides, it is a gift from Steve's cousin Bobby, you know, the one he was raised with. He's a fishing and hunting outfitter with exclusive rights to several lakes in Canada. It will be an adventure!"

To tell the truth, I was worried — about leaving the comfort zone of Spring Hill, about my non-existent fishing skills, about a bear breaking into the cabin, and about making love in a sleeping bag on a bunk bed. Had I rushed into this marriage? Would I wake up one morning to find I had made a terrible mistake and ruined my life? I was in love, really in love for the first time. I always followed my heart, and I was following it now. Wasn't it always the right thing to do?

Rounding a peninsula, Bobby cut the engine and the cabin came into view. Made from whole logs with a screened porch across the front, it was a rustic hideaway surrounded on three sides by tall aspen poplars dressed in my wedding colors with their white bark and light green leaves of early June. As we drifted toward the shore, the cabin seemed to emerge from some familiar primordial dream that I dreamt as a child, or even before I was born.

The cottage sat on a rise in this predominantly flat country, so the front side afforded a sweeping view of the water and both shorelines. Here the river looked more like a lake. It was well over a mile wide and two miles long, according to Bobby, with channels connecting it to other wide sections farther upstream and down. He also explained that there were numerous bays where the fishing would be great for large northern pike.

"You could hook into some big ones this week. Ice is out, and they're hungry."

I had no idea what a pike was or how big a "big one" was, but I knew I wanted to impress Steve by catching one.

The plane's momentum and the pilot's skill took us directly to the dock. Bobby stepped down onto the pontoon, rope in hand, jumped out onto the dock, and quickly secured the front and tail of the little aircraft. Steve released his seat belt and began handing bags, gear, and groceries down to his cousin.

"Honeymoon Heaven!" he said with a smile more in his gray eyes than on his lips, as both he and Bobby helped me climb out.

Well, for better or for worse, to repeat a recent phrase, here I was in the middle of nowhere to spend a week, removed from life as I had always known it, with a man I had met only a few months ago.

The air was crisp and clean. There was a slight wind, just enough to make the poplars rustle, like ancient voices whispering. I took a deep breath, feeling engulfed in something grandiose and pure yet edged with danger. And I wanted — I needed — to be part of it.

The guys, loaded down with our stuff, were already halfway to the cabin. I grabbed the two sleeping bags and hurried after them. The screened door to the porch was unlocked, but Bobby had to set the rods and tackle box down and pull a set of keys out of the pocket of his jeans to open the door to the interior.

"Why a steel door? Don't you think a wooden door would look better on a log cabin?" Steve asked.

"Helps keep the bears out," was Bobby's no-nonsense answer. "Hey, aren't you supposed to carry your bride over the threshold, Stevie?"

"I think that's for when we get home . . . but, what the hell! Drop those bags, girl, I'm taking you inside."

Up and over I went, accidentally kicking Bobby's shoulder with my hiking boot as I was hoisted. Steve tripped over the weather stripping, and we both landed on our backsides. Bobby thoroughly enjoyed the whole scene then helped me to my feet.

"We're off to a great start," I commented, "all of us wounded, bruised and battered. Susan and Phil must have had fun while you two were growing up. It's a miracle they survived it."

After seeing these two guys together I imagined that as kids they were probably little Dennis-the-Menaces, double trouble. Steve's parents, Susan and Phil Marsten, had taken Bobby in after the automobile accident in which Phil's twin brother and his wife died, but which their only child, barely a year old, survived unharmed.

I regrouped, took the sleeping bags into one of the two little bedrooms, and wondered if I really would have a bruise on my rump for the honeymoon.

The next half hour was spent getting oriented and settling in. I was happy to see a hot water heater and a shower in the washroom. Bobby explained how the butane appliances worked, then showed us the fish-cleaning shed, the ice bin, and the outhouse. We followed him back down to the dock where we were both given a quick lesson in starting and handling the boat motor. From his flannel shirt pocket he produced two photocopied maps of the river and pointed to some areas for good fishing.

"The portage point is marked by a white X on a boulder just opposite the tip of the peninsula. If things get dull here, there are some pretty feisty northern over in Buck Lake. It's about a fifteen-minute hike. You'll find a boat and motor moored right there where you reach the lakeshore. The underbrush is pretty thick, though. Wear heavy boots."

"Uh . . . I don't think things will get dull here," Steve grinned, as he put his arm around my shoulders.

Bobby untied the ropes and stood with one foot on a pontoon, the other on the dock. With a shy grin to me, he gave the plane a shove and hopped up into the cockpit.

"I'll check on you at midweek. Enjoy the fishing, Karen." His last words were nearly drowned out by the loud popping and chugging of the starting engine, but I could still detect a hint of ironic humor, probably intended for his cousin's benefit.

We stayed on the dock until the plane taxied to one end of the lake, turned around, and took off, flying directly over the cabin. As the sound of the engine faded, I became aware of the complete silence. The air had become perfectly calm, the poplars were mute. I felt entranced, unable to move because of the stillness. I let my eyes skirt the shoreline to the point of the peninsula. There it was. Perched atop a tall dead tree, white and black against the light blue morning sky, watching.

Steve took my hand as we trekked back up to the cabin. We put groceries away, pushed the bunk beds together in one of the two bedrooms, spread out our sleeping bags, and zipped them together to form one double-bag bed.

Steve looked really good in jeans, a dark gray T-shirt, and light gray hooded windbreaker. He was handsome — tall, muscular, tan, sandy blond hair — not at all the stereotypical English professor. He watched me slip on a long-sleeved sweatshirt, put my hair up in a quick ponytail, and pull it through the back opening of a fishing cap.

"There. I'm ready to go fishing."

As I reached down to pick up the tackle box, Steve took my arm and swung me around.

"Not just yet."

Drawing me to him, he removed my fishing cap and kissed my forehead, then between my eyes, then my nose. When he reached my mouth, my arms instinctively went around his neck. The kiss was deep and lasted forever. We were totally in love, we were completely alone, and the afternoon was not spent fishing. Neither was the evening, nor the following morning. Although to the detriment of my southern Protestant conscience we had secretly had sex a few times since we met in mid January, this was different. I wasn't sure whether it was because we were now officially husband-and-wife, or whether it was the exhilaration of the primitive and wild setting, or maybe both, but I felt free, free to explore and experiment, free to say what I wanted, what I felt. This was not just sex, it was true love-making — on the bunk beds, on the screened porch, and where I enjoyed it the most, on the dock, with the constantly-changing Canadian sky above, the cool wind adding its caresses to our naked bodies.

By noon of the second day we came up for air. And we were hungry. I made salami sandwiches and opened a bag of potato chips. We consumed our food as voraciously as we had made love. After demolishing a package of Oreo cookies, we loaded our gear in the boat. Steve climbed in and started the motor. I untied the ropes, gave a push with one foot as I stepped in — sort of like I had seen Bobby do with the plane, and I was off to learn the art of fishing.

After a few disastrous practice casts, I was ready to do nothing but sit back and enjoy the scenery. It was enough just to see Steve in the afternoon sun, the ends of his sandy hair sticking straight out from under his cap. I watched him reel in, take the fishing line and pull a fish out of the water, then release the first catch of the day. A glint of gold on his left hand caught my eye and went straight to my heart.

"You have to work fast. Remove the hook and get 'em back in the water. Do you know what kind of fish that was?"

"A golden fish — an angel fish," I ventured. "It was beautiful!"

"That was a walleye. Really good-tasting fish, but that one was a little too small. Come on. Help me catch a few nice ones for dinner."

"Still hungry, umh?"

"I caught that one jigging with a preserved minnow. Here. Let me rig you up. Jigging is easier than casting."

As Steve arranged my lure, I noticed that we were at the far end of the lake at the mouth of a channel. A shadow crossed my face. I shielded my eyes against the sun and looked up. Settling on a branch of a white spruce a few yards from the boat was the bald eagle. He turned his head and seemed to be peering at us, waiting for something. I was soon to learn what he was waiting for.

Catching my first fish was a sheer rush of adrenalin.

"It's a nice one, KK. Good work!" Steve seemed as excited as I was as he reached down, took my line, and pulled the golden beauty into the boat. He had picked up on the nickname my friends had made out of the alliteration of my name — Karen Kingsley. "It's a keeper."

And there were other keepers that afternoon. We had evidently hit a walleye "hole," or hide-out, and they were in a feeding mode. Almost every time we lowered our lines into the water one of us got one. Steve taught me how to do it all. By the end of the afternoon I was baiting my own hook and removing my own fish. I was becoming a pro.

Back at the campsite Steve showed me how to fillet the walleye. That was the bad part.

"It's terrible that such beautiful creatures have to give up their lives so we can eat."

Steve agreed, but assured me that one taste of freshly-caught pan-fried walleye, and I would forget my scruples. He was right. He picked up the bucket containing the remains of the fish from the filleting shed and headed toward the boat.

"We need to get this across to the other side of the lake and dump it on that big rock," he said.

"Why can't we just throw it in the garbage?"

"Bobby said it would attract bears to the cabin." No more needed to be said. I was in the boat. On the far shore Steve got the boat as close to the rock as possible. I stepped off onto the rock and dumped the fish skins, guts and all. As we headed back to the cabin, I turned and saw the eagle swoop down for his evening meal.

For the next two days our activities alternated between fishing and fooling around. In bed, lying with Steve's arms draped around me, I listened to the night sounds. Very early one morning I thought I heard the sound of something falling to the ground. Then snorting sounds. I shivered, pulled the sleeping bag up around my ears, and nestled closer to Steve's warmth.

Bobby flew in at midweek to check on us. Fortunately we were engaged in legitimate fishing when we heard the plane approaching. Since the water was calm, Steve had given me a few more instructions, and I was driving the boat. My heart pounded as I turned up the juice on the motor and raced to beat the plane to the dock. My navigational skills were minimal, but we managed to tie up to one side. The plane drifted directly into position at the front of the dock, with Bobby standing on a float.

"You two are actually fishing?"

Steve gave him a mock fist blow to the forearm then helped him moor the plane.

"What do you think we came all the way from South Carolina for? And I'm catching almost as many as *Stevie,*" I said.

"I taught her everything," was Steve's smug remark.

"I bet you did."

"Come on, guys, why don't you two have a beer on the porch?" I suggested, eager to change the direction of the conversation.

There was a case of beer in the refrigerator. I snapped open two cans of LaBatt's Blue and took them out on the porch.

"Aren't you having one with us?" Bobby asked.

"I've never had a beer, Bobby." In my southern milieu, men drank beer, ladies drank iced tea and, at Thanksgiving and Christmas, a glass of sweet wine.

He handed me his can. "Taste it. I bet you'll like it."

I sipped.

"It's cold and a little bitter, but it *is* refreshing," I admitted.

"Then I'll get you one," Bobby said.

So I drank my beer with the guys. We told Bobby our fish tales — about finding the walleye hole and the feeding frenzy, about trolling to pick up a few northern pike, and about an 18-inch walleye Steve had caught and released off the tip of the peninsula. I told Bobby my casting skills were improving, but we were not having any luck finding really "big ones." Steve dug out one of the maps and Bobby pointed to a spot where there were always large pike.

"Use a number four Mepps spinner or a Johnson silver minnow. Throw a big red and white Dare Devle at 'em," Bobby advised. "Just remember to crimp down the barbs. You may loose a few fish, but you won't tear any up getting them off the hook. Besides, it's the law in Manitoba."

Crimp down the barbs. It's the law in Manitoba. I now understood why Steve spent about an hour the night before we flew out working with a pair of pliers and the lure. And so far we hadn't injured any fish — other than the ones we had eaten.

After Bobby left, in his usual casual outdoorsman manner, we headed for the spot he had indicated. The big ones were definitely there. We fished until almost dusk, both of us pulling in several monsters that put up quite a fight. Getting that first large northern into the landing net was one of the most unforgettable moments of my life. I was completely exhausted from the effort but at the same time invigorated by the conquest of this dark, slimy denizen of the deep with his mouthful of miniature shark teeth. I came to think of the two species — walleye and northerns — as golden angels and black devils, the good and the bad, the beautiful and the ugly. But I loved them both.

That night we were too tired to fry fish, so we feasted on peanut butter and jelly sandwiches. We were even too tired for fooling around in the bunk. Instead we sat holding hands on the porch, sipping on soda pop. We said nothing for a long time. Then Steve brought my hand to his mouth, kissed it, and, with his heart in his eyes, said the three magic words. I leaned forward and kissed him slowly and gently on the lips.

But the evening wasn't over yet.

"Steve, look over there. What is that light in the sky that keeps getting brighter? Do you see it?"

Steve walked to the screen door and stepped out into the night to have a look.

"Sweetheart, come here!"

I was by his side in an instant. There above us was the most incredible spectacle of nature I had ever seen. Lights in the sky were growing brighter then fading, only to reappear in different patterns. Soon the whole dome of heaven was glowing with swashes of light.

"My God! What's happening? Judgment Day?" I was mystified, frightened, but mesmerized.

"The Aurora Borealis — the Northern Lights," Steve said as he moved behind me and enclosed me in his arms. We stood like that for a long while, watching in silence, awed by the mystery of light.

The next morning began with what had become our daily routine. One of us, usually me, would get up, go through the main room of the cabin into the little kitchenette, make coffee, and bring two cups back to the bedroom. Most mornings the coffee got cold while we got hot and heavy. However, this morning was different. After last night's special moment of bonding, I think we both felt a calm, an assurance in our relationship, something that did not replace, but transcended natural physical urges.

It was mutually decided that we would get out on the lake early. As we headed downriver to the walleye hole, I noticed that our "escort" was following us. The eagle had begun flying behind us whenever and wherever we went in the boat. Sometimes he would go ahead of us, settle in a tree, and wait for us to catch up. I'd swear he was trying to show us where the fish were.

"Don't worry," I said to him as he settled on a limb, "we'll give you your dinner tonight, that is, if the walleye are biting."

"Let's motor on through the channel to the next lake," Steve proposed.

"Fine with me." I was eager to explore a little more, too.

There were rocks in the channel, so Steve had to be cautious and motor very slowly. As the channel widened it grew deeper. I threw out my line to troll and immediately pick up a pretty nice northern. This part of the river was not as large as the area where the cabin was, but there was a little island in the middle which was surrounded by weed beds. Steve cut the motor and we began to fish them. I looked around for the eagle, but he was nowhere to be found. Yet I had the feeling he was near. I saw movement in the tallest tree on the island. The eagle was side-stepping along the edge of a large clump of small branches, twigs and weeds about three quarters of the way up the tree. Protruding from the top of the clump was another white-feathered head.

"Look, Steve. There are two of them, and they have a nest." I grabbed a small pair of binoculars from the tackle box and focused on the magnificent bird.

"That must be the female sitting on her eggs." I handed Steve the binoculars.

"Quite a sight, isn't it? I wonder when they'll hatch?"

"Just think, when we come back next year we may get to see them!"

"You mean 'Miss Spring Hill' actually *wants* to go wilderness fishing again?"

"Only if the same hunk of burning love will be here." I couldn't believe I had the nerve to say that. Mama and Ellen were the only people I would dare talk about sex with and even then in a rather proper manner. I guess I was getting pretty comfortable with this man I had just "upped and married," as one of the ladies of the Spring Hill Woman's Club had put it. Here in primitive nature old inhibitions were beginning to seem foolish. I began to see all social artifices and mores from a different perspective. Here I moved in the sphere of pure, natural life of which I was a part, a child of the universe, fragile and mortal, yes, but not tragic. Alive and sentient, I rejoiced in harmony with the world around me as it followed its predetermined course.

We fished a little longer, and Steve caught a real lunker of a northern. It took both of us working hard to land him. He got loose in the boat and had us scrambling. We finally got him back in the water, a little dazed at first — the fish, that is — but okay. Then it seemed as though the fish suddenly stopped biting. We had drifted quite a ways from the island during the struggle with the big pike. There was a low rumbling in the distance and dark clouds were forming to the south.

"We'd better head in, Karen. Could be a storm."

I reeled in my line, closed the tackle box, and slipped on my windbreaker. By the time we reached the narrow part of the channel a few raindrops were falling. Just then the propeller got stuck on an underwater boulder and the motor conked. As the rain came faster, Steve and I worked frantically with paddles to free us. Finally, Steve left his place at the control stick and stepped toward me to put more weight up front, and the propeller popped free of the rock. It took a few pulls of the cord, but he got the motor going again.

By the time we reached familiar territory, the rain shower had turned into a heavy squall. I could no longer see either shoreline. I couldn't even see Steve five feet from me in the boat. The temperature had dropped significantly. I was getting soaked through to my skin. Then I noticed the bottom of the boat rapidly filling with rainwater. I looked around in a panic to find something to bail with and saw the capped top half of a plastic gallon milk carton bobbing in the boat water. I realized in a split second its purpose. I grabbed the handle and began bailing furiously. I heard Steve yell something about "the shoreline," and noticed that he was turning the boat in another direction. Within a few seconds I could discern rocks and poplars. As the squall continued, I bailed and Steve followed the shoreline until finally we reached the dock. It wasn't easy, but we managed to secure the boat, get the rods, reels, and tackle, and dash to the cabin.

Once inside, I found myself trembling uncontrollably from the chill, the panic, and the exertion. I stripped off my soaked jeans and t-shirt and changed into dry things while Steve got a fire going in the little wood stove. Heavy rain continued to pound the roof of the cabin, and thunder echoed all around the lake, but we were safe. It took my body a while to accept that fact. We had been out on the lake since fairly early in the morning. By my watch it was then a little after three p.m. Now warm and dry, we gobbled down a very late lunch of ham and cheese sandwiches and sat sipping on hot chocolate, staring into the fire.

"I thought our time together on earth had come and gone," Steve said, breaking the long silence.

"So did I. But you saved our lives."

"Maybe a much higher power helped us out," Steve confessed.

It was the first time I had ever heard Steve allude to God.

"So you believe in God?" I ventured.

"Sometimes you just have to."

In my heart I agreed. Mama had asked me whether or not Steve was a Christian when I dropped the bombshell of our plans to marry. I really didn't know. How could I, a dyed-in-the-wool southern protestant girl, now the revered organist of the First Presbyterian Church of Spring Hill, rush into marriage with a man whose religious beliefs were not even considered before accepting his proposal?

"It just doesn't seem to make any difference, Mama. He's a good man, and I am totally in love with him. I just feel it's right."

"Well, honey, if you're happy, then it's okay with me. But I do wish you would wait. Just to be sure. You don't really know him yet. You could be making an awful mistake." Mama was a worrier, especially where her two daughters were concerned. But she was usually right.

Daddy always looked on the practical side of things:

"It's not exactly like she's marrying a drifter. The fellow's got a Ph.D. in English literature from the University of Iowa and a good job at our own Heyward College. She's met his folks and says they're fine people. You know they took in a boy that wasn't their own and raised him. The way I see it, Karen has always made good decisions — like going over to Spartanburg to get her degree in music from Converse College, and, contrary to what a few of our friends think, I believe she made the right choice when she decided to leave Julliard and finish her Master's degree here at Heyward."

It *was* the right decision to leave Julliard. My early training with Spring Hill's most qualified piano teacher, Mrs. Nona-Jean Williams, had given me a solid foundation. She was demanding and thorough, taught me theory and technique, and, above all, instilled in me a profound love for music. The four years at Converse had been a true joy. I was the pride of the music department. My piano professor, Dr. Matthew Cory, was not only an excellent teacher but also an aggressive promoter who networked to arrange numerous opportunities for me to perform — solo recitals in the private homes of donors to the music program and a concerto with the school orchestra. At first a scholarship to Julliard seemed like a dream come true. So did the first month or two in New York where I took in as much culture as possible on a student budget and without cutting into the many long hours of practice necessary.

I have never fully understood all the psychological factors that led to my decision to leave. Two things, mainly, I think. First of all, I got really homesick for Mama and Daddy and Spring Hill where I was a big fish in a little pond. In New York I was only one of many promising young talents, most of whom seemed to me to be a lot more promising than I was. Everybody practiced *all* the time. Although I was studying with a great teacher, the international Russian artist Ilana Irenakoff, she was away concertizing much of the time, so I often had to answer my own questions about technique and interpretation. She seemed pleased enough with my work, though, and even encouraged me to prepare for a series of piano competitions, assuring me that I had a good chance to win. I guess I just didn't like having *any* competition. At Julliard even my friends were my competitors. So when I heard that Heyward College had hired a new professor of piano, Dr. Jacob Lavinsky, a pianist who held a Doctorate of Musical Arts from Cincinnati Conservatory, who *had* won a number of important competitions, and who was enjoying a respectable career in performance, I knew he was my ticket back home.

I sent him a tape of my playing with a note explaining that I wished to transfer my Julliard credits to Heyward and asking for his help in getting accepted into the masters program. Within two weeks he had arranged everything. Before I knew it, I was sitting in LaGuardia waiting for my flight back to Columbia, South Carolina. I felt as if an enormous weight had been lifted from my heart.

"There's quite an impressive sunset out there." Steve's hand on my shoulder startled me out of my reverie. I followed him out onto the screened porch, and sure enough, there was my first real Canadian sunset in all its splendorous hues of fuchsia, orange, green, blue, and purple strewn out across the sky in deepening bands of color, like an immensely magnified drawing by a school child with a pack of colored crayons.

"Storms usually bring with them an aftermath of great beauty. That's the heart of Romanticism," Steve said, reverting to his role as professor of English literature. He often quoted lines from Wordsworth and the other Lake District poets, but rarely did he "teach" when we were together. He specialized in the Romantic Period, but his knowledge of literature extended far beyond that periphery into American, French, and Italian works of various periods. He was a voracious reader, and since I had become involved with him, I had discovered the joy of reading good novels, short stories, and especially romantic poetry. Great literature and wilderness fishing, seemingly two opposite ends of the spectrum, but Steve had opened them both to me, and I loved them equally, just like the angel and devil fish.

I slipped my arm under his, and we stood there for a few moments in what could well have been a scene from a romantic novel. Until Steve's hands began to roam over the now familiar territory of my neck, shoulders and breasts. I swung myself around to respond to his caresses. We somehow managed to make it back inside to the bunk beds without letting the heat of the moment subside. Our lovemaking was intense, deep, as though we had only that one night left in our lives. Here at Poplar River I was as natural as the wilderness itself. Here I let go of all apprehension and self-consciousness. Here time was not divided into minutes and hours, but cycles of light, cycles of life — rich, pulsating life.

Night was transforming itself into morning when I awoke, my head in the crook of Steve's shoulder. I knew it must have been around four a.m., so I settled back down. Then I suddenly realized that this would be our last day at the outpost. It was Friday, and Bobby would be coming in very early Saturday morning to fly us back to his base near Winnipeg where the van would take us to the Winnipeg airport to catch the commercial flights home. I eased myself from the bunk, slipped into my jeans and a flannel shirt, went into the kitchen and got the coffee started. I stood at the double kitchen window that looked out over the front steps to the lake. A mist was rising from the water, obstructing the view across the lake. Mother Nature was completely silent. By the time I had taken a trip to the outhouse, the coffee was ready, and I carried two cups into the bedroom where Steve was still asleep.

For a moment I studied this man, the man I had just pledged to spend my life with. He was handsome, yes, intelligent, and passionate. And my senses reeled at his touch. But what should I expect when we return to "normal" life? Would he change? Would I be different, too? I tried to envision our future, but only shadows filled my mind. Two of my closest friends from Spring Hill High had already married and divorced. I shook the apprehension from my head and bent to wake him with a kiss.

We went out on the lake fairly early. The mist had cleared, leaving a crystalline sky and the promise of a perfect day. The fishing was slow at first. We tried jigging and casting, but the fish seemed to elude our efforts.

"I think all the golden angelfish must be in heaven today," I mused.

"And all the slimy devil fish in hell," Steve concluded.

We fell silent. I continued to jig while Steve cast. A haunting theme from the Schubert B-flat piano sonata had just slipped into my mind when I felt a quick pull on my line. Setting the hook immediately I switched back to reality and began trying to pull in a fish. I could tell by the way it moved in the water that I had a walleye. It was not a very big one, but its golden skin glistened in the clear morning sun.

"All right, KK! First fish of the day."

I freed it easily from the barbless hook and held it out for Steve to admire.

"A thing of beauty is a joy forever," I smiled, glad to have found an occasion to use the one quote from Keats' poetry that I remembered.

"Its loveliness increases; it will never pass into nothingness, but still will keep a bower quiet for us, and a sleep full of sweet dreams," Steve continued the quote as he took the golden angel from my hands, leaned down and slowly released it into the water. As the fish swam away Steve looked up at me, his gray eyes more radiant than the day. This moment would take on more significance than I could ever have imagined.

I pushed the music and poetry from my mind and began to concentrate on my fishing. Now I understood what Daddy meant when I'd asked him what he thought about while he was fishing, and he answered, "Fishing. Fishing clears the head and the heart." Well, my head was clear, but my heart was full.

"Where's your friend?" Steve asked as we baited our hooks.

"What friend?"

"Your traveling companion who always seems to keep an eye on you. You know, Mr. Eagle."

So Steve had also noticed. I hadn't thought about the bald eagle today. I scanned the branches of the nearest trees. Then, as if on cue, the huge bird appeared out of nowhere, landing, with wings high, atop a jack pine. The timing of it was uncanny. I felt as though powers were conspiring, not exactly against me, but over me, or on my behalf.

"I think the two of you are in cahoots," I said, almost truthfully.

"We definitely are," Steve answered, as much with his eyes as with his voice.

The simplest words are often pondered later. In the coming months I would give much thought to this innocent conversation.

At lunchtime we finished up the peanut butter and jelly, then headed out again for one last fishing fling.

"You wanna try that walleye hole one last time?" Steve asked as I shoved off from the dock and jumped into the boat.

"Good idea." And it was. They were feeding again. We both picked up fish simultaneously every time we drifted across the area.

"Just like playing a duet," I laughed after about our third pass over the hole. "How many do we have on the stringer?"

"Enough for dinner."

"Good. Then we throw everything back from now on?"

Steve shook his head affirmatively, and we went on fishing for another twenty minutes or so until the walleyes shut down.

We cleaned the fish we'd kept, leaving the remains for the gulls and "my friend," who was perched high above the feeding rock, waiting.

After dinner we tidied up the cabin then went out onto the porch to watch our last Canadian sunset. The striations of pink, purple, blue, and gold reflected in the unusually calm lake turned sky and water into a double rainbow of color, a harmonious balance like that expressed with equal majesty in a Bach fugue: the divine and the human, heaven and earth, sacred and profane reconciled and, for a few moments, united.

The philosophical mood continued through the evening. Steve must have sensed it, for we scarcely spoke a word as we stood once again beneath the Northern Lights then slipped into our two-made-into-one sleeping bag. For some time we lay in silence while the curtain of night fell around us, both of us knowing that in the drama of our life together a new and very different act would begin with the dawn.

* * *

"Your suspicions are confirmed, Mrs. Marsten. You are indeed pregnant," Dr. Johnson announced as he came back into the examination room. “I would say you can expect to give birth around the first week of March. Congratulations to you and Steve. I know your parents will be thrilled at the prospect of a grandbaby, since your sister Katherine and Ted seem determined not to have any for a while.”

So I had conceived this child in Canada. It had to be on a night we saw the Northern Lights, when the whole universe seemed to be celebrating our union. That thought doubled the excitement of Dr. Johnson’s confirmation and helped to abate any latent fear.

“I will refer you to Dr. Phillips. He’s one of the best obstetricians in town. I’m going to give you a prescription to take for nausea in case you need it. In fact, I’ll go ahead and call it in to the pharmacist down at American Drugs so you can pick it up on the way home.”

Dr. Johnson took my hand and patted it in a fatherly fashion. A close friend of Mama’s and Daddy’s, a kind and caring man, he had been my doctor since childhood. I was on cloud nine when I left his office.

In the car I began to plan exactly how I would tell Steve . . . and Mama and Daddy. I imagined each one’s reaction to the news. As I turned into the drugstore parking lot, I brought the car to a sudden stop and drew a quick breath. In all my going in and out of Spring Hill’s oldest drugstore I had never noticed it before. But now I saw it quite clearly. There above the entrance, beside the red letters that spelled out “American Drugs,” was a very large black and white image of a Bald Eagle.

Chapter 2: The Year of the Bald Eagle

Cherra

"I will take care of you little whiteheads. I'll see that you learn to soar above the waters, to spot and catch swimmers, paddlers, and ground runners for food. I'll teach you how to find your life-friend and how to dance with your friend the coupling rite so that you, in turn, will have little ones to instruct."

It was my habit to talk to the shells beneath my belly, assuring them early on that Trosk and I would keep them safe and provide for them until their time for flight came. Trosk was perched a short distance above me, high atop the nesting tree, ever alert, keeping an eye on water and land creatures. Suddenly he lifted his wings, leapt out from his perch, and glided down toward the nest.

"The roaring bird is coming, Cherra!" he called to me as he passed. I, too, could hear the churning sound of the huge bird growing louder as it approached the water.

No doubt it will bring more uprights to glide across the water in their noisy water-skimmers. With long sticks with strings they'll pull swimmers out of the water then throw some of them back. In a strange ritual they will mutilate a few of them and leave the choicest parts on a rock at the water's edge.

Anticipating the tasty inward parts of the golden ones made me hungry.

I watched the roaring bird crawl slowly along the water surface until it reached its perch in front of the hilltop nest of the upright ones. Trosk followed the loud bird to its flatlog landing and settled in a lookout tree opposite the uprights' nest.

Good. He's watching. He'll report everything to me.

Since long ago, when Trosk and I first danced together, I had felt no fear. He was a trustworthy life-friend and a great provider. In the nesting season he would always see that I and the little ones were well fed, even when he himself was hungry. My first life-friend had disappeared when great flames spread throughout the forest destroying almost all the greenery and many of the forest creatures. The heat caused our nesting tree to fall, but one of the little ones, Lera, survived. I alone provided her food and protection. We almost starved.

The seasons that followed were lonely ones. One day Trosk landed on the branch where I was perching near the warm river of the south during the cold season.

"Fly with me to my birthplace in the north for the warm season. We'll dance the rite together and chose a spot high in a fine whitebark for our nesting place. You are a strong female whitehead, and you need a life-friend. I want to be with you." So I came north with him. And we danced. We built the nest that has held our young ones every warm season since then.

I shifted my weight on the shells and glanced with my long-vision toward the uprights' nest. One of the uprights had remained on the landing perch while the other two carried bundles toward the nest. The one that stayed behind seemed different from the other two. Trosk would explain that to me when he returned. This one seemed to be looking for something in the poplars. Trosk? Was the upright looking for Trosk? I could see that Trosk had focused sharply on the upright, who suddenly turned, picked up two bundles in its soft talons, and went up to the nest. What happened next even Trosk could not explain. When the lone upright reached the entrance to the nest, one of the two others lifted it into the air and threw it down into the nest then flung itself in through the opening. *The uprights have inexplicable rituals*, I mused.

Trosk landed on the nest behind me.

"I flew beside the roaring bird as it circled toward the water," he reported. "Inside I could see the upright ones: two males and one female. The female is smaller and more fragile. She saw me in the air and again on the check-perch across from the nest. She seems harmless, even innocent. I'll keep watch on her to make sure the other uprights don't harm her. It seems as though they're trying to. One of them threw her down. For our sake I hope these uprights will leave parts of swimmers on the water-edge rock."

So it was the female who stayed behind the others on the landing perch and who was thrown into the nest. Trosk was right. She seemed more fragile, like the shells beneath me. How like Trosk to become her protector, as he did for me, and as he has done for all our nestlings. Once he had even swooped down to warn a great antlered one and save him from the uprights who arrived with their fire-sticks shortly before the cold season.

Just then I felt movement under me. *Pecking. Yes, definitely pecking.* One of the little ones was about to come out of the shell.

I *must be careful to cover it completely yet give it room to emerge.*

I shifted my weight again. There would be a beak to feed by morning, and probably another one after two or three more light-dark cycles.

"Trosk! A nestling is coming out of its shell. I'm sure of it."

Trosk moved closer to the birthing hollow of the nest, peered in, and inclined his head to listen.

"During the next light cycle we are going to need food for this little one," I reminded him.

"Yes, I know. As soon as skybright comes I'll seize a swimmer or a water-paddler and coax the nestling to eat strips of it. You have no reason to be concerned."

"You're right, Trosk. I never have to worry." I felt the pecking grow more forceful.

With Trosk so near there was no need for me to be watchful. I could savor the pleasure of the chick coming forth. I closed my eyes to feel the cracking going on beneath me and drifted into sleep.

I was floating on the water, struggling to paddle with my wings toward the nesting tree. I felt the heat from the advancing flames and watched helplessly as the tree began to bend heavily. I wanted to fly to the rescue of my two little ones, but my wings were heavy with water. "Where is Karak? What has happened to my life-friend?" I tried in vain to move forward in the water. "I cannot let them perish! I cannot . . ."

"Wake up, Cherra. I've brought food for the new beak. It's a female. I'll watch over the nestling until she eats. The other shell is still whole. You've been spread over them for so long. Now go ride the winds before more pecking begins."

Trosk began depositing strips of a black swimmer into the nest. I was glad to have a chance to leave the birthing hollow for a while. Moving to the edge of the nest and extending my wings their full length, I caught a current of warm air that lifted me up and out over the waters. How good it felt to me! I soared upward, exulting in the spread of my wings in the warm air and the joy of being free.

While Trosk is with the little one, I'll fly over the uprights' nest to see if they come out to get into the water-skimmer.

Past the channel into the next wide water, over the peninsula with the check perch, I soared, circled the uprights' nest, and then found a good viewpoint on a tall stump of a whitebark that had been gnawed in half by a flattail. I fluffed my feathers and watched for any movement of the uprights, turning my head first one way then the other. The upright ones remained quietly hidden in their nest.

I was hungry. Using my long-vision I spotted a tiny squeaker darting out from beneath the uprights' nest. Within an instant I had descended, talons ready to grasp. But there were too many berry bushes for the squeaker to scramble to. I couldn't reach my prey fast enough. Disappointed but determined, I returned to the whitebark stump.

Trosk says I often descend too soon. This time I'll wait.

Meanwhile, I searched the water for a swimmer floating belly-up. I loved to glide on the winds, dive, and pick a juicy swimmer from the water. But I saw none.

I have to save my strength for the nestlings, I reminded myself. Besides, my curiosity was piqued: I had never before eaten a squeaker.

I sat motionless now, my vision focused on the underside of the uprights' nest. Before very long, the squeaker reappeared. This time I allowed it to venture farther from protective cover. My aim was precise, my flight path secure. I took the squeaker in my grasp with ease. Flying to Trosk's check perch, I tore into the meat, what little there was. So great was my hunger that I didn't even think of the little one. However, on my way back to our nest I saw I small black swimmer jumping to the surface to snap up tiny water-crawlers. A powerful instinct propelled me toward the water. Now, my young whitehead, you'll have food offerings from both your life-givers.

During the next light-dark cycle I scarcely left the nest. The second shell had pecked open earlier than expected. Trosk faithfully supplied all three of us with strips of food. He was an agile hunter. His descents were fruitful more often than not. And he always imparted his skills to our young ones.

From the nesting tree I could see the uprights when they finally emerged from their nest. Two of them — a male and the female — had remained behind, while the other male had gone with the roaring bird. I watched the two of them come down to the flatlog landing-perch and begin to strip off layers of body coverings. The female spread out something flat and lay on it. The male approached her and touched her with his soft talons.

Trosk suddenly landed on the edge of the nest.

"He's about to harm her! I'm going to descend and warn him away from her."

"No, Trosk," I said. "He's not going to harm her. Can't you see? It's the uprights' coupling ritual."

Trosk was silent for a moment while he studied the coupling dance of the uprights. He turned his great white head toward me.

"You're right, Cherra. You're very wise."

"And you're very brave, Trosk."

* * *

At last the uprights began moving about in their water-skimmer. We were both surprised to find them out in the early light with their sticks and strings, pulling swimmers out of the water. For the next few cycles we heard the water-skimmer starting up shortly after first light. Although the sound of it was not pleasant, it did signal to us that there would be abundant swimmer parts on the water-edge rock when the great light moved to the west. And there were.

Trosk and I took turns stocking the nest with morsels of golden swimmers for the two little ones. So far the older female nestling had made no attempt to destroy the younger male, although she did eat most of the food we provided. I knew she would like to remain the only object of our attention, but I wanted to see them both grow into mature whiteheads. I would do my best.

"What shall we name the new whiteheads?" Trosk asked, offering me a strip of swimmer.

I took the meat in my beak, then dropped it in front of me. It was my female prerogative to name the first-hatched.

"We'll call her 'Merron of the Winds.' And what shall we call the younger one?" I asked my life-friend.

Trosk shifted his eyes from long-vision which was focused on the water, searching for injured swimmers floating on the surface, no doubt. Looking down at the two fluffy nestlings, he spoke solemnly.

"He shall be called 'Vonce, Guardian of the Forest."

"Yes, like you," I responded softly, just before settling over the young ones to shelter them, for the time of dark sky was approaching.

* * *

Very early during the next skybright Trosk used the winds to rise, circle, glide, descend, and grasp swimmers, some of which he ate, most he brought to the nest for me and the nestlings.

"I've put food in the nest. You and the chicks may eat these," he said as he paused on the edge of the nest and cocked his head toward a large pile of swimmer strips. "There are still a few parts left on the water-edge rock. After checking on the female upright, I'll feed myself from them. The water-skimmer is at the landing perch, and the two uprights are in the nest." I loved the way Trosk liked to feel in control of all things.

After he left, I coaxed the nestlings to eat, and then I tidied up the nest, pulling fresh greenery supplied by Trosk over the old. The little ones pecked at each other, tried moving about in the nest a bit, then settled down for a nap. Setting my long vision on the uprights' nest, I spied Trosk high in a dark tree and saw that his eyes were locked on something. I followed the direction of his gaze. There was movement in the bushes. I sharpened my focus. A long-toothed-long-clawed prowler was headed toward the uprights' nest. His long black fur was unmistakable. As I watched him lumber through upright territory, I was startled by an object plummeting from the sky to the clearing in front of the uprights' nest.

What could fall like that? Then I noticed a dark wing protruding upward from the motionless black and white object.

"It's Trosk! What in the world has happened to him?" I cried aloud. Within an instant of the fall, the longclaw loped toward him.

"Oh, Great Spirit, help him. Please spare him from the longclaw."

Longclaw lowered his head to inspect the inanimate body. He raked his claws over it. Trosk did not move. Then suddenly he fluttered and hopped away from Longclaw, extended his wings, and flapped a short distance into the air. But he could not rise high enough to catch the wind.

"Higher, Trosk!" I screamed.

Just when I thought he was about to soar upwards, he plummeted again. Longclaw didn't delay reaching him. Again Trosk escaped the predator, only to fall a third time. By the fourth fall, even through my terror I realized that Trosk was drawing Longclaw farther and farther from the uprights' nest. He lured him across the small bay toward the peninsula. But was he really injured? I could do nothing but trust Trosk's strength and courage. Longclaw swam across, snorting with anger and determination. With his pursuer close behind, Trosk fell onto the water-edge rock, sending a group of hungry gulls into furious screeching flight.

How clever of Trosk! I now fully understood my life-friend's ploy. *Longclaw will certainly prefer the inward parts of swimmers remaining on the rock and abandon the chase of the 'injured' great whitehead.*

And he did. Trosk wasted no time flapping off the rock, rose in the wind and flew back to me and the nestlings. I stood to greet him.

"Cherra," he said faintly, and settled beside me.

"Are you injured, Trosk?"

"Not too badly, but I am weary."

"There is still food in the nest. You must be hungry. Do you want to eat?"

"No, Cherra. I want to sleep."

"Of course."

His great eyes closed. I rubbed his beak with mine then flew up to the look-out perch, leaving my brave Trosk to recuperate from his heroic mission.

While he slept, I assumed watch over our territory. From the high perch I could both see and hear the roaring bird's return. The male and female were in their water-skimmer, but made it back to the landing perch just before the male in the roaring bird stepped out. Then all three of them went inside the nest.

Why does the male not run off the intruder? I wondered, remembering the many times Trosk had to defend our territory, calling out warnings, giving chase, and once even diving to lock talons in midair with an aggressive male interloper.

Perhaps they'll go elsewhere, build another nest, and establish a new territory.

I didn't understand all the ways of the uprights, but I did know there was no need to fear those who came with the long strings to pull swimmers from the water. It was the ones who came at the end of the warm season with loud fire sticks that frightened me.

* * *

The great light was low in the east when the uprights next went out in their water-skimmer. Still worn from his adventure with the longclaw, Trosk had decided to remain on the nest while I went in search of food. I soared over the peninsula toward the uprights' nest and followed them as they floated through the channel from their wide-water toward ours. A well-leaved branch of a whitebark offered protective covering from which I could better observe their actions. I fluttered a bit as they came toward our island, then flapped myself back to the edge of the nest.

"The uprights are very close to our nest," I warned Trosk.

He opened his weary eyes. "They mean no harm, Cherra. They'll use their strings and perhaps leave some food for us on the water-edge rock. But keep watch, all the same."

Trosk obviously needed more sleep. I felt proud that he had entrusted the territory and our well-being to my keeping for a while. I swept my long vision both up and down the water flow. In the distance, above the falling water, dark forms were gathering in the sky.

I have to find food for Trosk, Merron and Vonce. Since I had seen no lifeless swimmers floating on the water surface, I headed for the falls where I could easily pick a swimmer as it fell through the water. Yet I was apprehensive over the dark sky-forms.

I must work quickly and return before the skywater starts coming down. This thought added urgency to my flight.

The uprights were grappling with a large black swimmer and drifting with the water flow when I soared over them. I wondered if they had noticed the darkening sky to the south. I called out to alert them, but they seemed not to hear.

On reaching the falling waters, I circled a few times then landed atop a drooping longneedle tree and waited, eyes fixed on the water at the upper edge of the falls. The instant I spotted a group of black swimmers about to go over I took my dive, grasped a long thin one in my talons, spiraled upwards, and turned my direction toward the nesting tree.

Then the skywater came — quickly and heavily. My wings were being soaked and weighted down. I struggled against the pounding drops, clinging desperately to the squirming black one in my grip until finally I was forced to drop the swimmer and seek refuge at the base of a longneedle. The skywater was so thick I couldn't see beyond the water edge. My long-vision was of no use in these conditions. I could only wait for the dark forms to pass, and for both the sky and my wings to lighten. In the distance I could hear the voices of the uprights as they called loudly to one another.

They didn't make it back to their nest, either. I wonder if they, too, lost their swimmer.

"Don't worry," I said softly, as though the uprights were with me, "we will be all right." Then my thoughts were silenced by the great sky-noises that have always frightened me. I took comfort in knowing that I was not the only one caught in the sky's anger.

The skywater and noises left almost as quickly as they had come. My wings were light enough now, and with a few hard flaps I was once again in the air headed toward the nesting tree. I thought of the released black swimmer and dreaded having to admit the loss to Trosk. We female great whiteheads are supposed to be better at finding food than our life-friends, but not so in the case of Trosk. I had perhaps come to rely too heavily on his protection and provisions. After the disappearance of Karak during the horrible fire that destroyed the nest and one of the fledglings, I had been very hesitant to accept another life-friend and to give birth to more whiteheads.

How strong Trosk has been for me, yet how gentle with me and all our little ones since that first warm season together here in his birth territory. I wanted him to know that I was well again, that I could effectively perform all my responsibilities. He should be able to count on me, just as I counted on him.

Landing on the nest I found Trosk, Merron, and Vonce awake.

"Cherra! I'm glad you're safe. I was afraid for you during the sky's anger." He approached me and softly rubbed my beak with his. The nestlings hobbled over, too, looking around me for strips of food.

"I'm all right, but I had to release a fine black swimmer I had seized at the falling waters. I am ashamed."

"There's plenty of food here, Cherra. Just before the skywater started falling, a paddler who had lost a paddle to a black swimmer managed to come ashore just beneath the nest. I took it effortlessly. But I haven't had time to tear it into strips."

He turned his head to indicate a clump of paddler feathers on the other side of the nest. I hopped over to examine the prize.

"This will be a feast! I'll shred it immediately so that we can all have our fill."

Happy to be of use again to the others, I began stripping the feathers and tearing out the meat. The chicks were impatient and started pulling on the strips. I nudged them away but they came right back. It was not easy work. I glanced at Trosk who seemed to be taking in the scene with his usual reserve. The sky brightness had returned, the wind was calm and cool, the air smelled of wet longneedles, whitebark leaves, and paddler flesh. I felt somehow purified by the soaking of the skywater, and my spirit was renewed.

There was more than enough for food the four of us. I discarded the hard structure of the paddler over the edge of the nest where I knew it would be consumed by tiny ground nibblers. Trosk stretched his wings and with a few flaps rose to the lookout perch above the nest.

"I'm quite rested now, Cherra. I'll watch until skydark," Trosk called down. I had settled down over the chicks and was too comfortable to stir.

"Are the uprights safely back in their nest?"

"They are," he answered. He was back in control of the forest.

With a sigh of relief I turned my head westward to watch the sky begin its dance of colors.

I must have slept for a while, but something waked me abruptly. I listened, but heard only the silence of the dark boreal forest. Nothing moved about in the underbrush, nothing called out to the night. I looked for movement on the water, and there I saw what had awakened me. Reflected on the water surface was the face of the night sky glowing with bright swirling lights, fading and reappearing in dramatic patterns. The ancient whiteheads used to say it was the sky celebrating the beginning of life. It was during one of these night-sky celebrations that Trosk and I had first performed the coupling rite. And the next light cycle we selected this whitebark as our nesting place. A short time afterwards we had our first little one. How happily I had spread myself over the shell, how joyfully we greeted the pecking. Of course, we overly concerned ourselves with the nurturing — the feeding, the cleaning of the nest, the watch for intruders, and the training of the fledgling for flight.

As I watched the changing skylights, memories of all our warm seasons together came back to me, the times of shell-laying, the feedings, the hatchings, the fledglings that were quick-to-learn and the slow-to-learn, the vacant nest seasons when I spent the dark cycles enjoying Trosk's warmth, savoring his devotion, feeling secure in his strength.

Yet I knew I had not been awakened just to reminisce over my life. There was something else happening inside me. Something instinctual was forming. I closed my mind's eye to the past and focused my inner eye on the present. Then I knew.

I will tell Trosk tomorrow: The female upright has conceived a shell and the sky has greeted the new life.

This realization gave me pleasure. It is good to carry life within you and to bring it forth.

The dark cycle is very short during the warm season. In fact, it never grows as dark as it does in the cold season. I heard the night creatures moving about and felt the calming of the winds as first light approached. I loved the stillness of the forest early in the new light cycle. The nestlings were beginning to stir. Trosk called down from the high look-out perch:

"Are you hungry? There is a floating swimmer that I can pick up easily in the channel for you and the young ones."

I nodded approval, and Trosk flapped away into the crisp early-light air. I watched him rise and use the sky currents to circle then glide toward the channel that separated our nesting area from the uprights'. He made a fast downward glide to the water surface, raised his wings just above the water, opened his talons and plucked the lifeless swimmer from the surface. I turned to prepare a place for the stripping of the meat and found that Merron had hopped to the edge of the nest.

So she, too, has been observing Trosk, I mused. *No doubt she learned much from this first lesson in procuring food.*

Trosk and I tore the swimmer into strips, eating a little ourselves as we did. The nestlings were both eager to fill their bellies. Merron devoured much of the food, but there was enough for Vonce as well. Then we began our routine of nest cleaning and clearing. I threw out as much debris as possible and covered the bottom of the nest with fresh greenery as Trosk deposited it. Tucking some stray feathers into crevasses of the nest, I thought about what I had seen with my inner eye during the dancing sky lights.

Many things we see with inward vision are secret things. I won't tell Trosk, I decided.

Early in the next light cycle, the two uprights appeared on the landing perch with bundles from the hilltop nest. In the distance the roaring bird churned its way through the air, headed toward our waters and, no doubt, the uprights' nest. The large bird landed on the water, slowed its pace, and glided to the flatlog perch. The lone upright inside the bird hopped out and, with the help of the other two, tied the bird to the landing perch.

"The uprights have such strange ways," Trosk commented.

"They do indeed."

After all the bundles had been placed inside the roaring bird, the two uprights that had been living in the nest climbed inside. The last of the three followed them.

Trosk watched the roaring bird speed over the water until it rose against the wind. He seemed proud of himself.

"There. She is safe now. They'll go to find a new territory, construct their own nest where she'll place her shells." He turned to me. "Like us, Cherra, they will be life-friends and life-givers in the warm seasons."

So Trosk, too, had experienced a similar inner vision. He understood that much. But I did not respond to Trosk's pronouncement. For as I watched them disappearing into the sky, I felt a growing uneasiness and sensed that something would go wrong.

Chapter 3: The Year of the Beaver

Karen

"Ice-out was late this year," Bobby said once Steve and I had climbed aboard the Cessna, "so you'll probably see white patches in a few places along the shoreline, but the river's fully navigable, and the water is high."

"Does that mean the fishing will not be so good?" Steve wanted to know.

"Just the opposite. The big northern will be grabbing just about anything you throw in the water."

"What about the walleye?" I piped in, eager to hold my first angel fish in two years.

"They may be a little slow at first, but you'll start picking up a few, especially later in the week after the females have finished spawning," Bobby informed us as he slid a set of headphones over his ears.

I settled back, clicked shut my seatbelt and waited for Bobby to get clearance for take-off from whomever it was he talked to through the pilot's headset. Within minutes we were speeding along Manitoba's Red River. As soon as I realized we were airborne, the same sensation I had experienced two years ago surged like an electric current charging every cell of my body: *I am headed toward an inscrutable destiny.* There was something about rising up off the water in this little plane going into the northern wilderness that provoked an intensity of feeling in me. It seemed as though the floatplane and its passengers had been grasped by the hand of Fate and set upon an appointed course, borne by the winds of change.

"Thank you for this, Mama and Daddy," I whispered to myself. They had volunteered to take care of Meredith, even though she was entering the toddler stage and had to be watched "with eagle eye." I had used the phrase deliberately when giving my parents detailed instructions, although no one in the world except myself had a clue to its mysterious significance. But the entire family understood the alliterative significance of the child's name, Meredith Marsten.

"You two need some time off. You've been so busy giving piano lessons in the afternoons and playing at church every Sunday. Steve's working night and day, grading all those term papers and compositions, writing stuff to publish, and running off to deliver papers at conferences, then both of you taking turns with this child. It's a wonder you haven't come down with some illness."

That was typical Mama, worrying, but this time Daddy agreed completely. Steve was reluctant.

"I really need to use this break before summer session to get some writing done, Sweetheart. I just don't think I can spare the time."

But Bobby had been persuasive, assuring Steve that he would find room for books, pen and paper in the floatplane. Steve could work at the cabin during any rainy days, and Bobby himself would take me out fishing for the day at midweek check. I really wanted this trip and was so grateful to Mama, Daddy, and Bobby.

"So those are patches of ice," I spoke the words aloud in the back seat of the plane, though neither Steve nor Bobby could hear me over the noise of the engine.

White spots had begun to appear along the edges of lakes as we flew farther north. Thank goodness Bobby had called a few days ago to suggest that we bring along some heavier clothes this time. I anticipated the warmth of a fire in the woodstove, steaming hot chocolate, and Steve's passionate embraces.

Morning clouds had grown thin, parting like a filmy curtain before the mounting sun. I watched the shadow of the Cessna as it glided alternately over forests and lakes through mile after mile of pristine wilderness. Many a sleepless night back in Spring Hill had been spent visualizing the poplars and pines and recalling the aroma of conifers, and even the smell of freshwater fish. I remembered the clean and crisp feel of the morning air. I could hear the call of the wind in the poplars and the cries of the loons and Canada geese. I imagined touching the angel fish and even the slimy northern pike. Over the past two years the Canadian wilderness had become a spiritual retreat in my secret moments.

Steve never really talked about it, only to say that it would be impossible for us to take the fishing trip for our first anniversary, since the baby was too young and he had agreed to teach a summer course of freshman composition. So we just went to the one fairly decent restaurant in Spring Hill, then came back to the apartment and watched a movie on TV. Mama had picked up Meredith that afternoon and kept her until the next day so we could have the evening alone. The meal, the movie, and the evening alone were, all-in-all, rather disappointing. Or perhaps it was simply the effect of my unfulfilled longing for Poplar River.

"There's the cabin," Steve called back to me.

And so began our second stay in what Steve had labeled "Honeymoon

Heaven."

Everything looked different. There was indeed a little ice here and there, and the leaf buds had not yet opened on the poplars, making the whole forest appear barren, forsaken. Standing on the dock while the guys unloaded the gear, I looked around for the bald eagle, but no sign of either the male or female, or any of the young ones that must have learned to fly and fish by now.

"Where are you hiding, my soaring friends?" I whispered into the chill of the air.

"KK, grab the two sleeping bags and go on up to the cabin. Bobby and I will bring the rest."

I had taken a bag in each hand and had started up the hill when a loud splash in the small bay to the right of the cabin got my attention.

"A fish jumping doesn't make that much noise," I thought. Glancing over my shoulder I could see expanding circles in the water. "I'll have to investigate that later," I decided.

Coming up the steps to the porch I noticed that the screened door was completely off the hinges and lying on the ground below. I went inside the porch and turned the handle of the metal door. It opened. *Wasn't it locked before?* I suddenly pictured the three of us at this door, Steve lifting me over the threshold, my foot kicking Bobby as he did, Steve tripping, the two of us falling flat on the floor, and all of us laughing like school kids on a playground. For some reason, the involuntary flashback made me a little sad, imbued as it was with a bittersweet flavor.

"What happened to the screened door?" I asked, as Bobby stepped onto the porch with a box of groceries.

"You really don't wanna know."

"What happened?" I insisted as I followed him and the groceries inside the cabin.

"Better get the perishables in the fridge right away." Bobby seemed determined to ignore the question. He turned to the food shelves where he picked up a hammer and screwdriver.

"A little bear got in through one of the back windows last week, probably looking for food. The cabin was empty, of course. He must have panicked, forced the metal door, and proceeded to demolish the screen door in his hurry to get out. But don't you worry, ma'am. I'll have all repairs done before I leave today," he finally answered playfully, pointing the screwdriver at me.

"A *little* bear?" I continued to follow him, forgetting the perishables.

"Seems to me like it would take a pretty big one to do all that!" I shuddered.

Bobby grinned at me as he got to work on the metal door latch.

"They don't usually come around when people are here, at least not inside — unless the people do something really dumb like leave food lying around. I had one party of six guys at the end of the season last year who put bacon and peanut butter and other food outside to *attract* the bears. Then when Bruno showed up, they took turns having their pictures made with him," Bobby huffed as he put some energy into tightening a bolt or screw or something.

"Trust me, Bobby. I'm extra careful to keep our food contained and the smell of it to a minimum," I assured him and myself at the same time.

Steve had piled all our gear on the porch during the reparation of the door lock and had started attaching the reels to the rods.

"Okay, Stevie. Give me a hand with the screen door so I can get out of here. I still have a couple of guys to fly up to Cinnamon Lake today."

I got so busy putting the groceries away — *really well* — that I didn't realize Bobby had left until I heard the sound of full throttle on the Cessna. I watched the lift off through the kitchen window. Then I lowered my gaze to follow Steve as he ambled up the hill toward the cabin.

"Please, God, let everything be okay this week. Don't let me do or say anything to upset Steve. Please let him be happy to be alone here with me," I prayed, then immediately felt embarrassed by such a personal and self-centered request. I heard the screened door close.

"KK, how about some of your gourmet peanut butter and jelly sandwiches? I'm starving."

"You're always starving."

I located the essential ingredients and had the sandwiches well underway when Steve came up behind me, locked his arms around me, and kissed the back of my neck.

"As soon as you feed me, I'd like to make up our bed," he whispered, then released his hold, letting his hands glide over my breasts as he moved away.

* * *

The early morning was cold and still. The water lay like a liquid blanket over the land. Nothing stirred. Up and dressed in jeans and a thick black turtleneck, I pulled on a pile-lined jacket and, carrying a cup of hot coffee, went out through the porch and down the slope to the dock. Morning clouds of light pink, blue and gray were reflected in the motionless lake. In my mind I could hear the pale arpeggios of Debussy's *Reflets dans l'eau.* I could even feel my fingers moving over the keys, creating the gentle flow of mellifluous sound.

As I stood there admiring the beauty of the inverted sky, a furry head suddenly appeared out of a pink cloud and began moving in streamlined silence through the reflected heavens, making an almost imperceptible wake. The creature was swimming parallel to the shore, passing directly in front of the dock. I took a step forward to get a better look, and the head went under. Then it popped up again a few yards to the right. This time I stood perfectly still, my eyes fixed on the animal. In a flash the head ducked under, a rather large brown furry body rolled forward and down in a dive exposing a big flat tail that slapped hard at the water surface, shattering the crystalline mirror of the sky, breaking the pure silence of the morning.

So that was the sound I heard yesterday. A resident beaver.

The sighting of any animal in the wild started my heart racing. I sat down cross-legged on the dock, took a deep breath, finished my coffee, and waited. But no more Mr. Beaver, or Mrs. Beaver. Yet I could still sense his presence somewhere under the water.

"I won't hurt you, my friend, or disturb you in any way. I just want to watch you swim and do whatever it is you beavers do." I spoke the words as though the animal could both hear and understand. Then, there it was again, very close to the dock this time, facing me. Two dark eyes looking directly at me. I dared not move a muscle or even breathe. He held his position for a few seconds then continued swimming in his original direction, apparently satisfied that I really wasn't a threat.

"Please come to see me again," I called out to two little round ears, as the head glided on its way through the liquid clouds.

"Hey! What happened to the coffee service in this bed-and-breakfast?" Steve yelled down from the porch.

He had been sleeping so soundly when I got up to light the butane stove and get the percolator going that I decided not to wake him with room service just yet.

"Not open for business yet. Too early." I retorted.

When I got to the porch I discovered that he had already poured his coffee and was dressed and ready to get out on the lake.

"Aren't you the early bird this morning," he said as I gave him a kiss on the cheek.

"I am. But the fish will get the worms!"

We had brought in a supply of earthworms to use with jigheads for walleye, despite Bobby's warning that we might not see any for a few days.

"Want some breakfast before we head out?" I asked dutifully.

"Just grab that box of doughnuts and let's get going, KK. The water's nice and calm, and I have a feeling your angel fish are hungry."

Unfortunately he was mistaken, and Bobby was right. We had a really slow morning, pulling in only a couple of skinny little northerns that Steve referred to as "fingerlings" and "ax handles."

Warmed by the mounting sun, I became drowsy, and we fished in silence for a while. Involuntarily out of my memory came the image of Steve quoting poetry to me as he released a golden walleye. The poignant flashback jolted me into a fully awake mode.

"Let's try up the channel around the eagle's nest before we call it quits," Steve suggested. I reeled in, secured my rod, pulled my cap down a bit, and swiveled my seat around to face the captain. Steve headed the boat up the west channel and out toward the island. I squinted against the sun, trying to sight a bald eagle.

"Look, Steve. The nest is still there. I know the eagles must be somewhere close by. I read somewhere that they use the same nest year after year."

Steve didn't seem interested in my discourse on the habits of bald eagles, for, while I was busy searching for eagles, he was trying to untangle the knotted fishing line in his bait casting reel.

"This is sure a helluva mess," he muttered. "Don't put your line back in the water, KK. We're going back to the cabin for beer. Fuck the fish."

And back we went. Steve was miffed at our bad luck, and I was disappointed at not sighting an eagle, but as we made our way back down the river, through the channel and out into the lake, my negative feelings seemed to evaporate like mist before the serene grandeur of Poplar River. Not the case for my fishing buddy.

Without a word Steve left me to moor the boat, and, taking only the rod with the knotted line, tromped up to the cabin. I removed the loose lure, straightened up the tackle box, and did some general tidying up inside the boat. Taking the empty doughnut box and the carton with the remaining earthworms, I started up the hill.

Splatt!

I stopped in my tracks. Turning slowly to look behind me, I saw the beaver's head come up a few yards beyond the dock. It began to swim in the same direction it was going the first time I saw it.

"It's time to investigate," I decided.

Walking as quietly as possible I made my way to the shore just past the dock. The footing was rocky and the wet moss was slippery, so I had to move cautiously. Even my heavy hiking boots could slip or sink into mushy spots. Just past a group of blueberry bushes I found a long flat rock jutting into the water. From there I had a clear view of the bay to the side of the cabin. I watched as the beaver made his way toward a high pile of logs and branches at the back of the bay, close to the shore. The head ducked under and the dark body was visible for a second. I waited. But he was gone.

* * *

"Steve, I think I found a beaver's house!" I was exhilarated as I came into the cabin. "Just around in the bay by the cabin!"

He was sitting at the big pine table in the center of the main room, a half-empty bottle of LaBatt's Blue on the table at arm's reach, and a mound of curled fishing line on the floor by his feet.

"I had to take all the line off this damn reel." He was tying new line to the reel barrel.

"Here, hold the line taught while I rewind," he said, handing me the spool of monofilament line.

"So, you were out exploring while I was in here cursing and drinking like a sailor. You could have fallen in the lake, you know."

"I was real careful, and the beaver was so cute. They are so quiet when they swim — except when they slap their tails on the water." I tried to concentrate on the tension of the fishing line, but I kept getting it too tight or too loose to please Steve.

Besides, my mind was on the beaver.

"Do you know why they do that?"

"Do what?"

"Slap the water with their tail."

"You'll have to ask Bobby. He's the woodsman when it comes to wildlife. Dad took us camping and taught us to fish as kids. That's the limit of my forestry training. But Bobby really loved that kind of thing. Majored in biology at Iowa, then took special courses in subjects like Wildlife Management and Environmental Science and such. Got his bush pilot license. Bought up rights to several lakes up here, refurbished the cabins, and makes a pretty good living at it. But it's rough work, to say nothing of the dangers."

"Like bears?" I asked, the destruction of the cabin doors looming in my mind.

"Mostly from the weather, you know, flying around in it all the time. And you've seen how quickly it can change. Thanks, KK. Now I'm good to go again."

Steve reattached the freshly-wound reel to a rod and carried it out to the porch where we kept about six of them neatly lined up, ready for use.

After a lunch of ham sandwiches and a can of split-pea soup, Steve settled down in the one comfortable chair in the cabin and opened a book about Mary Shelly. Sunshine was pouring in the cabin windows, warming the interior enough for me to trade my heavy jacket for a light-weight down vest. I sat at the table, leafing through the spiral notebook that served as the cabin logbook. Guests filled the pages with fish tales, records of how much beer was consumed, who fell in the lake, where they caught what and using which lure. I found one entry from last year in which a certain Ned Thornton from Akron, Ohio, described the activities of a family of beavers building what he called a "dam" in the south bay. I checked the position of the afternoon sun and concluded that Ned was describing what I had seen:

We motored a little way into the south bay looking for walleye. It was almost dusk. Nothing showed up on the fish finder screen, but we did spot what looked like a beaver dam. Russ had a pair of binoculars with him, and with them we could see the critters moving around, ocasionally pushing large twigs up onto the pile, but mostly coming up to the surface, then diving back down. Man! They sure can stay under the water for ever! Must have great lungs — or a set of gills. The guys got quite a laugh when we came in tonight and told them we had found some beaver.

I closed the notebook and tried to imagine what the cabin would be like with a bunch of guys in here for a week of hard fishing and hard drinking. A far cry from what I had experienced here in what Canadians call the "bush." I wondered if any of the male guests had joked about that term as well.

Feeling a little bored and neglected ("spoiled" was perhaps a more accurate word) I took a beer out of the refrigerator, went out on the porch and sat down on the old couch where we had enjoyed the sunsets on our honeymoon. Funny how I never drink beer at home. Never want one. Or much of any alcohol for that matter. But somehow in an isolated outpost in the wilderness it seemed to fit and tasted really good.

Wait a minute! Didn't Steve pack a pair of binoculars in his duffle bag?

I set the beer down on the floor and went in search of them. I wanted a close look at the beaver house, or "dam."

Steve had fallen asleep with Mary Shelly open on his lap.

"Sleep well, my dearest, while I go to see my furry friends," I whispered to his dreams.

Armed with the binoculars I had retrieved from Steve's bag, I walked out into the full afternoon sun.

* * *

Wednesday morning dawned in splendor, not a cloud in the sky. Crisp sunlight hitting the gently rocking water was breaking it into glistening tesserae of gray, silver and blue. Warmed by three straight days of sunshine, the buds on the aspen poplars had begun to open and tint the forest with a greenish haze that softened the brilliance of the morning sun. Everywhere there were sounds life. The commotion of Canada geese honking erratically as they flew over in vee formation. Gray jays making "chucking" sounds as they scratched about in the underbrush. The distant bellow of a bull moose. The wing flap of gulls swooping down near the dock to check for possible fish scraps. Standing next to the water, I let go of all my self-images and simply allowed my being to become a part of the natural life forms that were surrounding me.

Despite the ideal weather, we had not done much serious fishing — or fooling around. Our luck had not been great, even with the northern, and we hadn't caught a single walleye. I did find a surprise fish at the end of my line yesterday that Steve identified as a perch. It was too little too eat, but it was a fish. And I wanted to catch some more.

Steve's mind was on his scholarly work. After the knotted fishing line episode, he had come up with the idea of a book entitled "Ladies of the Lake," a study of the women associated with the English Romantic Period, especially with those writers known as the Lake District Poets. That evening I had listened with enthusiasm and admiration as he paced the cabin, verbalizing an outline for the book and detailing certain facts he planned to include. He was ecstatic, convinced that the book, when published, would assure his tenure and promotion at Heyward.

I returned to the cabin from what had become my early morning routine of having coffee with the beaver. He swam by about six a.m. each day, pausing briefly to look me over and reassure himself that I was harmless. I would ask Bobby what beavers eat. Maybe there was something I could try to feed him. Better get Steve fed first, I thought, and hurried into the kitchen area.

* * *

"What time do you think Bobby will get here?" I asked Steve, who was finishing up a plate of scrambled eggs and bacon.

"Any time. He's usually up and out early. Especially today, knowing that he has a date with you. I'm surprised he's not already here. I think he's always had a kind of crush on you ever since I took you home to Iowa to meet my family."

"Don't be silly." I swatted him playfully with a potholder and picked up his breakfast dishes. "He makes fun of my southern accent and probably thinks I'm nothing but a reformed redneck."

"Yeah. Sure."

We washed and dried the dishes and walked out on the porch.

"I think I hear the plane, KK."

I heard it, too. Bobby's midweek arrival was welcome last time, even on the honeymoon, but this time it was especially so. He had promised me all-day fishing. No coming back to the cabin for lunch, but a real shore lunch of fried fish, potatoes and onions at a picturesque spot he knew about. Steve would have all day to entertain his Ladies of the Lake, and Bobby would help me find some angel fish, or maybe a big northern pike.

Bobby came in like a whirlwind, grabbed a large frying pan from its nail on the kitchen wall, a knife and a spatula from the drawer, four beers from the refrigerator, four rods from the porch, and headed back down to the dock.

"Let's get going, Karen. It's prime time for morning fishing. The walleyes are starting to bite."

I was right behind him, tackle box in hand. I knew the procedure for untying the boat and pushing off as I stepped in, an action which merited a grin of approval from the captain. Steve gave us a formal salute as Bobby turned the boat toward open water.

The morning was refreshing, the fishing fast and furious. Bobby seemed to know all the walleye holes, and they were indeed biting. Mostly males, but hungry ones. I caught them jigging, casting, and trolling. Bobby, too. We vied for the biggest walleye, and Bobby won, except for the huge one I had on the line that threw the hook before I could net him. We fished and laughed almost to the point of exhaustion.

"I'm as hungry as the walleye, Bobby. Where's that breathtaking shore lunch spot you told me about?"

"We're on our way there as you speak, my dear."

We reached a peninsula of gently sloping land surrounded by a rocky outcropping.

There was a basic picnic table, a stone-ringed fire bed, and a stack of firewood logs, which Bobby began to split with an ax into small pieces.

"The ladies room is to the left, and gents to the right," Bobby explained as he chopped away, aware that the morning had been a long one.

When I came back from taking care of the necessary, Bobby was filleting the walleye on a board that had been set up across two tree stumps. He worked quickly, showing me how to cut the fish into perfect boneless fillets. He cut off a pair of fins from the underbelly of one fish and held them in the air, making them dart around.

"I'm going to fry you a 'butterfly' as an appetizer."

Then, reaching into his knapsack, he asked, "Do you like mushrooms?"

"I love them!"

He seemed pleased as he opened a plastic bag of sliced fresh ones.

"I thought you might."

Before long, a pan full of potatoes, onions, red peppers and mushrooms was sizzling, while a pile of breaded walleye filets and the butterfly sat waiting their turn in the hot oil.

After several hours of fishing in the chill of the morning, the aroma of the browning vegetables made me ravenous. I began nibbling on them as soon as they were out of the pan. Bobby's butterfly was a delicacy: the muscle that held the two "wings" was tender and succulent. I opened a couple of beers, handed one to the chef, and sat down at the picnic table. While we enjoyed the crisp, flaky walleye fillets, gray and white gulls began gathering around us and squealing in anticipation of human meal leftovers.

When we had eaten more than our fill, we cleaned up the site, washed the camping dishes in the lake, and stowed everything away in the boat.

"Don't put the fire out just yet, Bobby. I hope you don't mind if I ask you a few questions," I said, trying to find a somewhat comfortable rock to sit on by the fire.

"Going to give me the third degree?"

"Tell me what you know about beavers. What do they eat? What do they do? Do they really build dams . . . and live in them?"

Bobby sat down next to me, took off his fishing cap and ran his hands over his head of dark curls.

"*Castor canadensis*. That's the official Latin name. They were almost extinct from the fur trade, but they've made an impressive comeback. There's a beaver lodge in the bay by the cabin. That's where they live, in *lodges*, not in the dams they build.

"I saw the dam, I mean 'lodge,' near the cabin, and every morning I have coffee on the dock with one of the beavers."

"You what?"

"Well, he swims by while I'm having my first cup, before I wake Steve up."

"They are afraid of humans, and normally stay away from them. Even on a chance encounter with a fisherman, a beaver will slap his tail on the water to warn the others of danger."

"He did that the first couple of times I saw him, but now he just gives me the once over and goes about his business, whatever that is."

"Probably not building dams here on Poplar River. The channels are deep, even in the south bay near the lodge. In fact, the bay is naturally ideal for a beaver lodge. Right now the mating season is well over, and there are probably a couple of kits in the lodge's chamber. And maybe some yearlings. You might be able to spot them if you're approach the lodge slowly and quietly."

"Can I put out some food for them?"

Bobby smiled and shook his head. "Not really. They eat bark from twigs and leafy aquatic plants — things like that — and their food supply is plentiful right now. Why this sudden interest in beavers?"

A little self-conscious and hesitant at first, I told him that I felt somehow connected to the beaver, just like the bald eagles two years ago. I talked about my angel fish and devilfish and how I loved to touch them but not harm them. I even tried to express the inexpressable: my secret winter yearning for the wilderness.

"There's a name for it, Karen. The call of the wild. I know exactly what you're talking about. That's why I'm in this business. You know, you really amaze me. A sophisticated lady like you, who teaches and plays the piano, and yet you love to get out in this rugged country and fish all day."

Bobby stood up and held out a hand to help me up.

"And it's time to get back at it. I just might know where you can find a pretty good northern or two this afternoon."

* * *

"Steve! I caught a trophy! We could see it lying in shallow water near the shore. It was a monster. I used a silver lure called a 'redeye,' and he went for it. Oh, my gosh, it took me about ten minutes to bring it to the boat. And it weighed a ton. Bobby kept telling me to keep a tight line and give him time. It was forty-one inches long — Bobby measured it and said that it was big enough . . ." I was breathless from the excitement of the catch.

"Whoa! Slow down a minute, KK." Steve was helping Bobby moor the boat.

"It's true. She pulled in a trophy," Bobby confirmed and handed Steve the frying pan, spatula, and knife he had borrowed from the cabin. "I'm going to take off. Got to check on the guys up at Cinnamon before I head back."

I set my tackle box down and ran up to Bobby, put my hand on his shoulder and gave him a kiss on the cheek.

"Thank you soooo much, Bobby. It was great!"

"You're a good fisherman, Karen."

I could see Bobby stifling a smile as he turned to untie the floatplane. Feeling that maybe I had stepped a little out of line, I took Steve's hand as soon as he had given the plane a good shove away from the dock. We stood together and waited for Bobby to lift off and gain altitude.

"Did you get a lot of work done?" I asked Steve, hoping for a positive report as we climbed back up the hill.

"Some, but not much. I really need to be in a library. I brought only a few books with me, and now that I have thought of a topic, I can't do much with the materials I have here. Besides, I missed spending the day with you. I sat here envying Bobby, and, to tell the truth, a little jealous."

"And I missed spending the day with you," I said, slipping my arms around his waist, as he did the same.

There was no more mention of the Ladies of the Lake the rest of the week, and Steve and I both concentrated on the fishing. I spotted the bald eagles a couple of times and gained a sense of satisfaction from that, but my curiosity rested on the beavers.

On Friday, our last full day at Poplar River, the beaver didn't show up for morning coffee. Throughout the day I was disappointed and a little saddened by the lack of his presence. After supper Steve started preparing for tomorrow's departure. While he was dismantling the rods and reels, I took the binoculars and the camera and went down to the dock. There was still plenty of daylight left. I loosed the boat, stepped in, took the paddle, and began "slowly and quietly," as Bobby had suggested, making my way around the flat rock toward the beaver lodge. Through the binoculars I could see what looked like the kits in a boxing match at the shoreline. They looked adorable. I stopped paddling and let the boat drift directly toward the lodge. I was close enough to get a photo. I "slowly and quietly" stood up in the boat and raised the camera to my eye.

I would relive the next fifteen seconds a thousand times. I zoomed in on the kits and pressed the shutter of the camera. At that very instant a crosswind caused the boat to rock. My knees buckled and I lost my balance. Striking my shin on the rim of the boat, I fell headlong overboard. I felt the surface of the frigid water hit my face. Then I was completely under, hiking boots and jacket pulling me down despite my instinctive efforts to propel myself to the surface.

Something bumped my knees, projecting me into a horizontal position. Someone was under the water with me. Another bump at the midsection sent me forward in the water. I was now able to move my arms and kick my legs the way I had been taught in YMCA swimming classes in Spring Hill. I felt my hands touch mud. Then my feet found the bottom and my head came up above water. Gasping for air, I slipped, slid and fell onto the mossy shore. At first I could not move from the shock of having been submerged in the icy water. I turned my head to one side, and there he was, water still dripping from his quill–like outer layer of fur. The two dark eyes, the round ears, the rotund brown body.

"Thank you, my friend."

Hypothermia. I must get to the cabin and get warm.

I don't even remember how I made it back. All I remember is reaching the metal door. I remember Steve stripping off my clothes and zipping me into a sleeping bag. I remember hot tea, the fire in the wood stove. I remember feeling embarrassed and ashamed of myself. But most of all I remember Steve's tears. The only ones I would ever see.

"Oh, KK, I almost lost you! Thank God you're okay."

* * *

Our lives took an interesting turn on Thanksgiving Day that year. There were two surprises. The first one came by way of a phone call from Jacob Lavinsky.

"No, you're not interrupting anything, Dr. Lavinsky. I'm just keeping an eye on a green bean casserole in the oven. My sister and her husband and Steve and I are having dinner at my parents' house in a little while. . . . The Hofmann Piano Competition? No, I really don't know anything about it. . . . Yes, I know that my Masters degree recital was taped. . . . A finalist? . . . Well, I guess I could get the Schumann Concerto back in shape by March. Who would accompany me? . . . You would? This is so unexpected, I don't know what to say. You know I have a toddler and church responsibilities, and my private students . . . I just don't know where I could find the hours to practice every day. . . Yes, I realize what an opportunity this is, but . . . Okay. I'll talk it over with Steve and my family and call you tomorrow."

"Who was that on the phone?" Steve had come into the kitchen with Meredith in his arms — her favorite place these days.

"Professor Lavinsky, with some startling news. It seems that he submitted a tape of my Masters recital to the Josef Hofmann Piano Competition, and I was selected as one of five finalists. I'm supposed to go to Aiken for the finals in March."

Steve set Meredith down, but she immediately began pulling at his pants leg to be picked up again. "Who is Josef Hofmann, and where is Aiken?" he asked.

"Josef Hofmann was a world-renown Polish pianist, a child prodigy, who toured the world in first half of the twentieth century. I'm not sure what the connection with Aiken is. It's a nice little town in South Carolina which I thought was known only for its race horses."

"So what does all this mean?"

"It means hours of daily practice, which I just don't have. I'm going to tell Lavinsky that I can't possibly do it."

"Of course you can do it, if you want to. Is there a prize for winning?"

"Five thousand dollars for first place, a performance with the South Carolina Symphony in Columbia, and I think he said something about a recital at the Polish Embassy in Washington."

"You'd be crazy not to try, KK. I know you're good at the piano, better than most of the pianists we've heard at Heyward, or even in Columbia, for that matter."

"I think you may be slightly prejudiced, my dearest. But anyway, I'll toss the idea out to Mama and Daddy today, and we'll get their reaction."

Mama was thrilled and just knew I would win, Daddy was practical, declaring the competition an investment in my career, Katherine and Ted agreed with Steve. Everyone offered to help with Meredith. So that was that. I would go to the finals in March.

The second surprise of the day came from Daddy during the carving of the turkey.

"I was going to wait until Christmas, but I have a little gift for you and Steve. I've owned a piece of property up on Lake Morris for quite a few years. Was going to build a house on it for Mary and me, but we decided to stay put in this old place on Oakwood. I'd like the two of you to have it to build you a nice place. We know you're cramped in that apartment. Karen has to come over here to teach her piano lessons, and Steve has to go to his office to do all his work. Besides, Meredith needs a nice yard to play in, and a place where she can invite her friends as she grows up."

"But Mr. Kingsley, we couldn't possibly accept such a generous gift," Steve protested.

"Of course you can. In fact, I've already talked to a good friend of mine in the construction business. He's going to come by your place next week to show you some sample plans. He's a good builder — the best around here, and he'll give you a real break on the price."

And that was that. We would build a house.

On Friday I called Lavinsky to announce my decision and to set up a series of coaching sessions with him. On Tuesday afternoon, John Roberts, the construction guy, came by the apartment to drop off several books of house designs for us to look over. Steve had a class that afternoon, but had made a list of questions for me to ask. Roberts was a pleasant fellow, stocky and muscular, with just a hint of a beer belly. His answers were clear and to the point, and he seemed willing and able to deal with our need for a living room large enough for a grand piano and that could double as a small recital hall for my students, a quiet study for Steve with wall-to-wall, floor-to-ceiling built-in bookshelves, and — a screened porch facing the lake.

"I just built a house last spring that I think would be the perfect plan for you. As a matter of fact, I think I have some pictures of it in my truck. You wanna come take a look?"

Eager to see what our new home might look like, I followed him out to the street where he had parked his truck He opened the passenger door, rummaged around in the glove compartment and came up with a few snapshots of a two-story brick house with a screened porch on one side.

"Looks nice," I commented.

"The plans for it are in one of the books I gave you. You'll know it when you see it."

"How long will it take to build it, once we pick out a plan?"

"It depends a lot on the weather, but usually no more than four or five months. Once we start a house, we stay busy at it. We have to live up to our name."

He shut the door of the pick-up and smiled as he pointed smugly to the company's name and logo: "Beaver Construction Company" was written in a semi-circle above a drawing of my wilderness hero.

Chapter 4: The Year of the Beaver
Pruu

The air and water were cooler than usual for the beginning of the warm season. The whitebarks did not yet have their greens, but their white covering, and the brown one under it, were easy to eat, and there were plenty of tender young sprouts coming up from the earth. I was returning from an early-light search for water plants to feed the kits and Ghinn. Despite the lingering winterish chill, the four kitlings had been born about the same time as the two were last birthing season. Now the older kits had already begun helping out, gathering small branches for the dwelling, and grooming the new kitlings with Ghinn. But mostly they enjoyed their frolics. I liked to watch their mock fights, for they reminded me of the fun I had not so long ago, before my care-givers told me it was time for me to leave the dwelling, find a life-friend, and build.

Pruu, I said to myself, *you are fortunate to have found her. Ghinn is a good partner.* I was pleased with the way she had nurtured the kitlings of last season, her very first birthing.

She lays the logs and branches well, and she knows how to apply just the right amount of mud. She's a good builder and a good care-giver. I was carrying a mouthful of young branches as I rounded the peninsula that led from the wide water into our quiet pond.

The sound of the roaring bird made me drop my twigs and dive into the safety of the underwater, instinctively sending the warning noise with my tail. Last warm season Ghinn and I had been terrified of the bird's enormous size and tremendous roar. But it never tried to harm us or any of the forest dwellers. After a while we continued our lives as usual and actually became more wary of the noisy water-skimmers that carried the uprights around the surface.

"They don't seem to want to bother us flattails, just the finned swimmers," I had informed Ghinn, trying to reassure her that it would be safe to continue raising the kitlings in our newly-built dwelling near the uprights' nest.

"Are you sure, Pruu? Sometimes they come very close to us with their sticks and strings."

That warm season came and went, and we were not harmed. But then other uprights came with loud firesticks that took the life-force from longclaws and antlered ones.

"Best we keep away from *all* uprights," I told Ghinn and the older kits.

Under the water I changed directions and headed away from our dwelling. At a safe distance back around the tip of the peninsula I stood in shoreline mud and watched as three uprights took bundles up the hill. I saw them go in and out of their dwelling, saw them patching up the damaged parts, and wondered why everything they did made so much noise.

"They must not be afraid at all, not even of long-toothed longclaw," I concluded.

I found a tangle of twigs and had just begun to munch on them, when I heard the bird's roar. I continued to eat as it moved faster and faster over the water surface, then rose into the air. Two remaining uprights went inside their dwelling, the bird disappeared into the clouds, and I could return to Ghinn and the kits.

The next early-light shone through soft colors onto calm waters. I don't know why I swam so close to the roaring bird's flatlog perch. Curiosity perhaps. One of the uprights seemed different from the others, and I wondered about that. And there it stood on the flatlog structure. I ducked underwater, but for some reason did not send the warning. Still curious, I brought my head up out of the water. The upright was standing there, unmoved.

Better send the warning. I took a good dive and brought my tail down hard against the water's surface. *Maybe that will frighten the upright.*

I circled under the water, then came up to take another look. This time I looked and listened long and hard. I heard a soft sound coming from the upright's mouth. I was sure I had understood the tones of the sound. *This one will not harm me. This one is gentle. This one is interested in flattails.* Then I suddenly realized: this one was the female. The first female upright I had encountered. The one inside the dwelling was the male. I wasn't sure about the third one, the one that had gone away inside the roaring bird. I gazed for a few more moments at this gentle upright, trying to find a way to describe her to Ghinn. I felt perfectly safe letting her see me swim off toward our flattail dwelling, even wanting her to know about my dwelling, my life-friend, and my young ones. So I swam through the pond with my head above water until I had reached our dwelling. Just then I heard the male upright's voice calling to the female.

I must learn more about him. I dived toward the underwater entrance.

* * *

"You were gone such a long time, Pruu. I had to go outside to find food for the kitlings. I went behind the dwelling to the white barks we felled earlier, and found some bark strips. I also gathered a few twigs — some with greens. Our food supply must not get low."

"Don't worry, Ghinn. Our food store under the water by the shore across the pond is plentiful and will last all of us for a while. Besides, I think the kitlings are old enough to find food now . . . and to be left alone. You can leave the dwelling whenever you like."

"Oh, I suppose I do fret over them too much. But that roaring bird is back, and uprights will be going in and out of their dwelling and coming into the pond with their water-skimmers, strings and sticks. I'm still afraid."

"Listen, Ghinn. I think one of the uprights is a female this time. There's also a male. Anyway, the roaring bird has flown away, and you know the uprights with sticks and strings have never bothered us."

"How do you know one is a female?"

"She spoke to me."

"She did? What did she say? Can you understand the upright voice?"

"I think I can understand the female. She said she would not harm us and that she just wants to learn about flattails."

"I hope you're right, Pruu."

I convinced Ghinn to come outside with me to help mark the mudhills we'd made. I had recently seen a young flattail from the clan that dwells near the whitewater. If he came into the pond, I wanted to make sure he knew this area of the water was ours. Together Ghinn and I dragged our hind parts over all the mudhills, marking them with our scent. Afterwards we sniffed the air, satisfied that the aroma was strong enough. The older kits swam out of the dwelling to join in the outdoor activity. The great skylight was warming, and there were no odors of longclaw or any of the large thin-legged bushytails that can devour us on land. So we sat on our tails at the water's edge, oiling our outer waterfur with our back feet. I kept watch on the sky for any whiteheads or other broadwing flyers that might spot the kits from their lofty regions.

"Since you're here with the kits and kitlings, I'm going to find some whitebark logs for the dwelling. It should be made bigger, now that we have new flattails to shelter," Ghinn said.

Bloff, one of the older kits, insisted on going with her and climbed on her tail.

"No, if you are old enough to go with me, you must swim on your own. You're not a kitling anymore."

Then off they swam with Ghinn leading out of the bay giving wide berth to the uprights' dwelling.

"It's good that she still fears them," I decided.

The waters and winds were calm and, with the great skylight warming me through the waterfur down to the inner fur, I wanted to sleep. I wedged myself into a hollow at the base of a water-edge longneedle. From there I could see the other kit, Frell, in the shore water gnawing on a twig. In my inward ear I could still hear the female upright speaking to me, softly telling me that she would never harm me, that she wanted to know about flattails. Then I could see her with my inner eye, leaning close to the water, still speaking softly. I answered her.

Come, I will show you the dwelling that my life-friend and I built last birthing season. And the upright began swimming with me through the water. . . .

"Pruu! Wake up!" Ghinn was in front of me, droplets streaming off her waterfur. "Frell is missing! I've looked in the dwelling and all around the pond. I've called and called. Where did he go? Surely you know where he is!"

My sleep images vanished. I immediately sniffed the air for Frell's scent. A trace of it lingered at the shore where I had last seen him. But I could not find any on the land.

"He must have decided to follow you and Bloff. I'll find him, Ghinn."

I went into the water and started swimming out in the direction Ghinn had taken. I stopped at the end of the peninsula and began calling, using the distress sound. Nothing. I swam on, following along the shore line, looking, calling, listening. What could have happened while I slept? Did a broadwing swoop down to the water edge and seize him? No, Frell would have cried out to me for help. It would not have been possible for a longclaw or a thin-legged bushytail to have come near without my knowing it. Frell must have simply wandered off. I remembered how curious I was as a kit, eager to explore and discover for myself, not having developed sufficient fear or caution.

Wait! I thought I heard a distant flattail distress call. I stopped swimming and listened. There it was again. Turning in the direction of the sound, I swam hard, using all my feet, not just the back paddling feet, moving them as fast as possible. My caregivers had once told me the story of Thann, a flattail in our clan many, many seasons ago, who had a front foot caught in the sharp teeth of one of the uprights' snapmouths that they used to set along the forest floor. They say it is impossible to free a foot taken in a snapmouth. Thann knew the uprights would come and take his life spirit away if he couldn't free himself, so he began to gnaw at the trapped foot as though it were a whitebark he wanted to fell. The red lifestream started to flow, but Thann endured the pain. It didn't take him long to gnaw off his foot. Then, using his three remaining feet, he got himself to the water, and, although weak from the loss of so much of his lifestream, he had been able to swim back to his dwelling. When he felt well again, he abandoned the dwelling and traveled with his life-friend and kits until they came to other waters and started a new clan — our clan — the Clan of the Whitebark Waters.

What if Frell has a foot in a snapmouth! "Oh, please, Great Spirit of the earth and waters, let him be safe from the creatures of the forest and from the uprights. And please keep his feet from a snapmouth!"

I had never felt such fear and desperation. I swam harder, making powerful strokes with my hind paddling feet and moving the front holding feet in a circular pattern. I set my tail so that it would steer me toward the sound which had now become distinctively louder.

"Frell! I'm coming! Stay where you are," I called to the kit.

Ignoring the danger from longclaws and thin-legged bushytails, I went ashore and started through the underbrush, still following Frell's distress calls. I knew I was close now. I picked up his scent and followed it. It led me to a freshly felled young whitebark. The kit was pinned beneath it.

"Pruu! Help me! I can't get out!"

"Are you hurt?"

"I'm not sure. I just can't move."

I began to gnaw at the branches binding him. Working quickly, I soon had the larger limbs off so that Frell could now turn himself to help with the gnawing. Finally he was able to crawl out from under the whitebark.

"We've got to hurry back to the water edge, Frell," I told him, giving him a shove with a front foot, knowing that some longclaw or bushytail would be attracted by the distress calls and drawn by the prospect of a tender flattail for food. We moved as quietly and inconspicuously as possible back through the underbrush toward the water. Once we had reached the safety of the water, I turned to face the wayward kit.

"You are not yet ready to build on your own, Frell. You could have lost your life spirit when the whitebark fell. You must stay with Ghinn and me for another cold season. We have so much to teach you yet. Then you can leave us, find your life-friend and build a dwelling and perhaps even a waterblock. But for now, you must not leave our pond unless you are with Ghinn or me."

"Yes, Pruu. I understand. I'll do as you say."

The journey back to the dwelling was long and silent.

* * *

When she saw that I had not returned alone, Ghinn swam out to meet us.

"Frell! Where have you been? I thought you had been taken by a bushytail!"

The three of us dived toward one of the underwater tunnels.

"He won't wander off again," I told Ghinn as we surfaced, safe in the dwelling.

Ghinn came up to sniff me.

"Are you all right?" she asked.

"Yes, my friend," I assured her.

"While you were searching for Frell, the uprights went out in their water-skimmer but didn't stay for long. When they returned to their dwelling, in spite of my fear I swam up to roaring bird's flatlog perch and sounded a warning. I saw the female, and you're right. She is harmless and she does seem interested in flattails. In fact, she followed along the water edge as I swam to the dwelling. Look, here are some twigs I brought with me while she watched. You must be hungry."

The kitlings were already nibbling at the greens. As I gnawed on a small branch, I looked around the inner space of our dwelling. Frell had nestled up to Bloff and fallen asleep, exhausted from the fright he had endured. I turned to Ghinn.

"Frell thinks he is old enough to go out on his own," I explained. "Across the wide water, near the water-edge flatrock, he was able to fell a whitebark by himself, but he couldn't judge the direction of its fall. He was trapped in the branches."

I could see the fear in Ghinn's eyes.

"He may be injured!"

She went over to the sleeping kits and with her front holding feet began to examine Frell. For the first time I noticed the swollen feeders on her belly. I could hear the kitlings chewing at the food she had provided. I sniffed the aromas in the dwelling: each kit and kitling had its own distinctive smell, but more than these, I smelled Ghinn. I remembered our two seasons of dancing the coupling rite together. I thought of how she refused to let me enter the dwelling when each of the birthing times came. In my inner vision I could see her feeding the first two kitlings from her belly, and now these new ones who were just beginning to gnaw and chew. I felt the warmth of the dwelling penetrate my own lifestream and flow throughout my being.

This is good, I thought.

Satisfied that Frell was whole and unharmed, Ghinn returned to me.

"I don't think we need to fear for the kits or kitlings anymore for a while, Ghinn. Together we'll find some logs and branches to enlarge the dwelling. As you said, we need more space now that we have increased the clan."

* * *

The next few light cycles were busy ones. The roaring bird came and stayed through almost one whole light cycle. At each early light I swam past the roaring bird's flatlog perch to see the upright female. She was always there, waiting for me. I sensed that she wanted to see the dwelling and the little ones. I wondered why the uprights never went in the water themselves. They always got into water-skimmers. Perhaps they couldn't swim.

But even longclaws, bushytails, and the antlered ones swim — not under the water as we flattails do — but they can swim. No, the uprights cannot swim, I concluded.

Nor can they fly. That's why the roaring bird brings them and takes them away, just as the water-skimmers move them on the water.

I was beginning to understand more about the uprights.

They are very limited creatures, relying on noise, strings, and firesticks for food and protection. It is much better to be a flattail.

* * *

The enlargement of the dwelling was proceeding well, as Ghinn and I took advantage of the long light cycles to gnaw the logs and push them over the water. Even the kits joined in what they seemed to think was fun time, often hindering more than helping. Frell was happy to stay within the bounds of the dwelling pond and to help with the twig gathering. He and Bloff liked the mud application to the dwelling most of all. I knew it was mainly for the fur cleaning they received from Ghinn afterwards.

"They are old enough to clean themselves," I chided Ghinn.

"I know. But they don't clean themselves well enough to suit me," she offered in defense.

We were settling into our now more spacious dwelling as one light cycle was fading. Ghinn had allowed the kitlings to feed from her belly. She, Bloff, and the kitlings were already asleep. Only Frell and I remained awake, listening to the sounds of the approaching dark cycle. Frell's experience with the felled whitebark had stirred in him the beginning of the wisdom and ways of older flattails. He observed and imitated me constantly. Although he still occasionally frolicked with Bloff, he worked with me and kept watch with me, as he was doing now.

The night light appeared at the water edge then began its slow rise toward the dome of the sky. We could hear the sound of the water in soft wind riplets slapping ever so gently against the shore. A female paddler followed by her little ones swam by on the way to their nesting place near a water stream that flowed into the dwelling pond. I listened to their low cooing noises and the swish of their paddle feet as they passed.

There was a long period of silence. Suddenly we were all jolted awake by the snorting of a longclaw. Standing up on my swimming feet, I peered out the upper air-opening of the dwelling. A longclaw was making his way along the shore. He reached the channel and entered the water, swimming in the direction of the water-edge rock. I knew he was in search of swimmers' parts left by the uprights.

"Don't make a sound," I warned the clan in an almost imperceptible tone. "Longclaw is hungry, and the gray-and-white flyers and great whiteheads have devoured all the swimmers left on the rock. He'll be back."

The four of us gathered over the kitlings, pressing our bodies together. I could feel the kits trembling. Inwardly I was trembling, too. We waited in the darkness. We heard the longclaw emerge from the water and shake his head. We heard the cracking of twigs under his heavy feet, as he followed the shoreline toward our dwelling. We began to hear his breathing in short snorts, as he sniffed the air of the pond. His foot noises stopped, and I knew that he was standing on the shore nearest the dwelling. He could surely smell us inside. Longclaw stepped into the water. Another step. And another. More short snorts.

As in the earlier light cycle, I felt great fear and desperation. This time there was nothing I could do short of swimming out of one of the underwater tunnels and offering myself to the longclaw. But I waited. If he came any closer I would do it. The sound of a dwelling log being pushed aside into the water made me move without further thinking toward a tunnel opening, slide into the water and swim down the narrow tunnel to the bottom of the pond. I turned and let my body float, pushing upward with my back swimming feet.

"Great Spirit of the sky, the waters, and the forest creatures, here is my life spirit. Keep my clan of flattails safe without me," I spoke with my silent inner voice as I rose toward the surface.

My head came out of the water. I was ready for Longclaw. But Longclaw had decided otherwise. The large dark body was stepping back onto the shore. I quickly ducked under. When I came up again, Longclaw had waddled into the brush of the forest and was gone from sight, although his aroma was still strong.

I made the decision to wait in the water to see if this creature that could devour us all would return. Standing in the shore water, I waited. No sounds came from the bushes. No sounds came from the dwelling. I knew Ghinn and the young ones were terrified, but I had to be sure of their safety before going back in to them.

After a long while I swam up through the tunnel to the open space in the dwelling.

"Longclaw has gone back into the forest. We're safe now," I could at last announce.

"Come, sleep," Ghinn said.

Curling my body into a round, I nestled in among my clan and slept.

* * *

The great sky light had already ascended to the tops of the whitebarks when I awoke. I swam outside and found Ghinn, Bloff and Frell on the shore grooming themselves in the warm light. Ghinn slipped into the water and came to meet me.

"Stay with the kits while I feed the kitlings, Pruu," she said as she dived under.

The kits, freshly-oiled outer fur shining, began chasing each other in and out of the water. I examined the damage to the dwelling made by longclaw. It was worse than I had expected: several outer logs had been knocked away and lay on the shore, leaving only one set of smaller branches, mud, and twigs to protect the inner space.

"I must rebuild this before the next dark cycle," I decided, speaking to myself in an audible voice. "I'll need help from Ghinn and the kits. Longclaw may return. The damaged dwelling is no longer protection, not even from a small thin-legged bushytail."

Frell had come up beside me and heard the last part of my grim pronouncement.

"I will help rebuild the dwelling, Pruu, if you show me how. I'll do whatever you tell me."

"Good, Frell. We must work hard in order to finish before the dark cycle arrives and the longclaws begin their search for food. You can start by putting more mud on the exposed twigs and branches. Then together we'll replace the logs of the outer cover."

Frell was pleased to be my partner in this important project. He went under immediately and came up with his holding feet filled with mud. I swam around the dwelling to the shore and gathered the logs stripped away by the longclaw.

Repairs took all of us working together steadily throughout most of the light cycle, but when the work was completed, there was still enough light remaining for the kits to amuse themselves in mock fights. Ghinn went back in to the kitlings, while I rounded myself into my favorite hollow on the shore by the dwelling. In the distance I could hear the movement of an upright coming down the slope from their dwelling. It must be the female. She had doubtless looked for me at early light. When I glanced in the direction of the flatlog perch, I saw the water-skimmer, with one upright, quietly entering our dwelling pond. Yes, it was the female, and she was using large sticks to guide the water-skimmer toward our dwelling.

"She is coming to see our dwelling and our clan," I realized.

The kits, busy with their frolicking, had not noticed the silently approaching water-skimmer. The upright put the large sticks down in the water-skimmer, stood up on her back legs the way uprights usually move, and, directing her vision to the kits, brought a small dark object up to her eyes.

Before I could take a moment to ponder this object, both it and the upright went into the water. I knew immediately it was not a dive, and at the same time I remembered my earlier conclusion that uprights cannot swim.

Instinctively I went into the water. Swimming below the surface, out past the dwelling, I saw her at the pond bottom, rear legs bent. I sensed her fear and knew she was in danger.

She must push out with her back feet!

I swam toward her, and diving under her, I hit the folded part of her legs with my body, straightening them into a swimming position. Still she was not moving forward. I knew I had to act fast. I circled around and came back beneath her. With all my strength I pushed her up and out in the direction of the shore. Her long body was straight now, and the long front and back legs were making an effort to swim.

There! She has reached the shore mud.

I swam beside her, watching her use all four feet to come out of the water onto the earth. I came out as well, and stayed beside her, waiting to see if she still had her life spirit. I could see her sides moving in and out rapidly, so I knew that the air stream was still flowing inside her.

She hasn't lost her life spirit. But I'll wait here with her to be sure.

The kits had swum to the safety of the dwelling once they had become aware of the presence of the upright and her water-skimmer. The only sound was that of the air going in and out of the upright's motionless body.

Then I saw her eye coverings go up. She focused her vision on me, but she did not move. Nor did I. But I think I understood what her eyes spoke: "Thank you, my friend."

I answered with my inner voice: "Yes, my friend."

She resumed her upright position, and I instinctively moved away and slid back into and under the water. When I came up in the deep water of the pond, she had reached the flat rocks about halfway between the uprights' dwelling and ours. Her movements were still unsteady, but she made her way to the nest.

She will be all right now. She's young and strong.

Thus assured, I swam down to a tunnel entrance.

I'm glad that she didn't lose her life spirit. And I'm glad that I could help her.

As I swam up toward the inner space of the dwelling where my clan waited, a strange and terrible sadness filled my inner being. Somehow I knew it was *her* sadness I was feeling, not a sadness of this season, but a deep one of a season to come.

Chapter 5: The Year of the Moose

Karen

"Welcome aboard Air America's flight 1216 non-stop to Minneapolis-Saint Paul. At this time we would like to acquaint you with the safety features of the aircraft."

The flight attendants had begun their routine. The clicking shut of seat belt fasteners, the whir and thunder of starting turbine engines, and the smell of jet fuel signaled the beginning of our annual pilgrimage to Poplar River. The two commercial flights from Columbia-to-Minneapolis-to-Winnipeg were dual portals to the wilderness world that had become a part of me, and of which I could become a part, even if for only one magical week of the year.

Secured in a window seat, I reached over to give Steve's arm an excited squeeze but discovered that he had dozed off while we taxied to the runway. Through the plane window I watched the airport out-buildings speed past and become smaller and smaller as we gained momentum and rose into the air. I realized how quickly the year had gone by. Steve had worked incessantly. He volunteered to teach overloads, presented several professional conference papers, and generously gave of his time to students needing help. But his most intense effort went to the Ladies of the Lake. Evenings of research in the library and, when it closed, hours of writing at the computer in his office left him precious little time to spare. And that was devoted to Meredith.

My life had been just as demanding, if not more so. Each day began early, with six hours of practicing the piano. Then, lunch and a little play time with Meredith, piano students in the afternoon, weekend church organist obligations, and a weekly extensive coaching session with Lavinsky on Fridays filled my days, and time flew by. I don't even remember much about Christmas festivities, which had to be kept to a minimum this year.

Our house by the lake was due for completion in April, but John Roberts had to take a back seat to Josef Hofmann.

"Honey, you've got to get some rest. You and Steve had better slow down," Mama worried. Mama always worried.

"Karen's young and strong, she'll make it all right, Mary," Daddy reassured her. "I'm glad you're performing again, Baby Girl. I hated to see you using your talent only on the church organ. You're going to make us proud, no matter how the competition turns out," he reassured me. Always the positive thinker.

At the Winnipeg airport Steve waited with the carry-ons while I perused the airport bookshop and made a purchase: *Manitoba's Wildlife*: *Principle Flora and Fauna of the Province* by Chester Wilkins. On the front cover was a photograph of a bald eagle pulling a fish out of a sparkling lake set amid quaking aspen poplars and white spruce. How could I resist? Standing in the shop I quickly flipped through the pages. There were internal color shots of beavers, snowshoe rabbits, martens, moose, and, my nemesis, black bears. I recognized some of the vegetation depicted, but knew very few of the names.

"Look what I found, Steve! This will be our field guide. We'll take it in the boat with us along with the binoculars."

"Yes, *bwana*." Steve gave my pony tail a little tug before picking up the reel case and my carryall. "Now can we go get our luggage and find Fred?"

Fred Eaton, a friend of Bobby's who lived in Winnipeg, operated a van shuttle from the Winnipeg airport and various hotels to the float plane bases at North Falls about an hour's drive north of the city. The area consisted of a few small houses, a service station, a 1950's-style motel where we spent the night, and a grocery store that catered to outpost fishermen. We had mailed our grocery order to the store well in advance so the food would be packed and waiting for us the next morning on the dock. Bobby's base camp was a little five-room bungalow that doubled as his office and home. An arm of the Red River branched out practically at his back door.

"All he has to do is go out the door, walk over a few yards to the water, get into his plane, and take off. Just like we do when we go to the apartment parking lot and get into our cars at home," Steve said as we stood in the yard about 5:30 a.m. watching Bobby and a newly hired pilot named Paul Guilford load the floatplane.

"Guess I'd better give them a hand." He sauntered off toward the two men on the dock.

I, too, wanted to make myself useful, but, not knowing what to do, I sat down on the back steps, took the Wilkins' wildlife book out of the carryall, and read at random:

> Moose. *Alces alces*. Largest of Manitoba's mammals. Males can weigh as much as 700 kg, females are smaller. . . . Only the males have antlers which they grow during the spring and shed

after the fall rutting. The male will leave the female after mating. The female usually has one calf in the late spring, although twins are not uncommon. The care of young calves is solely the responsibility of the mother.

Wonder why we've never seen a moose at the outpost?

Moose are solitary animals and usually avoid any contact with human beings. They are normally very gentle. However, a mother with her calf or a male during the rutting season can be quite aggressive. Males have been known to charge at cars and trucks on the highway. To be safe, keep a respectful distance from all moose.

"Would 'KK,' the Princess of the Piano, care to come aboard?" Bobby stood in front of me with a hand extended to help me up. "Paul's going to fly you up to Poplar River this morning, but I'll come up for the mid-week check."

"I don't know if I can fly with anyone other than the Captain of the Clouds," I continued the alliteration game. "I guess Paul goes to Poplar while Bobby goes Back to Bed."

"No, Bobby is going to Baldwin. Seriously, I've been offered a pretty good deal to take over the management of Baldwin Lake Lodge about 50 air miles north of Poplar. At least it's worth looking into."

I climbed up the familiar rungs of the floatplane's struts and slid into the tiny back seat. Then Paul got in and took the controls.

"Hand this to Karen," Bobby said, passing my carryall containing the camera and wildlife book to Paul. He slammed the door tightly shut.

"Are we all ready? Seat belts on?" Paul checked. The new pilot was the silent type, and no further words were spoken during the forty-five minute flight.

The boreal forest land below me was dotted with a seemingly infinite variety of lakes like pieces of an enormous jigsaw puzzle spread out on a cloth woven of different shades of green, brown, white and gray, each piece taking on the shape of my imagination: a snail with its head thrust out of a round carapace, complete with antennae formed by two streams, a slender mink with tail curving around short paws, a human-like footprint as if some giant of heaven had once stepped upon the earth. The magnitude of it all so permeated my being that I ceased to be a wife, a mother, a musician, or even a person with a name, a separate entity. Individuality fused with the whole of creation, the same way it is absorbed in the performance of great music.

* * *

Lavinsky was the only person I wanted backstage with me. Not Mama or Daddy or Steve or Katherine or Ellen. I needed the presence of someone who understood the agony of pre-performance nerves, and, more precisely, the frightening self-doubt and the desperate search for self-confidence that beset the psyche of the player waiting her turn to walk out to the piano, sit down and compete. One of the finalists, a classmate of mine at Julliard, had completed her doctoral degree there and had already won a competition in her native Japan. I knew she was good. What I had heard of the others when I passed by the practice rooms made me wonder how I ever reached the finals. How could my little Schumann Concerto hold a candle to the powerful Brahms First Concerto the audience had just heard the Russian fellow perform, even if I played it to perfection? What was I, a South Carolinian, doing in a competition with three Asian women and a Russian guy?

"Our third finalist is a native of our own great state. Please welcome to the Josef Hofmann Piano Competition, from Spring Hill, South Carolina, Karen Kingsley!" The emcee walked off stage and motioned for me to walk on. Lavinsky followed me, placed the orchestral reduction score on the second piano, and sat while I took the initial bow.

"The opening chords can make or break this work, Karen," Lavinsky had warned me. "There is no orchestra or second piano behind you. It is like an opening cadenza — your debut solo. It has to be grand, dazzling, and under complete, authoritative control."

I sat down, adjusted the stool, discretely placed a handkerchief inside the piano under the fully open lid, and glanced away from the audience at Lavinsky on my left. He was ready. His words of admonition repeated rapid-fire in my mind. I closed my eyes and shut out all thought, then placed my hands on the keyboard and played the opening chords.

* * *

It was raining when we landed at Poplar River, a light but chilly drizzle. We had to work quickly and efficiently in the transfer of supplies from the plane to the cabin. While Steve helped Paul get the floatplane off, I located some dry wood under the cabin and brought an armload inside. I emptied a small box of groceries and tore the cardboard into strips to use as kindling, the way Steve always did. By the time he came in I had the beginnings of a nice fire in the little iron woodstove in the central room of the cabin.

"Great idea," he said, rubbing his hands together then holding them out toward the fire. "Where'd you find the dry wood?"

"Under the cabin, at the back. There's lots of it."

"I'd better get some more. Looks like the rain is really moving in."

"I'll help." I slipped my windbreaker back on, showed Steve where I had found the wood, and each of us gathered up an armload which we piled on the floor by the iron stove. Then Steve decided that we should move the couch from the porch into the cabin and position it in front of the fire. It wasn't easy, but we lifted, pulled and pushed it in.

"Looks like no fishing for a while, KK. What in the world shall we do for entertainment?"

Evidently making love on arrival at the outpost had now become a family tradition.

"I brought a deck of cards," I suggested with an innocent-as-a-dove look.

"I'm so glad," he whispered as he ushered me to the couch.

There was always more abandon in our love-making in the wilderness, as if that was our purpose on earth, our one responsibility to which we were to give ourselves without reservation, with no distracting worries in the back of our minds that at home we reluctantly put on hold for a few minutes and resumed afterwards with a sigh of relief. Here in the rain or sun or snow of the remote Canadian wilderness there was no piano or organ, no students, and no Ladies of the Lake — Steve had learned that lesson last year.

"This time, KK, it's just going to be food, fishing, and fooling around" was the way Steve had put it one day last February when he came home with *Cabela's Spring Fishing Catalog.*

"No Ladies of the Lake?"

"Only one: the lady who fell in the lake," he answered smugly, sat down at the kitchen table, and opened the catalog.

* * *

In an unexpected reversal of roles, Steve got up before I did and made the coffee. The early morning was misty and calm. The kind of morning I loved best at Poplar River. We had not been fishing long when the walleye started to hit our yellow split-tail lure. Steve caught two in rapid succession, then I caught one, took it off the hook and asked Steve,

"Shall we put it on the stringer?"

"If you are willing to fry fish tonight, then hand it back and catch a couple more."

Yes, I did want to fry fish tonight. In fact, I had been waiting all year to do so. These delicate golden fish were unknown in South Carolina where catfish was the king "fin" and, more often than not, the only seafood item on the menu in most of the local restaurants of Spring Hill.

"I wish I knew how to cut out the butterflies like Bobby did last year," I whined to Steve. "I'll get him to show me how when he comes."

"Cut out butterflies?"

"Yes, I can't remember whether they come from the top or the bottom of the fish, but they are so cute — and delicious."

The wind picked up, but we continued to fish. Steve killed the motor and let the wind do the driving. The choppy water created a rocking action of the boat that actually made it easier to jig. We simply held our rods steady and let the boat move them up and down. The walleye seemed to like that kind of motion, for we began catching them simultaneously in rapid succession until they shut down.

"I guess they eventually get spooked," Steve surmised, "but it was sure fun while it lasted."

I had never seen Steve in such a vivacious mood. He was funny, even silly, and more loquacious than I had ever known him to be. He even attempted to cut butterflies when we filleted the fish.

We put the fillets in the refrigerator and made ham and cheese sandwiches for lunch. Steve cut a happy face in a slice of cheese which he deposited on top of my sandwich. I wanted to keep that piece of cheese like a souvenir and guard the moment forever.

Fishing was slower that afternoon — a few northern caught trolling with Mepps spinners, but the walleye dinner was divine. Bobby had stuck a jar of his homemade tartar sauce in with our groceries, and I fried the potatoes, onions, and mushrooms the way he did last year. Steve ate heartily.

"You're getting to be a pretty good camp cook. I love the butterflies," he said, picking up one of our pitiful attempts from the plate of fried fish on the table.

As usual, we sat on the porch after dinner.

"Have you noticed that I haven't mentioned my book even once since we've been here?"

"Believe me, I have. You've certainly kept your promise. But I wish you would tell me a little something about it. I don't like being in the dark."

"It's off to a great start. But it's going to require tons of work. I hope you have lots of patience!"

"I do — for some things . . . but not for others," I said, pulling at the waist of his jeans. He got my not-so-subtle hint.

* * *

Thursday, the day after Bobby's midweek visit, I decided to check on the beaver. So at dawn, with a mug of hot coffee in one hand and Wilkins'

Wildlife in the other, I went down the slope to the dock. We had spotted one bald eagle on the nest and another soaring high above it, but I had not yet seen the beaver again. I sat cross-legged on the dock.

"Why didn't I think to bring something soft to sit on?" I chided myself.

I could hear a few Boreal Chickadees softly flitting about in the young poplars and pines around the cabin, otherwise there was neither sound nor movement. I closed my eyes for a few moments, absorbing the stillness. Then I turned my attention to Wilkins:

The calves stay under the protection of their mothers for the first year After that, when a new calf is born, the mother will chase the yearling away The yearling will make numerous efforts to remain with the cow, but afte repeated rejections, it will finally go its way alone.

Something was moving in the water near the peninsula opposite the cabin. Thinking I was about to renew my acquaintance with my beaver friend, I sat up straight and inched forward almost to the edge of the dock. I felt my heart pick up the pace. The animal was heading straight toward me.

"It must be the beaver," I said audibly. The color was right, the direction it was swimming was right, but the shape in the water was wrong. The head was too big, the speed too fast.

"There's another one swimming behind it!"

The two animals were headed toward the shore a little to the right of the dock. I froze as a large horse-like creature emerged from the water. Then a second much smaller one came ashore. I was looking at a moose cow and her calf.

The two disappeared into the brush without a sound.

For two or three minutes I could not stop my body from trembling. I was barely breathing. I had no idea moose could swim. And how could such a large animal move through the bushes without making any noise? How bizarre that these moose should appear just as I was reading about them, and precisely about cows and calves.

When my astonishment had somewhat abated and I was convinced that mother and child were not going to reappear, I grabbed cup and book and hurried back to the cabin to wake Steve and tell him what I had witnessed.

* * *

The Schumann Concerto took about one-half hour to play. After the first movement I remember picking up the handkerchief, wiping my palms, and putting it back. I did not want to take much time between movements lest I lose the transcendent state of mind I had reached in the first movement. I nodded to Lavinsky that I was ready, and we began the delicately playful intermezzo of the second movement. There was no pause between the second and third movements, and I liked the fact that the concerto, which had started in A minor, ended with a series of triumphant chords and arpeggios in A major. Sadness into joy, darkness into light.

Lavinsky, normally reserved with his emotions and sparing with his compliments, was beside himself. The minute we came offstage he threw his arms around me, kissed me heartily on the cheek, then stepped back, held me by the hands and said:

"Great! Karen, you were great!" He made no effort to contain his pleasure and excitement over the performance.

"Now, go back out there and let the audience recognize you."

I went out for three curtain calls. After the third bow I found Mama, Daddy, Steve, Ellen, Katherine, and Ted waiting in the green room. Even Dr. Johnson had driven over for the competition, as had Matt Cory from Converse. When all the hugs and complimentary remarks had been extended, I told Steve that I wanted to go out and sit with the family to hear the last two competitors. As I turned to exit the green room I had quite a surprise.

"Bobby! My gracious, I never thought you would be here."

"You know I wouldn't have missed this for anything, Karen. You were sensational." He gave me an awkward hug.

"Well, I hardly recognize you in a suit and tie."

"He had to borrow one of mine," Steve chimed in. "Looks pretty good, even though the shoulders are a little too broad for him." Steve couldn't resist starting a little light-hearted verbal war, but Bobby let it pass.

A section of orchestra seats had been reserved for friends and family of the contestants, and the Kingsley-Marsten clan took up most of them. The other two players were quite good. I thought my friend from Julliard played the Mozart K. 488 exceptionally well, and, despite a memory slip in the Prokofieff Third, the performance of the final contestant was also commendable. But I already knew that the Russian who played the Brahms First was by far the winner, then probably the Julliard girl. Maybe I would have a chance at third place. But I hadn't heard the performance of the first contestant.

The evening that had begun at 7:30 was to be a long one: five major concertos with fifteen-minute intermissions between each one, then the judges' deliberation which could take forever. The Aiken Women's Club had set up a large spread of finger food in the lobby for the crowd to enjoy while waiting. People nibbled on fruit, cheeses, brownies and cookies, exchanged their opinions on the performances, and told each other what they thought the outcome would be. I had no appetite for the food or the chatter, but I was pleased to have so many positive reactions to my playing. It was after midnight when blinking lobby lights signaled the audience to return to their seats. The emcee stepped to the microphone.

"Ladies and Gentlemen, may I have your attention, please. The judges have made their decision."

* * *

Friday was our last full day at the outpost, since Bobby always picked us up early on Saturday morning. "The week always goes by too fast," I said to Steve as we put our fishing rods in the boat. "I wish we had another week or even a month to spend here."

"We'd have to eat fish every day, and you'd have to cook it," Steve said.

"If I can learn to catch 'em, you can learn to cook 'em."

"You're right, my beauty. Maybe next year."

"The weather is so perfect, could we just drift fish for a while?" I asked, once we motored out a ways.

"Tell you what. I'll put us in the middle of the water and we'll see where it takes us."

The wind was from the west and took us east, of course, around the cabin's promontory.

"Look, Stevie. There's a little bay beyond those rocks that we've never fished. Let's try it. I'll help paddle around behind the rocks."

With both of us paddling, we found the bay to be longer and wider than it appeared at first.

"The fish-finder shows fish in here," Steve said, after a glance at the new gadget he had ordered from Cabela's.

"Well, it's right, 'cause I've got one on my line right now."

The day was warm with a light breeze. Steve put his rod down and leaned back in his seat with his feet propped on the edge of the boat. I was at my usual place in the prow seat, dead serious about fishing.

"Wouldn't it be perfect if we could see another moose? A male, with antlers," I said after a while.

We drifted in silence. Then Steve slowly brought his feet down and leaned forward.

"KK, what's that up on the ridge in the trees?" he whispered.

I scanned the ridge but saw nothing.

"More toward the rocks," he said. I followed his gaze.

Then I saw it, too. The animal's head was lowered as if he were eating. He lifted it, displaying his already well-formed rack. The binoculars were in the boat. I took them cautiously from the case. I had only a few seconds to focus on him, but it was long enough for me to see the moss-like covering of his antlers, the long bell of skin and fur hanging from his chin, and his short, stubby tail. He stopped chewing and held the pose for an instant before disappearing down the other side of the ridge.

"I can't believe it. I spoke the words and he appeared."

"It is uncanny. Like the cow and calf you saw at the first of the week."

"He probably won't come back out, will he?

"I doubt it. He heard us, smelled us, and saw us. That should be enough to scare off even a bull moose, which I think he probably is. He had a nice rack."

We had drifted all the way to back of the bay up against the shore.

"Take a paddle and push us back out, KK."

I did, reluctantly. Steve gave a couple of pulls on the starter cord, got the motor going again, and we headed out of the bay.

* * *

"Before I announce the various winners and prizes, I would like to bring all the contestants onstage."

The five of us went out in the order we had played.

"We want to express appreciation to all of you. All the performances were outstanding. And I speak for the Aiken Chamber of Commerce, the Aiken Women's Club, and the Josef Hofmann Foundation: thank you for giving us the privilege of hearing you."

The applause was long and hardy and gave the emcee the chance to pull a slip of paper from his pocket.

"When I call your name, please come forward to receive your prize from Karl Skabicki, President of the Josef Hofmann Foundation."

A tall, slender, stoop-shouldered man took his place beside the emcee.

"Fifth prize of one thousand dollars: Jin Lee!"

The Chinese girl who had played the Prokofieff stepped forward to receive an envelope.

"At least I didn't finish last," I thought with a sigh of relief.

* * *

"You know, Stevie, we haven't had a single peanut butter and jelly sandwich this trip."

We had come in from our morning of fishing and moose-spotting ravenous as wolves.

"Well, that situation can easily be remedied," Steve said, swiping the jar of Squirrel Peanut Butter off of the grocery shelf and setting it in front of me.

"The big question is, who gets the nut?" I wanted to know. The Squirrel brand always had a whole peanut kernel sitting on top of the peanut puree, something I had never seen in any American peanut butter. The first year I had given the nut to Steve, but on our next trip he insisted that I eat it, and now it was a toss-up.

"We'll split it," he said with his mischievous-little-boy look that I had come to adore. However, it was a rare occasion when he let me see it.

Steve took a knife, the cabin's well-worn cutting board, and proceeded to saw on the tiny nut which popped out and rolled all the way across the cabin into the bedroom.

"I think Mickey Mouse gets it this year," Steve said, as he went off in search of the obstinate peanut.

I opened a bag of potato chips, and we gobbled our lunch like two true woodsmen.

"Let's take a short nap, KK. What do you think?"

I knew what that meant.

"I'd like to counter-propose a long, hot shower instead," I said with a sensual tone that I would never use at home. Here in the wilderness I was another me.

The cabin's butane water-heater provided hot water to the kitchen sink, the washroom basin, and tiny shower cabinet. It was close quarters for two people, but we managed.

Steve's upbeat mood had lasted all week — no periods of fading into his own distant world of despondent romanticism, no afternoons when he preferred to sit in the cabin and read, no attitude of being in the wilderness just to indulge my whim. He seemed to be really enjoying himself — "the food, the fishing, and the fooling around." He even seemed to get excited about the moose.

"I wish I had seen the cow and calf yesterday," he admitted during our après-sex afternoon fishing outing.

"Well, you did spot the bull moose this morning," I said. "Something I probably would have missed otherwise. I'm always so busy fishing."

"But you're quite a fisherman, KK. I'm afraid you can out-fish me."

"That's because you're always driving the boat. You never give me a chance at it."

"Okay. I promise: next year you can do the driving. But for right now, put a big red-eye on your line and let's see if we can find you another trophy."

We fished downstream past the west channel to a wide area with which we were unfamiliar. In one small bay we had luck with a few northern, but nothing spectacular. For a while we just sat in silence as we drifted wherever the boat wanted to take us. We heard sounds from the forest we could not identify, but that was okay. Steve's next words that afternoon, the calm water, the softness of the forest murmurings have become etched in my memory, a petroglyph defying the passage of time:

"KK, if you never hear me say it again, I want you to know that you are the love of my life."

"More than any of the Ladies of the Lake?" I regretted my superficial answer as soon as I had spoken the words. But I did not know what else to say. His joyous spirits over the past week had been most welcome but totally unexpected. I worried that I might do or say something to change his frame of mind. How many times I have wished that I had answered something more appropriate, more loving, more sincere — something more profound.

* * *

"The fourth-place prize of five thousand dollars goes to Yumiko Ikeda." My Japanese colleague from Julliard stepped forward.

"And in third place . . ."

I was ready to receive my prize.

"Jung Joo Woong."

The Korean contestant, whose performance I had not heard, took her envelope.

I could not believe it. I had actually come in second. Lavinsky must be ecstatic.

"Now, ladies and gentlemen, before I announce the next prizes, I have been asked to explain that the judges' decision in this case is unique in the history of the Josef Hofmann Piano Competition. However, the judges, the competition committee, and the president of the Josef Hofmann Foundation, after some debate, have concurred on the following."

I turned slightly to look at the Russian, but he kept his gaze straight in front of him, and from what I could tell his expression was impassive.

He knows he has won, I thought. *He knows I'm not on his level.*

"There is no second place winner. The judges have awarded two first places to Karen Kingsley and Dimitri Adanov."

There was enthusiastic applause, then photographic flashes, envelopes, hand shaking, hugs, and what seemed to me general mayhem before the emcee managed to quiet the audience.

"The prize money of both first and second place will be divided equally between Ms. Kingsley and Mr. Adanov. Ms. Kingsley will play her concerto with the South Carolina Symphony Orchestra, and Mr. Adamov will play a solo recital at the Polish Embassy in Washington. The members of the Hofmann Committee thank all of you for your patience and support, and we bid you a very good night. Until next year."

* * *

Bobby had asked us to have all our gear packed up and on the dock ready to load by 5:30 a.m. Saturday. We packed everything we could Friday night, broke down the rods, put all the reels in the reel case, and got our traveling clothes ready to jump into. All we had to do was dress, roll up the sleeping bags, and stow all our toiletries in my carry-all bag that doubled as a purse. We awoke early, decided to forego our coffee routine, and had everything on the dock by 5:00. I took a broom and started sweeping the cabin floor.

"Here," Steve said, taking the broom handle from me, "let me do that. You go on down to the dock to listen for the plane. Maybe your beaver buddy will come to say goodbye."

"Thanks, Steve," I said. Slipping the binoculars around my neck, I hurried down the slope. Instead of going onto the dock, I carefully walked along the flat rock outcropping from where I could see the beaver lodge. I located it through the twin lenses. No visible activity. Then I began scanning the shoreline behind it. I spotted a few of their scented mud hills then panned toward the little inlet that fed into the pond area. What came into view so startled me that I almost did a repeat performance of last year's dunk into the water. I let the binoculars fall back onto my chest. The little moose was standing in the stream looking directly at me. It was not big enough to be the cow, and it was definitely not the bull. The calf alone? I swung the binoculars up again. No, it was too big. It stood perfectly still in the shallow water of the streamlet, staring in my direction. I had the distinct feeling the little animal was trying to figure me out, or tell me something, or ask me something. I wanted to call it to me, but I knew if I made any noise it would dart away into the brush. During those few seconds with our gazes locked I remembered Wilkins' words: "The yearling will make numerous efforts to remain with the cow, but after repeated rejections, it will finally go its way alone." I was looking into the pleading eyes of a rejected yearling.

The screened door of the cabin slammed as Steve came out with the sleeping bags, and the yearling instantly disappeared into the thick brush.

"Any sign of the plane, KK?" Steve asked, setting the bags down.

"Nothing yet."

"How about the beaver?"

"Ditto for the beaver."

I didn't want to mention the little yearling to Steve. How could I explain to him what I had felt and understood about the creature? After the eagle and the beaver connections, it would really be stretching things to expect him to accept this incident. So I kept it to myself. I would tell Bobby when I got the chance. I joined Steve on the dock.

It was Paul who flew the Cessna in to pick us up, and the three of us began loading the floatplane.

"Bobby's back up at Baldwin. Looks like this lodge deal is gonna go through. You guys been up there yet?" Paul asked as he angled the rod case into the rear of the plane.

"Not yet. Really haven't talked much about it with Bobby," Steve answered.

"I went up with him last week. It's real nice. First class. With a dining room and guides and all. I bet your wife would sure like it." He had switched me out of the conversation and into the third person and was obviously speaking only to Steve, as these guys often do. A female in a remote fishing outpost was a rarity that some men didn't know how to handle. It probably made them feel self-conscious, perhaps because they thought they had to watch their language and weren't free to urinate anytime, anywhere. But they seemed to appreciate a wilderness woman, and I rather liked being that rarity.

We taxied to the east end of the lake and took off close over the cabin. I pressed my forehead against the window trying to get a last glimpse of the beaver pond and the yearling. As we flew over it, I had the distinct feeling that I was leaving a child behind.

* * *

"First things first, KK," Ellen said as she stripped off the top of a packet of Sweet'n'Low and poured it into her cappuccino. "What dress are you wearing to play in?"

"Dress? For heaven's sake, Ellen, I'm so nervous about the performance and so desperate for practice time, I can't even think about what I'll wear. Besides I don't want to practice. Ellen, I don't even want to play with the orchestra, that's not what I want to do with my life. Otherwise I would have stayed at Julliard. I like playing the piano, but for the music, not for the glory and praise."

We were sitting at our favorite table in The Coffee Bean, Spring Hill's only gourmet coffee shop. With my obligations to the church, my piano students, Meredith, and Steve, and Ellen's duties and odd hours as head reference librarian at Heyward, the two of us had little time to pal around anymore. An occasional coffee together and a more-or-less weekly phone conversation had replaced our regular shopping sprees and girls-night-outs.

"You know, we're moving into the new house next week," I went on, "and since we got back from Canada I've done nothing but pack box after box. I had no idea Steve and I had accumulated so much stuff. I think I could fill a truck with nothing but Meredith's clothes and toys! I wish Lavinsky had never sent that tape in."

"Be that as it may," Ellen dictated, "you have to go through with this performance — for the music, and you and I are going to Columbia next Saturday to find you the perfect evening gown. So put that down in bold letters on your calendar."

"I'll try, Ellen," I said with a sigh, genuinely hoping that it would all work out.

"There's a great little shop called *Chicki's* that carries gowns to die for. It's *the* place to get formals."

I smiled at Ellen. My friend ever faithful since the first grade. No conditions, no complaints, no jealousy. A true friend through the years.

"Do me a favor, KK. Between now and Saturday, would you think about what it is you *do* want to do with your life? I'd like to know."

After making a firm commitment to the Saturday shopping trip, I left the coffee shop, drove to the apartment complex, and stopped at the mailbox. The usual ads and bills and an unexpected letter from the Josef Hoffmann Foundation. What if the judges have changed their minds and altered their decision? With a mixture of dread, hope, and anxiety I tore open the envelope.

Dear Ms Kingsley,

Plans for your appearance with the South Carolina Symphony Orchestra have been finalized. You will perform the Schumann Concerto with the orchestra at their opening concert September 23rd in the Coggins Art Center. As you know, this program is being made possible by funds from the Josef Hoffmann Foundation and by a matching grant from the South Carolina Arts Commission.

The conductor, Maestro Tomaso Montero, will contact you to set up a rehearsal schedule.

You will be pleased to learn that a block of tickets has been purchased and set aside for the residents of the State of South Carolina Home for Adolescents as a gift to the community by the Columbia Chapter of the Loyal Order of Moose of South Carolina.

We are very proud to sponsor you, and we look forward to your performance.

Very Truly Yours,

Lucas T. Whisnant, Chairman
The Josef Hoffman Foundation

Chapter 6: The Year of the Moose

The Tova

"I don't understand, Noda. Why won't you pay attention to me anymore? Why don't you lick me, or nuzzle me, or call me to follow you?"

She didn't respond, but continued to lick the face of the cuva, the new little hooved-one.

"Can't you hear me calling to you? Don't you know I'm hungry?"

The cuva wobbled up into a standing position, nuzzled Noda's belly until she found the milk spout, and began to feed.

I moved closer, and as I did, Noda raised her head high, widened her eyes, and gave me a frightening glare.

"Stay away," she said with a shrill tone that made me trot back to the edge of the birth clearing.

"Noda," I whimpered.

Again she glared.

I turned and began munching the tender greens of some brush food. Of all things, I did not want Noda to be angry with me. But what had I done to displease her? Ever since the arrival of the cuva she had changed. I thought at first she was too busy teaching the cuva to stand, walk, find food, and swim — things she had taught me long ago in the last warm season. She warned me about the soft white water that floated down from the sky at the beginning of the cold season and showed me how to walk with care through it and how to find the edible stalks and stems beneath it. She taught me to identify all the smells and sounds of the forest. I closed my eyes and recalled the smell and warmth of her underbelly where I had been cuddled between her front and back legs during the coldest dark cycles. We had always been together.

When I opened my eyes, Noda and the cuva were moving away, headed in the direction of the flattail pond.

Noda is going to teach the cuva how to find the edible plants on the water bottom.

I followed them at a distance that would not provoke Noda's glare.

It was a short downwind walk to the streamlet that led to the pond. I knew to move quietly, listening for the crushing sound of a longclaw and sniffing constantly for his pungent aroma. From time to time Noda glanced around to see me following. Her eyes were not kind.

When they reached the flattail pond, I hid myself in the thick brush and watched them dip their heads underwater. Sounds came from the uprights' nest, and Noda and the cuva moved back into the brush covering, then went farther out onto the peninsula. I remained in my hiding place.

An upright came down to the roaring bird's landing perch, folded its legs beneath it, and sat motionless.

"The uprights who come with water-skimmers, sticks, and strings are not to be feared," Noda had explained to me. "But always keep far away from the ones who carry loud firesticks. They come to kill longclaws and kodas, especially the big kodas with large headbones. Very soon you'll become a tova with little knobs on your head, then a koda with your own headbones. And they'll seek to kill you, too."

I studied the upright on the landing perch.

She is a noda, I know she is. And I watched her. She seemed to be searching the pond with her long and short vision, but she sat perfectly still.

After a while Noda and the cuva reappeared at the water edge across from the uprights' nest. Noda entered the water, and the cuva followed.

Is Noda showing the cuva how to swim? Or are they swimming away from a longclaw?

They seemed to be headed toward the upright. They came ashore close to the landing perch and disappeared into the brush. The upright noda remained still.

Keeping myself hidden, I moved in the opposite direction, past the flattail nest, toward the upright noda.

She'll help me if a longclaw comes.

I stopped at a safe distance, listened and smelled for Longclaw, but there was no sign that he was anywhere around. The forest became still. The upright noda unfolded her legs and stood.

How amazing that she can stand on only two legs!

I had once seen Noda do that when another noda came into our territory looking for a koda. Noda glared with anger, raised the hair on the back of her neck, stood on her back legs, and kicked hard with the front ones until the invading noda retreated into the brush. Although her anger had surprised me, I was proud of Noda.

The upright moved quickly up the slope to the nest and went inside.

I went closer to the nest to sniff her aroma.

Yes, she's definitely a noda, I confirmed, *and she's inside the nest with her upright koda.*

The first and only time I ever saw my koda, he had come looking for Noda just before the white skywater floated down. When I heard the sound of his headbones pounding the brush, I was frightened and ran to Noda, but she told me to stay back. Then the great koda emerged from the bush, his mighty headbones lowered and his ears back. He made strange sounds that seemed to please Noda. He stamped his hooves hard on the earth, forming a little pit. Then he squatted, filled the pit with his body water, and bathed himself in its mud. When he moved away, Noda went to the pit and bathed herself in it, too. I watched Koda put his head on Noda's hind parts. She moved around slowly, and Koda stayed behind her, his head still lying on her rump. After a while Koda stood on his back legs at Noda's rear. She began making low noises, saying things I couldn't understand. As scared as I was, I didn't run away. I had to learn.

I dared not stay long near the uprights' nest lest the ones with firesticks come out or Longclaw surprise me from behind. I made my way back past the flattail nest and into the streamlet. I was hungry. After sniffing again for Longclaw, I ducked my head under to graze on some water plants and found some of my favorite greens, soft and tender. I lifted my head and chewed for a while. When I went to duck under a second time, something about my image on the water surface startled me.

What is that?

I leaned closer. There were two little knobs above my eyes.

My headbones! My headbones are forming! Just like Noda said they would. I'm becoming a koda. I must run to tell Noda. And show her the knobs.

I ran as fast as I could back to the birth clearing, knowing that Noda and the cuva would have circled behind the uprights' nest and would be there by now. And they were. But when I ran toward Noda, she reared and kicked at me. I barely had time to escape the blow of her hooves. Her eyes were fiercer than ever.

"Noda!" I screamed. "Why? Why are you trying to hurt me? You're my noda!"

The cuva, who had been lying on the pressed grasses turned her head slowly and spoke to me for the first and last time.

"No. Not *your* noda. *My* noda now."

I don't think the uprights' firesticks or longclaw's blows could hurt me as much as the cuva's words. I could not speak. I could not move.

"You must go," Noda said. "You must leave us. You are a tova."

She was calm now, but her eyes were compelling.

I turned around and left the birth clearing, not knowing where to go or what to do. I went back to the streamlet and tried to eat more of the greens, but I could not. Lifting my face from the stream, I closed my eyes. The ancient voices of the poplars repeated in sibilant whispers, "She is no longer yours!" Dropping my eyes to the water, I peered at my reflection and hated the knobs on my head.

A tova. What is a tova? A nothing. Not a koda yet, no longer a cuva, and certainly not a noda. A nothing, a nobody.

Strange sensations formed in my inner being.

"I hate the cuva! I hate Noda! She probably said the same thing to Koda, and that's why he didn't stay with us through the cold season. That's why he is not here now. I'll go and find him. He'll take care of me."

That notion brought me back to right thinking. I had seen Koda only once, and he frightened me. The way he tossed his huge headbones from side to side, the way he widened his eyes, stamped the ground, reared up behind Noda and put his hooves on her back, I thought he was going to kill her and probably me, too. I was scared to go near him. A koda could never be a noda. I knew that.

I needed to rest, so I folded my legs and lay down on the mossy grass still damp from the melted white water. In my inner vision I kept seeing Noda's threatening glare and hearing the cuva's words. I could not silence the inner voices.

I wonder if I will grow headbones as big as Koda's? Will I stamp the ground, too? And cover myself with body water? Then maybe Noda will want me instead of the cuva.

At once I knew what I had to do.

I must grow into a koda as fast as I can in order to have Noda again.

The inner pain caused by the cuva's terrible words began to subside. I was calm now. And I slept.

* * *

The sound of the uprights' water-skimmer woke me. I had been sleeping by the streamlet not far from their nest.

Longclaw could have found me here. Since Noda is not watching over me, I've got to be more careful about where I rest.

I walked through the streamlet to the flattail pond to check on the upright noda. She and her koda were in the skimmer moving toward the wide water. Taking the path out onto the peninsula where Noda and the cuva had gone to swim, I entered the water. I swam toward the nest and came out of the water exactly where they had, near the landing perch. I stood there listening and sniffing. Nothing other than the distant noise of the water-skimmer.

But the aroma of the upright noda was sweet and pervasive. I didn't like the way it mingled with that of the upright koda. I wanted only the rich, warm scent of a noda. I moved in different directions, seeking a spot where the aroma was pure, hers alone. I found it on a rocky strip that jutted out into the lake on the side of the landing perch nearest the flattail nest. I inhaled deeply and felt safe.

If only she would come back without the koda.

With my inner vision I could see her walking beside me through the forest, teaching me more about the forest creatures, showing me good things to eat, and finding streams for us to drink from.

She will choose a safe place for me to lie down, and nuzzle and lick me until I fall asleep.

I went back through the clearing in front of the uprights' nest and into the forest. I wasn't sure where I was headed or what I was going to do. There were abundant tender shoots sprouting from the earth. I nibbled here and there as I wandered through the dense underbrush, disturbing several long-eared hoppers who seemed frightened of me and jumped away when I approached.

I always found the hoppers amusing.

They must think I'm a longclaw or a large bushytail.

I stopped eating and watched a hopper disappear into a burrow. At that moment I realized that the noise of the water-skimmer had ceased. The water edge was close by, so I went to take a look. The water-skimmer was floating in a bay that was almost hidden by a ridge of rocks. I could see the upright noda holding a stick and string. Farther back along the ridge, at the far end of the bay where the trees and bushes grew, I thought I saw something move. Yes. It was a large dark figure. There were quick movements in the water-skimmer. The creature swung its head up.

"It's Koda!" I said aloud.

I was upwind and couldn't smell him, but the massive headbones were unmistakable. Despite my fear, I was in awe of him. He was a magnificent koda with huge headbones, large eyes, and a fine skinflap hanging from his chin.

I'll look like him soon. Why should the uprights want to kill him?

The thought scared me.

The uprights in the water-skimmer may have firesticks as well as the sticks with strings!

But they sat still, watching Koda disappear down the back side of the ridge.

Koda is not afraid of them, but he is careful to avoid all uprights. When the upright female becomes my noda, he will not have to avoid her.

The water-skimmer began making its loud noise again.

Without understanding why, I went back through the forest to the uprights' nest. Approaching it from the forest side, I noticed that there was space under the nest. I walked up and peered in. Except for a few stacks of wood and some strange objects, there was nothing in the space.

Here's where I can sleep safely! A big longclaw can't get under here, and my upright noda will be in the nest above me. Even if the koda is with her, she'll still be near me. And if I call to her, she will hear me.

It wasn't easy to get into the space. I had to drop my belly close to the earth and crawl under. I couldn't stand up, but I felt safe. I folded my legs and lay down. A few squeakers started scurrying around. I detected the odor of a ringtail as well as other aromas I couldn't identify, but they didn't frighten me. I heard the water-skimmer land at the perch, then upright voices in the nest — the low sounds of the koda and the soft, high tones of the noda, tones that pleased and comforted me. I lowered my head onto my front hooves, closed my eyes, and dreamed of Noda and the cuva for the last time.

* * *

"Come, Tova. It's time for you and Cuva to learn more about feeding beneath the white skywater when it covers the earth."

I stopped drinking from the milk spout and took my head out from under Noda's belly. She turned and began licking my face. The regular pattern of her long, gentle strokes soothed me. I felt no fear, no distress. I had no thoughts. I existed only in the sensation of her tongue gliding over my muzzle and over my eyes, pulling ever so slightly.

"Me, Noda! Lick me!"

The cuva's voice was like briars in a mouthful of tender greens.

Noda seemed not to hear the cuva.

"You have beautiful knobs, Tova. You will make a fine koda with grand headbones."

"Will the cuva also be a koda?"

"No, she is a noda, like me."

Noda's voice was soft, as were her eyes. She turned and walked into the forest with the cuva following close behind.

"Wait, Noda! Don't leave me!"

I tried to go after them, but I couldn't move. My hooves seemed to be stuck to the earth.

"Stay back." The cuva's raspy voice came from the forest. She emerged from the brush and ran toward me. The cuva was instantly transformed into a full-sized noda, much larger than me. She reared and kicked at me with her front hooves. Her eyes blared.

"Not your noda! My noda now!" she bellowed.

I wanted to run. Still I could not move. I wanted to call out to Noda, but I could not speak. Then I heard the water-skimmer . . .

* * *

The uprights' nest was quiet when I awoke. The sound of the water-skimmer at the landing perch must have saved me from the horrible dream-cuva.

The uprights must be going onto the water with their sticks and strings.

I crawled out from under their nest and shook myself to be sure I was awake and able to walk. I was hungry for some bottom greens, so I treaded gently through the brush beside the cabin until I came to the flattail pond. Two young flattails were cleaning themselves at the water edge. They scampered into the water, swam toward the flattail nest and went under, flapping their tails on the water surface.

"I don't want to eat you flattails!"

I liked flattails. I admired the way they worked hard to build their nest and keep it in good repair. And I liked the way they all lived together. I enjoyed watching the young ones play with each other.

I wish I were a flattail.

I waded out into the pond, put my head under, and soon found the greens I was craving. I stayed in the pond for a long time, eating my fill, chewing slowly, as Noda had taught me to do. In the distance I could hear the water-skimmer and an occasional upright voice. The uprights had strange ways that I did not understand, but I liked them, especially my new noda.

The flattails had come out of their nest, convinced that I was harmless, and had begun swimming around and eating the twigs and branches they seemed to like. They even ate the covering and hard parts. I preferred the greens.

Something startled the flattails, and they all ducked underwater.

I lifted my head and sniffed. The wind coming from the wide water brought with it the smell of the flattails and the peculiar smell of the water-skimmer.

I had eaten my fill, so I turned around toward the water edge to leave the pond and found myself looking straight into the eyes of Longclaw.

He was standing at the water edge with his two front feet in shallow water. His aroma hit my muzzle just as he made a circular motion with his head, opened his mouth and made that dreaded growling noise that I knew meant "I am going to eat you."

Instinctively I turned back toward the deeper water and began to swim with all my might.

"A strong koda can outswim a longclaw."

Noda's words repeated inside my head. I knew not to look back. I concentrated on moving forward in the water. My legs moved in swimming circles as fast as possible. Longclaw splashed in the water behind me. Past the landing perch I scrambled out of the water and ran toward the back of the uprights' nest. Longclaw loped after me. I crouched down and thrust myself into the safe place. Longclaw pushed his head in, but his thick body prevented him from entering. He snorted with fury. I backed into the center of the space under the nest and did not move. My body pounded from fear. My legs trembled. After several attempts to push himself into the underspace, Longclaw withdrew his head, gave another growl of anger, and moved away.

I waited.

Longclaw circled the nest, came back to push his head in again, his long teeth bared. He reached in with a front foot, curling his deadly claws at me.

I did not move.

He withdrew again.

I waited.

A terrible stench reached my muzzle. Longclaw had relieved himself near my safe place.

I wanted to get away from the hideous odor, but I dared not move.

Finally I heard the crunching sounds of the longclaw trudging back into the brush. I listened until his heavy footsteps faded.

Still I waited. I waited until my fear was gone and the trembling stopped. Finally I felt it was safe to come out again. I stuck my head out, looked around —just to be sure, then crawled out. I stood up straight.

"I outswam Longclaw! I found a safe place that he can't enter!" I cried out for all the forest creatures to hear.

It was good to outsmart a longclaw. In the elation of the moment I ran fast circles around the clearing in a dance of joy.

"I'm really becoming a koda! A koda! I'll tell my upright noda all about it."

With that thought, I hurried off to the water edge to check the size of my knobs.

* * *

With the great light low on the horizon I fed at the streamlet close to the flattail pond, in site of the safe place. I knew now not to keep my head under too long without lifting to sniff and listen for a longclaw or a big sharp-toothed bushytail with long, thin legs, or uprights that might have firesticks.

The water-skimmer had brought the uprights back to the nest. The scent of swimmer parts wafted from one of the structures near the nest. Then the two uprights got back into the water-skimmer and went to the water-edge rock where they always left the inner parts of golden swimmers.

Why do they mutilate the swimmers, leaving parts on the rock?

Shortly after their return from the rock, the wind began to smell of burning swimmers.

What if they do the same to tovas? I shuddered, remembering Noda's warning that the uprights with firesticks come to kill kodas and longclaws. I didn't care that they killed the longclaws — I wished they would kill them all. But why kodas? Because they were frightening when they bellowed and stamped and thrashed their headbones around?

I wonder if longclaws and kodas will hurt uprights? A longclaw probably, but surely not a koda. Kodas eat greens, not creatures.

I was having serious doubts about my choice of an upright for a noda when she emerged from the nest and came down to the landing perch. I watched her from behind the brush. She stood looking at the colored strips that the great light makes before it disappears. Occasionally she swung her vision to the flattail pond.

Is she looking for me? Can she smell me?

Of course not. She had never seen me, and she was upwind.

Just as I mustered the courage to step out into view, she turned and went back up the slope into the nest.

I'll sleep in the safe place during the dark cycle, but at first light I will let her see me.

* * *

There were sounds in the nest at first light. The uprights were awake and moving about. Lots of strange noises came from above me. A little wary, I slipped from the safe place into the brush and went around to the flattail pond where I could eat in the streamlet and watch the entrance to the nest. When it opened, I took cover in the brush. Both uprights came out carrying bundles that they took down and deposited on the landing perch. They repeated this action several times. Finally the upright noda emerged alone and came out onto the flat rocks closer to the flattail nest.

This is it. My chance to show myself to the new noda.

I stepped out into full view at the mouth of the streamlet.

The upright noda held something up to her eyes. *Another set of eyes?* I had never seen her with them before.

It could be her long vision, and she's searching for me.

She turned her head slowly first toward the flattail nest then moved her long vision toward me. She saw me. She released her long vision eyes then held them up again, and this time the two rounds were definitely fixed on me.

Noda! Please be my noda. I'm all alone now. Call me to you. Please.

I waited for her call.

A loud noise came from the swinging entrance to the nest. The upright koda came out with two more bundles, and I ran for cover.

Go away! Go back into the nest.

But he didn't go. The noda went to meet him on the landing perch. When distant sounds of the roaring bird became louder, the two uprights began searching the sky for it.

I backed farther into the brush as the huge bird glided down to the water surface and turned in the direction of the uprights' nest. When it settled at the perch, another upright koda came down out of the bird. The other two uprights gave him the bundles to put inside the roaring bird.

Still I hoped. *The two kodas will go inside the nest. Then Noda will call me.*

But when Noda climbed up into the bird, I knew she was leaving me. Her koda climbed in after her. Then the other koda pushed the bird out a little way from the perch and climbed in last.

The bird made popping noises as the feelers on its head began to spin around faster and faster. It turned and glided back into the wide water, went downstream, turned around and began to fly over the water surface and up into the air.

I did not move until the sound of the roaring bird faded away.

I trotted back out to the mouth of the streamlet and looked at the uprights' nest.

I remembered my escape from Longclaw and my dance of joy in circles. I thought of the squeakers scurrying around in the safe place and recalled the sounds and smells of the uprights above me.

"My safe place. My new noda. No. I don't need a safe place. And I will never have another noda. I'll go away, too. To become a koda. To swing my headbones, to stamp the ground, to rear up on a noda, and to frighten tovas."

With my inner vision I could see it all. I held my head high, as though my headbones were already as large as Koda's, and strode away from the uprights' nest, back into the forest.

Chapter 7: The Year of the Ojibwe

Karen

"Looks like we won't be getting out anytime soon," Bobby said.

The heavy rain mixed with icy particles was being blown sideways by an unrelenting wind.

"You guys might as well relax and enjoy a leisurely breakfast."

Steve, Bobby, Paul and I sat at a booth in a diner that was part of a Husky gas station, the only station in North Falls. As soon as I arrived in Canada, my appetite always increased dramatically. I ordered two eggs over easy, bacon, pan fries and toast with coffee and orange juice. Bobby had already eaten at his base camp before joining us and just ordered coffee. But the rest of us really chowed down. I started to leave a few potatoes, just to be lady-like, but ate them anyway.

"What's the latest report from the weather tower?" Paul asked.

"They say the storm should pass on through in a couple of hours. Then conditions will improve enough for both of us to take off."

While Bobby went into more detail about the weather forecast, I was distracted by the framed artwork hanging on the wall above our booth. A flat piece of something resembling parchment was etched with an intricate symmetrical pattern. The geometrical figures and swirls fascinated me. It seemed to be expressing something deep.

"That's a photocopy of an Ojibwe birch bark biting." Paul had noticed my interest in the work.

"I've never heard of that. What is it?"

"There's an aboriginal woman from a First Nations village near North Falls who makes them. It's traditional Ojibwe art. She prepares the bark from a birch or poplar, folds it a special way, bites the pattern into the bark, and then unfolds it. She's pretty famous — sells her work all over the country."

"I'd love to have one. Are they expensive?"

"I'll see what I can find out for you," Paul said.

Bobby, who was explaining the trip arrangements to Steve, noted my exchange with Paul and brought the conversations together.

"Paul was born and raised in Winnipeg and has lived in North Falls for the past few years, so he knows the region. And he's a good bush pilot. Never takes chances. I'm lucky to have him working with me. He'll take you two to Poplar River. I'm taking a group of lodge guests up to Baldwin in the Otter."

I glanced at the counter where five or six men wearing fishing caps and heavy clothing were obviously enjoying their breakfasts and each other's company.

"Those guys?" I asked. Bobby nodded.

"What's an Otter?" Steve wanted to know.

"It's a larger two-prop plane made by the good old De Havilland Company. It'll carry eight to ten people, depending on how much cargo you have. This one's equipped with wheels to land on a hard surface, but it could take pontoons as well. It belongs to the lodge. Takes about three trips when we have a full house up there. You two should consider it for next year."

"Oh, you'll never get KK to give up Poplar River," Steve said.

"Maybe we could do both next year. Take a two-week vacation," I proposed.

"That's a possibility," Bobby said.

I realized I had presumed on Bobby's generosity.

"Bobby, you'd lose too much money — we'd pay for the lodge."

"We'll work it all out. Right now you just concentrate on deciding which lure you're going to try first and what part of the river you'll head to. I need to get back to the base. Finish your breakfast and go back to the motel. Paul will come to get you when it's safe to take off."

Bobby stood, picked up the check, gave me his familiar grin, and went to the cash register. Paul followed him.

Steve had been rather quiet during breakfast, leaving most of the talking to the rest of us. I hoped he would not lapse into one of his serious and silent phases this week, as he had several times during the year.

"I've just got a lot on my mind," was always his explanation. He certainly needed a week away from work. He didn't even take time off when we moved into the new house. Daddy, Mama, Ellen, Katherine, and Ted helped with the transfer of breakable items and the unpacking of boxes; Steve spent the time in his office and in the library. But he had been so happy last year at Poplar River. Maybe this year would be the same. I was trying to be optimistic.

"Well, it seems that we have about two hours to spend in a motel room, Sweetheart. Whatever shall we do?" he asked in a husky voice.

That was a good sign.

* * *

The storm lasted longer than expected, and we didn't take off until one in the afternoon.

"Better safe than sorry," Steve said as he buckled his seatbelt. "Don't worry. We'll still get in some fishing today."

The weather wasn't great. The rain had stopped, but the sky still looked menacing to me. I kept reminding myself that Bobby and Paul knew their business, and their business was flying in all sorts of weather. We bumped around a good bit, flew through a few rain showers, but had no problem landing. It wasn't our most enjoyable flight to Poplar, but once I stepped down onto the dock, all was well with my soul, to put it in a southern protestant church musician's vocabulary.

"Oh, wait a minute. I almost forgot."

Paul was in the cockpit and had started preparations for takeoff. He opened his door, reached down into the map pocket, and pulled out a bulky little envelope.

"Bobby said to give this to you, Karen."

The floatplane door slammed shut as soon as I had taken the envelope and backed away from the plane. Steve let go of the mooring rope and with a gentle shove on the tail, sent the floatplane on it way to wider water as the propeller began to whirl.

The envelope was sealed and there was something hard in it. I tore one end off and slid the object into my hand. A lure. A silver spoon-like lure with a faceted bead of red glass secured in a hole near the top. A treble hook hung from the bottom. The body was shaped somewhat like a snowman, with the words "Lucky Strike" imprinted on his belly. A silver snowman with one red eye in the middle of his head.

I put the lure back into the envelope and noticed a folded piece of paper inside.

"Karen: Try this spoon. The northern went crazy over it up at the lodge last week. It should get you some big ones. You and Steve might check out Buck Lake this year. Till Wed. Bobby"

Since the Poplar River preliminary ritual had been performed at the motel this morning during the storm, Steve and I got busy right away attaching reels to rods and tying steel leaders to the ends of the fishing lines to protect fingers from the teeth of voracious northern pike that sometimes hit like torpedoes then fight like mad when you try to get hooks out of their mouths. I loved this first ritual as much if not more than the preliminary. I was proud of the evenness of my knots and proud of the fact that after the first year, I had rigged and handled my own equipment independent of Steve's help. I could get a "bird's nest" out of my line quickly and deal with all the usual problems fishermen encounter. Strange how success as a fisherman meant more to me than success as a pianist. At least, that's the way I felt at the moment.

"All set, KK?"

"Ready and eager."

I checked the boat for a bailer, a landing net, a spare tank of gas, and life vests. The clouds were still a little dark and reminded me of the squall our first year — bailing in a panic and not knowing if we would survive. I thought of the chill of the water when I fell into the beaver pond. Remote outpost fishing was risky business, but there were precautions one could take.

We headed upstream toward the eagles' nest.

"What's that orange thing?" I pointed toward the north shore.

"I don't know."

Steve squinted and slowed the motor to get a better look.

"A jacket?" I guessed.

"Looks more like a boat cushion to me."

I opened the tackle box and took out the binoculars.

"It *is* a boat cushion — hanging on a limb of that big bush. That's really weird. Who do you suppose put it there? And why?"

"We'll investigate on the way back. Right now, let's go fish around the eagles' nest."

I closed the tackle box, tightened the hood of my sweatshirt, and sat facing Steve and the motor, turning my back to the wind. The air was cooler than usual, and the sky was covered with clouds of every shade of gray.

There will be a beautiful sunset this evening.

Steve caught the first fish. It was always a contest to see who would. We kept score.

"Okay. Now we're 'even Steven,'" I quipped.

It was a rare occasion when I could be witty at home, but here in the wilderness there was a lightening of the spirit at the same time there was a deepening of the soul. I would have to talk to Bobby about that.

Fishing was fair that afternoon. We both caught two or three northerns, but no walleye.

"Guess we'll eat your delicious canned beef stew tonight, KK."

"Wrong, darling. There's a new propane grill on the screened porch, and I requested a couple of T-bone steaks on our food order. They're in the fridge."

"We're heading home right now! I'm famished!"

Overhead the clouds were spacing themselves apart, making room for sunset colors to appear. We would have our steaks and beer on the porch and watch the show.

"Where's the boat cushion?" I yelled to Steve over the noise of the motor.

He twisted the drive stick, slowing the motor.

"What?"

"The orange boat cushion. I don't see it anywhere."

He looked up and down the north shore.

"Neither do I."

"Wasn't it on that big bush right above that rock?"

"I thought so."

The rock. I noticed something about the rock. There was the faint outline of a white X-mark on it.

"That's the rock that marks the portage path to Buck Lake. See the white on it?"

"You're right."

Steve thought a minute.

"In that note he wrote you, didn't Bobby suggest we try Buck Lake this year?"

"He did."

"Then he must have put out the cushion to make it easy for us to find the portage point."

"Yes. But who or what took it down while we were fishing?"

* * *

The mysterious orange boat cushion was a serious subject of speculation over our steaks on the porch, while the Canadian sunset brightened and faded. We concluded that Sasquatch, a.k.a. Bigfoot, was the culprit.

* * *

Ellen wanted something bright and flashy; I wanted black and simple. So we compromised and chose a floor-length navy blue chiffon. The top was fitted and delicately beaded with pearls and glass, the skirt draped gently from the hips. When I modeled it at home for the whole family, everybody loved it, especially Meredith.

"I'm going to learn to play the piano. Then can *I* have a dress like that?"

"Do you really want to learn to play, or do you just want a pretty dress, Pumpkin?" I asked.

"Both!"

"Then maybe we should start practicing everyday and having regular lessons."

"I will, Mama. I promise."

"Okay. So now I have a new student."

And off she ran to torture the keyboard and our ears.

My main concern was getting through the evening. The dress was comfortable and I could move my arms freely in it. But my stomach wasn't cooperating. I threw up in the backstage bathroom while the orchestra opened with Mendelssohn's *Fingal's Cave*. I tried some deep-breathing exercises and said my usual pre-performance prayer: "Dear God, Please help me through this and I'll never do it again!" This time I meant it.

The green room door opened. Lavinsky. He was the only person I would allow backstage with me. Somehow having my teacher there gave me a little dash of courage. He had absolute confidence in me, and he had been through the same agony many, many times. He knew what I felt.

He took my hands and looked me square in the eyes.

"Karen, lose yourself. Only the music exists. Not the orchestra, not the audience, not even you. Only the music."

He spoke softly, but something in his voice was commanding, almost hypnotic.

We waited together in silence until Maestro Montero tapped on the door.

"We're ready for you, Miss Kingsley."

* * *

Bobby's Lucky Strike lure worked magic. It was heavy enough to travel a good distance when cast, but light enough not to get snagged too often on rocks or tough underwater weeds. I caught dozens of northerns, mostly small and medium-sized ones, but a couple in the mid-thirty-inch range. My arms got tired.

"Here. You fish with it for a while and I'll handle the boat." I handed my rod to Steve. He cut the motor and we traded places.

Within less than one minute I regretted it. Continuing to cast into the shoreline right where I had left off, Steve hooked into a giant. I could tell he was huge by the way he moved in the water — more slowly than the smaller ones, creating large ripples on the surface. A dorsal fin appeared, then the tail fins. He took a deep dive and swam away from the boat.

"Whoa, fellow!" The fish was taking a lot of drag, but Steve kept the line taut.

"Let him tire himself out. Don't try to bring him in too soon." Here I was giving Steve advice on how to fish. I had my hands full keeping the boat steady and in deep enough water so the fish couldn't seek refuge in the rocks and weeds of the shoreline and get the line snarled in them.

"He's coming up. Get the net."

I clicked the motor into neutral and stood with the landing net poised, ready to scoop him up.

"Look how he's hooked! In the skin of his back." Steve said when the fish neared the surface.

After several aborted attempts to nab him with the net and another of the pike's efforts to escape out to sea, I finally had him, a tremendous u-shape in the net. It took both of us to pull fish and net into the boat. The treble hook had fallen out of his back, but he was ours! At least for another minute, before we released him.

"Let me get a picture, Steve. Hold him up like they do in fishing brochures."

"You brought a camera?"

"A little one. In my vest pocket."

I took the picture: Steve without his fishing cap, his golden hair mussed, his face joyous as he held up a glistening forty-inch northern pike. If a photograph could be worn away from being looked at, this picture would have disappeared long ago. It was to become my most treasured possession.

* * *

Time seemed suspended during the performance of the concerto. Lavinsky's words, "only the music exists," inspired me to make my entrance onstage, approach the Steinway concert grand, and take the initial bow with confidence — in the compositional skills of Robert Schumann. I loved the work, and I wanted the audience to love it, too. Apparently they did. The applause continued for five curtain calls. I was glad I had not disappointed Lavinsky or embarrassed my family and friends. Mostly I was glad it was over. But I was not prepared for what awaited me backstage.

"Congratulations, Miss Kingsley. A stunning performance. I'm Amos Stahl, manager of the Charleston Symphony. We'd like to invite you to perform with us next year. Here's my card. Please call if you're interested."

"A moving rendition of a beautiful concerto, Miss Kingsley. I hope you will consider playing with the Greenville Chamber Orchestra next season. Perhaps a Mozart?"

". . . the Carolinians in Concert series in Charlotte next year . . . ."

"The Augusta Symphony . . . ."

". . . a solo recital at the university . . . ."

". . . an interview on South Carolina Public Television as soon as possible."

And the offers continued over the next few weeks by phone and by mail. I wondered how they could get either address or phone number, since I performed under my maiden name but we were listed under Marsten. The offers came from all around the Carolinas, Georgia, Tennessee, and even from states outside the southeast. One from a music festival in New Hampshire. And there were invitations to act as judge for various piano competitions.

"Well, 'Miss Kingsley' is certainly in demand." Steve bit into his morning toast a few days after the concert.

"Mama is a star!" Meredith announced.

"Mama is a mama and a wife, and Mama is exhausted from the thought of all this other stuff," I said in no uncertain terms. "Besides, I haven't accepted any offers yet."

I was carrying my plate of bacon and eggs to the table when the phone rang.

"Good Morning, Karen. This is Carlton Miller. I'm Dean of Performing Arts at Heyward College. I hope I haven't called too early."

"Not at all."

"I wanted to catch you as soon as I could. The president of the college and I met with the Board of Trustees yesterday afternoon, and we are in agreement. We'd like to offer you a full-time position on the music faculty as artist-in-residence. Would you be interested?"

"I'm quite honored, Dr. Miller. But I would need to know a little more in order to make a decision. And I would have to discuss it with my husband and family."

"Of course. If possible I'd like to meet with you and the chair of the music department today. Are you available for lunch?"

"Why, yes, I suppose so."

"Fine. Come by my office at noon, we'll work out all the details over lunch. Goodbye, Karen. See you shortly."

Meredith was helping her daddy clear the table. I was holding my cold breakfast in one hand and the phone in the other.

I've got to go someplace where I can think. I hung the receiver back, sat my plate on the table, walked through the living room and out onto the screened porch.

* * *

"What do you think about Bobby's suggestion of portaging over to Buck Lake? Would you like to try it tomorrow, if the weather's good?" Steve was sitting at the large table in the middle of the cabin's main room studying the map under the butane lamp that hung from a log beam.

"It's okay with me. We could take along some sandwiches and a thermos of coffee for lunch."

The morning dawned fair and bright, so we put on solid hiking boots, packed our lunch, and embarked on a new adventure. We had no trouble finding the rock with the faded white x-mark, but there was no orange cushion anywhere around. We pulled the boat up as far as we could onto the shore and secured it to the trunk of a poplar. Each of us held two rods, Steve took the tackle box, and I carried the substantial lunch bag containing the thermos, a bottle of water, the sandwiches and a few snacks. If we were going to hike through the bush then fish on a lake all day, I wanted to be sure we wouldn't go hungry or thirsty.

"You lead the way," I said.

"So the bear will get me first?"

"Oh, Steve, don't say such a thing! What'll we do if we see a bear?"

"Run like heck back to the boat. Do we have a first aid kit with us?"

"There's always one in the tackle box. But I don't think it will help much in case of a bear attack. And I don't even think we would make it back to the boat."

With that encouraging thought, the two intrepid fishermen forged into the unknown.

The path was easy to follow, for slash marks had been cut into the trees fairly recently. At first the footing was tough, but soon we were walking along a rocky ridge that seemed to be leading in the right direction. I kept listening and looking for any sign of my nemesis.

What would we do if we encountered a bear? A mother with her cub is supposed to be ferocious.

"Need a rest, KK?"

We had been hiking for about fifteen minutes, and my arms were tired.

"A short one. I don't feel too comfortable hanging around in the woods."

"We should be close now. Didn't Bobby say it was about a twenty-minute portage?"

"I don't really remember."

We sat our gear down, found a rock big enough for two backsides, and sat.

"Want a sip of water?" I handed Steve the bottle.

He took a rather long drink, and as he did, I had an uneasy feeling that we were being watched. By whom? By what? The same questions we had asked about the orange boat cushion.

It was another ten minutes of hiking before we could see Buck Lake sparkling through the trees. The sight of it gave impetus to our forward progress.

Steve was still in front. "I think I see the boat! Over there to the right.

It's pulled up on shore."

I couldn't see it at first, but Steve led us directly to it. A smaller boat, no swivel seats, just simple wooden planks, but it looked to be in good condition. We cleared out the accumulated leaves and other debris, found a full plastic gas container, a bailer, a first aid kit — and two orange boat cushions.

"Let's put everything in the boat then work on getting it into the water."

I was glad Steve had taken charge. We were tired from the hike, still we mustered the energy to put our backs to the prow and push the little boat straight back into the water.

Steve got in while I held the front rope.

"Hope I can get this thing started."

Steve lowered the motor from its tilted position and began pulling the cord. I hadn't even thought about the motor not starting. I usually covered the whole gamut of things to worry about, but that one had escaped me. It would have been another needless worry. The little nine-horsepower motor caught on the third pull.

"Good old Bobby. I guess he checked out the motor before recommending the portage," Steve said.

And we were off to explore Buck Lake and find some big pike. This time I had Bobby's Lucky Strike on *my* line.

"You work the shoreline for a while. I'll run the boat. If you don't pick up anything we'll just troll around the lake until we find the fish."

After about ten minutes of steady casting but fruitless fishing, I sat back down.

"I think we'd better troll."

As far as I could tell, the lake was oval shaped, with a rounded bay at one end. A snowman shape, like Bobby's lure. I settled back to troll with the little red-eyed snowman. But I wasn't thinking about the lure or the fish. I was sitting on an orange boat cushion, and I knew we were being watched.

* * *

Mama compiled a list of all the performance offers I had received, complete with contact information for each and all the details. Steve was hesitant to advise me about which ones to accept — my inclination being to turn them all down. Why put myself through all that stress again? Raising a child, keeping house, playing for church services, and giving piano lessons was enough.

"KK, it's your career. You have to decide. Accept all, some, or none. It's up to you. In a couple of years I'll get my tenure and a promotion with a substantial salary increase, and you won't have to do anything. We'll even be able to afford a housecleaning service."

"I don't mind cleaning house."

"That's not the point."

"What is the point?"

"The point is . . . oh, I don't know any more. I've got to get back to my research."

So I turned to my kin. Mama, Daddy, Katherine and I sat down in the living room of the family home and went through the list. It was decided that I should accept the offer from the New Hampshire Music Festival and take Steve and Meredith with me. It would give the child a chance to see another part of the country, and it would give Steve a break, if he could take a few days off. Make a short vacation out of it. We also thought the Charleston Symphony was a good idea, since they wanted the Schumann again. I didn't have time to learn a new concerto or an entire solo recital program, so all those offers bit the dust. All adjudication offers were accepted. The pay wasn't great, but judging auditions and competitions was stress-free.

Daddy picked up the list. "Okay. That leaves the job offer from Heyward."

"The salary's good," Katherine said.

"It may be too much on you." Mama, the worrier.

"Dean Miller said I would have a few students of my own to teach each week, take over for Lavinsky when he's away performing, and give a recital every two years. I would have to drop some of my private students — and I have one or two that show no promise."

"Sounds like you want the job." Daddy said.

"I'd be in the place where Steve spends so much of his time and energy."

And the family council adjourned to the kitchen for coffee and Mama's caramel apple cake.

* * *

"Fish on the line!" I jumped to my feet, keeping the rod tip up.

Steve cut the motor and began reeling in so we wouldn't get our lines tangled.

"Feels pretty heavy."

It was a nice northern, one of a number we had caught trolling the "head" area of the snowman-shaped lake. I pulled the fish up to the side of the boat, held the leader in one hand, took a pair of pliers with the other, clamped on the treble hook, and turned it upside down. The barbless hooks slipped out, and the fish fell back into the water.

"Great release!" Steve said.

"And I didn't get any northern slime on my hands."

"I'm about ready for lunch. How about you?"

"I was ready for lunch by the time we got the boat into water!"

The sun was warm. We sought out a shady spot along the shore, not too far from where we had found the boat, and tied up to a sturdy-looking bush. I set up our in-the-boat picnic while Steve went to the little boys' room.

We sat facing each other in the boat, eating ham and cheese sandwiches on our laps. "Go ahead and drink your coffee. I'm going to find Mother Nature's ladies' room."

This part was never much fun. When the weather was cold I had to bare a lot of skin to the chilly air; and when it was warm, I got insect bites in places I couldn't scratch in polite company. I unbuckled my belt.

I wonder if I'm still being watched.

I listened. Nothing but the pleasant sound of the water lapping against the shore. Prying eyes or not, I had to go.

"Look what I found." Steve was on one knee at the water edge a few yards from the boat, motioning for me to come there.

Several stones were stacked carefully one on top of the other, the larger ones on the bottom. The top one was wedge-shaped and seemed to be pointing up the shoreline toward the spot where Bobby had moored the boat.

"It has to be Native American," I said. "Do you think there may still be some aboriginals living in the wilderness?"

"This far from civilization? With no roads for at least a hundred miles?"

"Well, here's mystery number two. And have you thought about our orange boat cushions we've been sitting on all morning?"

"I did notice them. But we didn't hike our way through the bush to solve mysteries. Let's get back out on the lake, Nancy Drew."

Any uneasy feelings I had evaporated in the afternoon sun and fun. We caught a number of northern pike, a few walleyes, and even a fish that neither of us could identify.

"I guess we'll call it Mystery Number Three," I told Steve.

Steve glanced at his watch. "It's after five o'clock, KK. I think we'd better get the boat moored up and head back in."

"Aye, aye, Captain Steve." I reeled in, closed the tackle box, and looked at the sky. The sun seemed awfully low for five o'clock. We were at the opposite end of the lake from the snowman's head. Steve opened the motor to full speed. A good swimmer would have passed us.

"Can you see the mooring spot?" Steve asked as we neared the area.

"Not really. I should have paid more attention."

We rode slowly, paralleling the shoreline, until we found what looked like the place we had found the boat, and Steve turned inland and cut the motor. I stepped down into the water with the front rope in hand. Steve tilted the motor up out of the water and got out. After pulling as much of the boat onto shore as possible, we put some large rocks as weights in the front end and tied the rope to the trunk of a pine.

"What time is it now?" I asked.

"It's . . . still a few minutes after five? My God, my watched must have stopped!"

"I think it's a lot later than that. Look — there's already a sunset."

"Get your rods, Karen. We need to get back. I think that's the path over there."

But it wasn't the path.

"Isn't that the little rocky ridge over there?" I pointed to the right.

But it wasn't the rocky ridge.

"Don't we have a compass in the tackle box?"

At that suggestion, Steve set the box down and searched it. But there was no compass.

"I wouldn't know which direction to head in even if we had one," he said. "The best thing to do is to keep going in the same direction. Descartes said if you did that, you would eventually find your way out of the forest."

I don't think Descartes had ever been in the Canadian wilderness.

We had lost sight of Buck Lake, the footing was deep, and the light which had seemed bright enough on the water was dim in the bush. The farther we went, the darker it got. It was impossible to continue in one direction, for there were impasses created by fallen trees, rocks, and brush too thick to penetrate. My two rods were lightweight, but I knew the tackle box was heavy.

"Steve, let's take a short break. Then I'll carry the tackle box for a while."

"It's no problem." And he kept going. And going. And going.

I must have tripped over a rock or log or who-knows-what. I fell flat on my face, snapping one of my rods as I went down, and cutting my chin on the half-a-rod left in my hand. Steve stumbled his way over to me as best he could and pulled me to my feet.

"You're hurt!"

He went back for the tackle box and found our first aid kit.

"Hold still. This may sting. I think it's alcohol."

"I wish it were the drinking kind." I really meant it. I was exhausted and getting a little put out with Steve and Descartes.

"I think we're headed in the right direction, KK, but it's too dark to keep going. We'll find a place to build a fire — I've got some matches in my pocket — and rest until it starts getting light again."

I looked down at my broken rod and felt like I had lost a good friend. I unscrewed and removed the reel.

"I'll try to keep my chin up, I said with intentional sarcasm, fingering the awkward bandage Steve had concocted.

I slipped the lonesome reel into my jacket pocket and followed along again.

How could I be humorous at a time like this? The situation has become serious. We have no food, no compass, no sense of direction, no weapons. Why didn't I think to bring the filet knife? There are bears in the woods, and I'm sure something or someone has been watching us. Please, Lord, forgive our foolishness and help us out of this difficulty. Amen.

We came into a little clearing that Steve thought would be a good place to establish camp, so we set about gathering firewood. It was an easy task, since there were sticks and leaves a foot deep everywhere. Before long, we had a decent fire going and sat down by it. The highlight of the evening was a little package of crackers I had stashed away in the other jacket pocket and forgotten. We shared them and drank what was left of the now lukewarm coffee.

"Is that bear scat?" I pointed to a pile of pellets.

"It looks more like moose to me."

"I hope you know your poop." I lay down, carefully avoiding the pellets, and curled up my side.

"Go ahead, Sweetheart. Get some sleep. I'll stay awake and keep the fire going."

* * *

A crunching noise. I opened my eyes. Steve lay facing me, asleep. The fire had long been out.

More crunching noises. Coming from woods straight ahead. Something was moving toward the clearing. I sat up, terrified. My whole body began to shake uncontrollably. A large dark figure emerged from the foliage and stood in the clearing.

My scream was probably heard at the North Pole.

"Do you people need any help?"

It took me a minute to comprehend. The animal spoke English, American English. The animal was a human being. A *man* was asking if we needed help. Steve and I jumped to our feet.

"I'm sorry I frightened you, Miss."

"Who are you?" Steve had enough composure to ask. I was still frozen.

"My name is Tom. I saw you as you came through the bush this morning and also while you were out in the boat on the lake. Then tonight when I saw your fire I thought you may be in trouble."

"We . . . we got lost," I finally managed to say.

"What in the world are you doing out here?" Steve asked.

"I live in this area during the summer. I am Ojibwe. This is the land of my ancestors."

"We're just here to fish. Staying at the cabin on the river." Steve said, pointing into the woods — as if he had any idea which direction it was.

"Yes, I know. You're Americans. Most of the guests are."

My eyes had adjusted to the semi-darkness of the Canadian night, and I studied the stranger. His dark hair was pulled straight back and woven into one long braid. He wore jeans and a suede-like jacket over a faded flannel shirt. A buckskin pouch decorated with small cylindrical beads hung over one shoulder. His face had the strong bone structure of a Native American. He walked over to our defunct fire. *Moccasins.* He was wearing moccasins.

"The night air is pretty chilly. Let's get the fire going again. When there's enough light, I'll take you back to your boat on Poplar River."

He squatted and began arranging the charred remnants of the fire. Steve and I were slow to come out of our state of shock, but we managed to gather a little wood from around the clearing, with no concern for the moose poop, and pile it beside the fire. Tom was obviously much more adept a fire steward than either of us, and soon a blaze lit the clearing. Strands of gray hair extending from his temples into the braid reflected the firelight.

"I have some dried meat, if you're hungry."

He took the bag off of his shoulder, pulled out several little packets, and handed two of them to each of us. I recognized birch bark as the wrapping.

We sat together around the fire eating the smoked meat in silence. I wondered if I might not be eating one of my beaver or moose friends.

Forgive me, my woodland brothers and sisters. I thank you for being my sustenance.

Not exactly the kind of prayer I was taught to say before meals at home, but it was what I felt and what seemed right.

"Tom . . . ," I was hesitant, unsure of the Canadian terminology, "do most . . . First Nations people wear . . . moccasins?"

"Not normally," he said with a little chuckle. "Only at powwows and during tribal ceremonies, when a lot of Anishinaabek wear traditional clothing and accessories."

"What are 'Anishinaabek'?"

"It's an Ojibwe word that means 'first people.' It's what we call ourselves. Actually it refers to the first people of creation, sort of like Adam and Eve."

Tom stuck a foot out in front of him and pulled the jeans leg up a bit.

"You'll notice I'm wearing the moccasins with socks — U.S. army socks, as a matter of fact. That's certainly not traditional."

"I don't see how you get through this underbrush without boots," Steve said.

"It took me quite a while to get used to them. It was rough on my feet at first."

"Then why do you wear them?" I was bold enough to ask.

"It would take a long time to explain. You'd have to know my whole life story."

For someone who had just about scared the life out of me, Tom was becoming a reassuring presence. I was curious to learn more about him.

"Tell it to us. Really. We have nothing to do but sit and listen."

"She's right. Go ahead. I'd like to hear it, too. Besides, time always passes faster when you're engrossed in a good story," Steve said.

"Well, okay, I'll tell you a little bit. But then each of you must do the same." He turned his face toward the fire and stared into the flames for several minutes, and began softly chanting in another language, no doubt a native tongue, before he began his remarkable story.

Chapter 8: The Year of the Ojibwe

Tom's Story

"Great Spirit, you who created all things and blessed the Earth and Sky and Water with beauty, I thank you for my life and for the desire you have placed within me to walk softly among your creatures and plants. I offer to you and to these, my brother and sister, the story I am about to tell."

I did not translate the prayer I had spoken in the Anishinaabe language for the couple waiting to hear what I had to say, but I did explain:

"That is an Ojibwe prayer to Gitchi Manitou, the Great Spirit, that Nokomis — my grandmother — always said before she told us kids stories around the lodge campfire. It is an ancient tradition among my people to recount the legends of the Anishinaabek to our children, and so to preserve them. For many generations the stories were only transferred orally. Now, of course, quite a few have been written down and even published. But campfire story time is still popular in many aboriginal villages. Like the one in which I was born. It's called Red Arrow and is located south of here.

"We are a tribe of what you in the United States now refer to as 'Native Americans.' Believe it or not, we once inhabited the Atlantic shore. But natural forces and the encroachment of white people drove us farther and farther inland until we reached an island in Lake Superior that became our home for generations. The place is still considered sacred by many traditional Ojibwe. There we prospered and proliferated and were able to defeat all our enemies, especially after friendships formed with French traders and explorers who supplied our people with firearms and 'firewater' in exchange for beaver pelts. And we spread out in all directions. Red Arrow is located in the northern-most region of migration on what became Indian reserve land.

Poplar River was — and is — our hunting ground. Most of the men in Red Arrow, like my grandfather, made their living as hunters and trappers, while the women made hand-crafted items that went to larger towns along the eastern shores of Lake Winnipeg from where they were transported to Winnipeg and the tourist markets. My father operated a local general store that provided basic supplies for the villagers. We lived in a small government-built house with my grandparents and my older brother, Tim. My mother liked the similarity of the names — Tim and Tom."

"My mother did something like that, too. She gave both her daughters names starting with 'K' to match our last name 'Kingsley.' I'm Karen, and I have a sister Katherine. But please go on," the young woman said.

"First Nations people still have unrestricted use of the land around Poplar River. Not too many bother with it anymore, though. Most of our young people want to become part of the white world, or at least blend in with it — the way I did. Unlike my brother, I was a good student in the First Nations elementary and high school in our region and managed to get a scholarship to college. I could have attended the University of Winnipeg, but I wanted to study in the U.S., so I accepted a partial scholarship to the University of North Dakota.

A few weeks before I was to leave Red Arrow, my dad and I were making our way through the bush to check his trap line up near the river. As we came to the top of a little rise in the land, Dad stopped walking and stood perfectly still for a moment.

'There's a fire somewhere, son. I think we'd better go back.'

I inhaled deeply and noticed a faint burnt aroma in the air. As we retraced our steps, the odor grew stronger. A little haze soon became a dense fog of smoke. I remember a feeling of panic as we pushed ourselves forward through the underbrush. We had left home at dawn and were at least a three-hour walk from the village, but we made it back in less than two. We heard screaming and confused shouting. The whole village was on fire. We rushed first to one side then the other, but in the end there was nothing we could do but stand and watch complete destruction. The little wooden government houses burned like kindling. About two-thirds of the population of Red Arrow perished. I lost my mother, Tim, Nakomis, and grandfather. Nothing remained of Dad's store."

"How horrible. What in the world caused the fire?" the lady asked.

"That's the worst part." I looked into the campfire and saw again images of a village in flames. The answer to her question was not easy for me, but I had started the narrative and felt obliged to continue, although I could recall very little of the ensuing days.

"The Provincial Police took charge of the investigation. Fire inspectors from Winnipeg determined that the fire started from a lighted cigarette in *our* house. Tim had a habit of smoking in bed. He would often drink beer until daybreak then have a cigarette before falling asleep. I was totally ashamed — ashamed of my brother, ashamed of my family, ashamed of my people. So I left, firmly convinced I would never return. I was going to the U,S. I was going to become an American."

I have never admitted this to anyone before. Why am I telling these people I don't even know? The campfire tradition, perhaps. Or maybe I just need to tell somebody, to go through it one more time, and get it out.

"But you're back in your home territory now." The lady seemed genuinely interested in my story.

"I worked hard, finished my pre-law degree at North Dakota, and was lucky enough to get into Stanford Law School. That's where I met Maureen: green eyes, dark hair, perfect figure — and smart. We moved in together. I thought I was on top of the world. A great school, hard as heck, though, and a beautiful American woman in my bed."

"Did you get your law degree? Did she?"

I was flattered that this Karen woman wanted to know more.

"We both did. But things didn't work out between us."

"Why not? What happened?"

"Well, one day I came home to the apartment and caught her with another guy. That pretty much ended it."

"I guess it would kinda mess things up. So then you decided to come back to Manitoba."

"Not right away. I tried to act tough and make myself believe it didn't matter about Maureen. But I couldn't get her out of my mind —out of my system. I had thought we made a great couple. I was happy, and she seemed to be, too. Yet, afterwards, I realized that the warning signs were there all along. I just chose to ignore them.

"Like what?"

"Like studying together. At first that's what we did. Then she started wanting to go to the library when I wanted to stay home, and vice-versa. 'I can concentrate better when I study alone' was her perfectly plausible excuse. After we split up, I *had* to know *why* and what I had done wrong. I found out when and where she was to take the bar exam and confronted her as she came out to get in her car. That encounter eventually led me to return to my people."

Karen leaned forward and touched my arm.

"It must have been very painful for you to face her."

"It was what she said that changed my life, and I'm grateful to her for it."

The pain of that last meeting with Maureen, although dulled by the passing years, became a persistent ache floating atop a deep pool of sadness that drained ever so slowly, drop by drop, from my heart.

* * *

"We need to talk, Maureen." I knew I had caught her by surprise.

"Tom! . . . What are you doing here? I thought you'd already passed the bar exam." She removed the car key from the latch and opened the door.

"I have to know, Maureen." I took her thin shoulders in my hands and turned her squarely toward me. She was petite, and I loomed over her. She stiffened.

"This is making me uncomfortable."

"Of course it's making you uncomfortable, but I need to know."

"Know what?" She was becoming defensive. With an index finger she slid a strand of dark hair behind an ear.

"What went wrong between us? Why did you need someone else?"

She turned away and started to get into the car, but I took her shoulders and held her firmly this time.

"Be straight with me. I know it's over between us, so go ahead and tell me."

She had trouble looking at me.

"It's . . . your background . . . your race."

"What about my race?"

"You're an Indian, for God sakes, and I'm white. You need to be with your people, and I need to be with mine."

"That didn't matter to you in the beginning!"

Her eyes sharpened. "You were just . . . a curiosity."

I released her shoulders and turned away, stunned by the impact of her words. I felt outrage and impotence at the same time. I wanted to strike her, but I couldn't move, I couldn't even speak.

An 'Indian' . . . you called me an Indian? I'm not from India, I'm from Canada. I dress and think the same way you white Americans do. I speak English the same as you do, I eat, sleep, and make love just like any man. What the hell do you mean??

I wanted to hurl all that at her, but my throat closed, and I felt tears welling up. I curled my hands into fists and walked away without looking back. And that was the last time I saw her.

* * *

I gave the young couple at the campfire a short version of what had transpired between Maureen and me, then resumed the story.

"My first reaction to the break-up was to change my persona. I actually dyed my hair blond. It turned out to be sorta reddish, but I thought it looked pretty good. I took a position with a law firm in Minneapolis and began my new American life. I bought some rich-guy-looking clothes, businessman shoes, and an expensive watch — part of being young and foolish, I guess. Rented a little bachelor pad and started hanging around with one of the other junior partners in the law office, guy named Harry. We both had the same goals in life: climb the law-firm ladder and *cherchez la femme* — go after women. We worked late every night doing all the grunt work for the boss, Richard Marks, then we hit the bars and hit on the ladies.

* * *

"Send another round of drinks to the two ladies at the table over there," Harry told the bartender, motioning toward a booth in the back corner. "Tell them it's compliments of the two handsome gentlemen at the bar."

He pulled out a twenty-dollar bill to cover his generosity while we waited to see if they would invite us to join them. This time they didn't indicate any interest.

"Win some, lose some," Harry shrugged and ordered two more beers for us. 'These are on you, Tommie!"

"I wonder if Little Richard ever goes out honky-tonking," I used our pet name for the senior member of the firm. He was rather short and full of energy like the legendary rock 'n' roller, but he always kept his distance from the juniors.

"I think he's a happily married man with a trophy wife. Not the kind to play around. Besides, *two's company, three's a crowd*." Harry loved platitudes.

"Yeah, but just think, we could become *every Tom, Dick, and Harry*!" I was proud of my platitudinous joke.

"Speaking of Little Richard, I noticed you spent some time in his office today. What was that all about?"

I took a hefty swig from the bottle of Bud Light. Harry had touched on a subject I was trying to avoid talking, or even thinking about.

"A new case he wants me to handle."

"Solo?"

"It's not a big deal. A job discrimination case."

"African-American?"

"No . . . Native-American."

"Oh, okay. That makes sense. You can relate. Your background."

It's your background . . . your race.

I stood up and excused myself. In the men's room I splashed cold water on my face then looked at myself in the mirror over the basin. A crack in the glass cut a diagonal line across my face.

"*Makwa, why have you left us?*" It was Nokomis' voice, distinct in my head. She used my Ojibwe name, the one she and grandfather had given me when I was a child — at the naming ceremony. They had chosen 'Makwa' — bear — because I had such thick black hair and was larger than most of the kids my age. Now I was a red makwa, but still a makwa.

I pulled down a paper towel, dried my face, and lumbered back to the bar.

"I'm calling it a night, Harry, ol' man. Need to be at work early."

I left Harry looking rather puzzled and walked the eight blocks home. Tomorrow I would start on the case. I would not disappoint Little Richard, the client, or myself.

* * *

"Did you win in court?" Karen's husband asked.

"Yes and no. The company really didn't want the negative image of being discriminatory, especially in a state with a considerable Native-American population, so they offered him a substantial severance pay and other enticements if he would settle out of court. In the meantime, he took a position at a higher salary in another company. I advised him to accept the deal from his former employees, and he did."

"You must have prepared your case well, if you were able to scare the defendants into a nice settlement," Karen said.

"I worked hard. Yeah, I was satisfied with the outcome and so was Little Richard. He moved me up a notch in the firm, but by then I knew what my life was all about. I had to go back — back home to my people. There was so much that could be done for them, legally and culturally. I realized that as an attorney I could make a difference.

Education was the key. First I had to educate myself, so I enrolled in a special program at the University of Winnipeg. I saturated myself in First Nation culture, concentrating of course on the Anishinabek. I took Ojibwe language courses and then went out into the remote villages to talk with the *medewiiwin* — the shamans. I wanted to learn everything, our history, traditions, and myths."

"I know so little about all that," Karen broke in, "but I'm fascinated by the things I have recently seen and heard, particularly the birch-bark bitings."

"For a long time people had Hollywood images of Native Americans and their lifestyles — the 'cowboys and Indians' version. Even a lot of First Nations people were influenced by them. At the university in Winnipeg I found other men and women like me, with the same goals. We formed an alliance group, solicited financial backing from a number of large corporations, small businesses, and individuals. We founded the First Nations Cultural Center in Winnipeg which offers free language and history classes to aboriginals. That's what I do in the winter. I teach there."

"Are you still a practicing attorney?" the man asked.

"Yes, I am. I'm called on to handle cases all over Manitoba that involve aboriginals and their rights. But I prefer to concentrate on my teaching. I've witnessed dramatic changes in individual lives as a result of our work at the Cultural Center."

"Did you ever marry?" Karen asked.

"I did, not long after settling in Winnipeg. A woman in the alliance group. She was a social worker, an Ojibwe, who became a counselor at the Center. We worked together for over twenty-five years. She was my wife, my co-worker, my constant companion, and my lover."

"You're using the past tense in talking about her," Karen noticed.

"She died three years ago. We started spending our summers here in the wilderness after our two children were grown. She became a real wilderness woman. Knew how to cook game and fish over an open fire. She could build a fire better and faster than anybody. Every year we put up our *mudookwan* — that's a kind of wigwam house — on the river bank, upstream past the rapids, out of Bobby's fishing area.

Images of Tarla are all so beautiful now. That was her name —Tarla. Things were not always perfect between us, but somehow memory holds fast the good and dismisses the rest. When I'm alone in the wilderness, I have visions of her skinning and cutting up a rabbit, smoking fish, or mending a tear in my deerskin jacket. But mostly I see her face lit by the campfire light, like tonight, as we sat on summer evenings, reliving the events of the day, retelling traditional stories, or just listening to the night sounds of the forest."

* * *

"Come, Makwa, it's late." She spoke in Ojibwe, reaching for my hand as she stood. The camp fire shone in her eyes, love fire in her body, and spiritual fire in her soul.

So many nights like that. In the mudookwan we made love, then slept, breathing the same woodland air and dreaming the same tribal dreams as our ancestors.

* * *

"You obviously loved her very deeply," Karen said. She seemed to see beyond my limited words.

"Yes."

"And you continue to come here alone every summer?" Steve seemed to have become intrigued.

"It's the only way to understand who and where I am in this life. It keeps me both alert and humble. I'm part of all nature — the earth, the sky, the water, the plants, and the animals. It strengthens my body and prepares my spirit for the great passage beyond."

As I spoke these words, Karen's eyes intensified.

"You may not believe me, but that's exactly the way I feel when I'm here each summer, even though it's only for one week."

I smiled at this young American woman whose nature seemed so akin to that of my people.

"I do believe you."

I had finished my narration and answered their questions as best I could. Then the three of us slept for a while. The late-night forest creatures had ceased their roaming, and the early-light ones had not yet begun to stir. Tarla called it "the silent time." It was all too short.

"Okay, you two. Gather your gear. We'd better get going. We're pretty far off course."

Steve had slipped off his jacket and laid it across Karen's upper body. He gently pulled it back from her shoulders.

"Wake up, my beauty. The fish are calling your name." He spoke with love in his voice.

Karen winced a little as she sat up. Not used to sleeping on the ground. I once knew those pains.

"It's not the fish calling, it's nature. Excuse me, gentlemen."

She ducked into the bush.

"It's not easy to be a woman in the woods," Steve grinned.

"They can adapt pretty quickly." I thought how easy it was for Tarla.

* * *

"I can see our boat!" Karen called back to Steve who was bringing up the rear of our little party.

"Oh, Tom, thank you so much for getting us back. We would have never found it ourselves."

Karen was a lot like Tarla: an intelligent, sensitive, and joyous creature, full of love and life. Being around her this night had rekindled the longing for my companion and brought back the ache of her absence from my life.

When we reached the boat, Steve took the helm, and, after a few pulls, got the motor going.

"The cabin's only a five-minute ride away," I told them. "Do you know how to get back from here?"

"Please come with us, Tom, and have some breakfast. You fed us last night. Let us reciprocate this morning." Karen didn't have to twist my arm.

At the dock I helped Steve moor the boat, and we both followed Karen up the hill. She sat her rod down on the porch, went into the kitchenette, and checked the food shelves.

"We have coffee, hot chocolate, or raspberry tea. Which would you like?"

"You have raspberry tea?"

"I do. It's my favorite kind."

"I believe you have an Ojibwe spirit. Raspberry tea is the perfect gift for an elder. It takes the place of tobacco for those who don't smoke. And I think you know why I don't smoke."

"You aren't elderly, Tom."

"Actually, I am an elder in my tribe. One more year and I'll be an official senior citizen."

"That's hard to believe. Raspberry tea it is, then."

Karen filled a pot with water and lit the stove.

"You're in great shape," Steve said. He tore open three packs of instant oatmeal and poured them into small bowls. "Make that three teas, KK."

We sat at the large wooden table eating oatmeal, toast, bacon, and eggs with the vigor of hungry seagulls that swoop down to the rock for the fish scraps.

"What do you do for food all summer? Do you eat mostly fish?" Karen refilled my mug with hot tea.

"Fish, rabbit, duck — whatever I can catch with hooks and traps. Bobby flies me in right after ice-out, and I load up the plane with non-perishables. I try to eat mostly traditional foods like wild rice and preserved meats. Usually fish and game is plentiful, and there are a lot of edible plants.

"How did you learn all that?" Karen asked.

"Mainly from my grandparents and the medewiiwin. Nakomis knew the vegetation, and grandfather was a great hunter. My father was good with traps. And I think I learned to fish before I learned to walk."

"When do you go back to Winnipeg? Sorry, Tom. We don't mean to give you the third degree," Steve said.

"It's okay. A lot of people ask me those same questions. In fact, I give talks about my summers in the bush, and there's always a question-and-answer period afterwards. Fall Semester classes at the Center begin in early September, so Bobby comes to pick me up about the third week of August."

"What would you do if you got sick out here?" Karen asked.

"Thank goodness I've never had anything I couldn't handle with our tribal medical practices. Tarla was good with herbs and roots. She knew how to make natural medicines for just about anything and everything. But, to tell the truth, the last couple of years I have brought in a radio phone with me, in case of a real emergency. I can get somebody to fly in less than an hour."

"That's probably a smart thing to do," Steve said. "Bobby has talked about putting one in each of his outposts. I'll feel better when he gets one in this cabin."

"Tom, there's one other thing I'd like to ask. Earlier this week Steve and I saw an orange boat cushion hanging on a bush by the portage entry. Then it suddenly disappeared. We've been baffled by this mystery. Do you know anything about that?"

"I'm the one who put it there. A student of mine from Winnipeg was planning to fly in with Bobby's guests this week to spend a few days with me — and learn about wilderness living. When he didn't show up, I returned the cushion to the boat on Buck Lake in case you two decided to portage over." The young couple smiled at each other, glad to have the mystery solved.

I looked at Karen and Steve. They were young, happy, and obviously in love. I envied their youth and the years awaiting them. But as I started to envision their future together, something like the huge wing of a dark bird covered my mind, and my envy turned to compassion.

* * *

"KK, looks like you got something special in the mail," Steve called out from the kitchen. He had come home early for once. I was in the living room practicing like mad the Chopin sonata I was to play for the Columbia Music Club next week and hadn't taken time out to bring in the mail — or even eat lunch.

"I saw this tubular thing sticking out of the mailbox when I drove up. It's for you."

Closing the well-worn sheets of the sonata and dropping it back onto the stack of "urgent practice" music, I went into the kitchen. Steve was standing at the breakfast table shuffling envelopes of mail like a poker hand. I picked up the tube.

"Must be from Bobby," I said, noticing the Winnipeg postmark.

I popped off the plastic end-cap and pulled out a sleeve of brown paper. Something was rolled up in it. Pushing aside the sugar bowl and salt and pepper shakers, I carefully unrolled the paper.

A birch-bark biting. Exquisitely intricate, balanced in its quadruple symmetry. A small piece of white paper had been slipped into the middle of the birch scroll.

For a kindred spirit.
Boozhoo. Gigawabamin Menawah.
Tom

I lay Tom's gift on the table, walked back through the living room out onto the porch, and looked out at the lake. I saw again the campfire, heard it crackle, and smelled the aroma of burning wood. I could hear Tom's voice telling his story. I felt the wind of the river.

For a kindred spirit.

Greetings. I will see you again.

Tom

Chapter 9: The Year of the Mouse

Karen

It had been five years since our honeymoon at Poplar River. The past season I played concertos with the Charleston and Greenville symphonies and accepted an invitation to perform a Mozart concerto next January on a special Saturday morning "Coffee Cup" series with the Atlanta Symphony, my most prestigious engagement so far. There had been the usual music club appearances around the state where I struggled with out-of-tune pianos in peoples homes and afterwards ate little round tuna salad sandwiches and drank sweet red punch with oohing and ahhing senior citizens.

Meredith celebrated her fourth birthday in March with a party to which she invited her entire day-care class. I stayed up half the night before, making a chocolate cake with marshmallow icing — her favorite — and decorating it with edible pink rosebuds and tiny green leaves that Ellen had concocted for the occasion. I managed to write out "Happy Birthday" with the help of some canned pink cake frosting that came with a decorating tube. I wish I had named my daughter "Pam" or "Jane" or anything shorter than "Meredith." The party was considered a great success, since only one child threw up, and there were no injuries other than a skinned knee during the outdoor games. Thank God the weather was too chilly for swimming in the lake. The birthday girl slept blissfully, with all the gift toys piled on the bed beside her, a giant teddy bear, "Pooh Bear," a present from her father, in her arms.

This year the trip to the wilderness was different. Bobby had arranged for us to fly directly from the Winnipeg airport to the lodge at Baldwin Lake. An upgraded hard-surface landing strip at the camp now allowed all the guests to fly in via Big Bear Airlines, a commercial company that serviced fly-in fishing and hunting lodges in the north. From the lodge either Bobby or Paul would pilot us in the float plane over to the outpost on Poplar River.

The Big Bear aircraft was a comfortable De Havilland Dasher 8 — I learned the name from Bobby's detailed letter explaining the new set up — which eliminated multiple trips in the Otter. I sat next to the window holding the video camera ready to record as much of the trip as possible. I wanted Meredith, Mama, Daddy, and Ellen to experience the wilderness adventure that had become an essential part of my life.

As the plane lifted off the runway I began filming. Almost immediately we were above the checkerboard farmlands that surround Winnipeg. The black-soiled fallow fields alternated with squares of fresh green crops. Farm roads and irrigation canals cut angular geometric forms. Within minutes we were over Lake Winnipeg, a huge expanse of water that mirrored the sky and clouds. For a while it seemed as though the Dasher was suspended between two heavens.

Soon the regularity and precision of the human landscape gave way to the irregular figures of Nature's whims. Clusters of dark evergreens sprang out of the white calcareous earth. Lakes became more and more numerous until the land seemed like a cloth perforated to reveal the sky beneath.

"Would you like something to drink?" Steve repeated the flight attendant's question to me.

I shut off the video. "Coffee with cream, please."

We had not had a bite of breakfast. The Baldwin Lake van picked up the lodge guests and outpost-goers from the hotel in Winnipeg at 5:30 a.m. and took us to the airport. I really needed my morning coffee.

No sooner had I started sipping than the attendant was back with a tray full of assorted muffins. I chose a cranberry-walnut, Steve took a blueberry. We ate, drank, and slept until the captain announced our initial descent to Baldwin Lake Lodge. Bobby was waiting to greet us when we came down the retractable steps of the Dasher.

"Welcome to Baldwin Lake. How was the flight?"

"We slept through most of it, so it must have been okay," Steve answered.

"They served great muffins and coffee," I chimed in.

"I'd like to show you two around. Paul's going to shuttle some fishermen to a couple of outposts. That'll take a while. Then we'll get you down to Poplar."

"What about our luggage and gear?" Steve asked.

"Don't worry about it. One of the guides will take care of it. Let's go on up to the main building."

I was wide-eyed at the place. The lake was enormous. The airstrip was drawn on a peninsula with the main building and cabins laid out in a straight line paralleling it. The main building consisted primarily of a kitchen and a large guest dining room with a bar, a huge stone fireplace, couches, and overstuffed chairs at one end. A bearskin, a stuffed lynx, and mounted fish provided the appropriate room decorations. Large windows allowed guests a maximum view of the lake.

"We can accommodate about twenty-eight guests," Bobby told us. "And when I'm not in the office, I hang out here in the back."

He ushered us down a hallway, past an office on the left and a little tackle shop on the right. The door at the end of the hall opened into a small apartment across the back of the building. Nothing more than a bedroom with a sitting area and a bath. From the sitting area Bobby took us into a dining room behind the kitchen.

"I eat with the staff back here. It's also our meeting room."

"How big is your staff?" I asked.

"We have fourteen guides, and four of them have wives that work as housekeepers. The guides double as handymen and baggage handlers. Plus there's Paul, my pilot, one cook, and a waitress."

"Where do they all stay?" I asked.

"In the cabins to the west of this building. The ones to the east are for the guests. I'd show you one of those, but right now they're all occupied. They're real nice — all with a private bathroom and shower."

"This place is fabulous, Bobby! And you live here all summer now?" I sounded like one of the oohing-and-ahhing seniors.

"That's right, I do. Weather permitting, mid-April through mid-September. I sold the cottage and airbase in North Falls. Bought a cute little house in Winnipeg for the rest of the year."

"I imagine you stay pretty busy here at the lodge." I hoped I wasn't being a pest, but Bobby seemed proud of his lodge and happy to answer questions.

"Well, I admit I don't have much solitude once the lodge is open, but, don't worry, I still find time to go fishing now and then."

"We have a lot of solitude at the outpost. And that's one of the things I love most about it."

Bobby gave me one of his charming grins and pointed to a table in the staff dining room. "Sit down and I'll have the cook make you some breakfast." He disappeared behind a swinging door to the kitchen.

As if the muffins weren't enough, we wolfed down two large pancakes each, with butter and Canadian maple syrup, bacon, and a glass of juice. *Why do I eat like a hungry animal every time I come up here? Survival instinct, maybe.*

While Bobby was in the office taking care of the business of the day, Steve and I wandered around the grounds. There were wooden cross-slat ramps as walkways. One provided the guests an easy walk to the cabins. Another led down to the pier where guides and guests were preparing for a day on the water. The lake fanned out in all directions from the camp. There were two islands directly in front of the lodge, and beyond them the far shoreline was so distant it was barely discernable.

Steve and I ambled around the whole camp, in awe of everything.

"I never dreamed it was so luxurious," I told Steve.

"Nor did I."

"You folks ready to fly down to Poplar?" Paul had obviously delivered the other groups to their outposts and was now free to take us.

Bobby was waiting on the float plane dock and helped me climb up the rungs and into the back seat. Then he turned and said something to Steve, handed him a brown paper bag, and helped him into the aircraft.

"What's in the bag?" I asked Steve, buckling my seat belt.

Paul hopped in and started the engine.

"Tell you later."

The flight in the Cessna took only about twenty minutes. When Paul circled and banked to descend into Poplar, I looked for my eagle. And as we taxied up to the dock, I glanced toward the beaver lodge and beyond it to the shore where I hoped to see my moose child again.

Nothing stirred. Even the air was still. The sun had already burned away mist and low clouds and was working to warm the surface of the water. The minute my feet touched the dock I was in another world, a magic world, an enchanted forest that awakened my soul. I was not being naïve. I knew there were critters out there killing and eating one another in the woods and in the water. I would certainly eat my fill of fish, so I guess I was in sync with nature, despite vestiges of civilization. Like groceries and clothes. And if tradition prevailed again this year, I knew I would be shedding the latter not long after Paul's departure.

* * *

The settling in process had become an efficient team effort. We each knew what to do with what. Food was stored on the shelves, kitchen drawers were lined with paper towels, the flatware and plates washed and put back in their place, reels attached to rods and set ready on the porch, beds pushed side by side, and sleeping bags zipped together.

Once I had done my part, I plopped myself down on the bed, stretched out, and began to absorb the reality of where I was. And the freedom. No piano practicing, teaching, or performing. Here in the wilderness I was neither mother or daughter, teacher or pianist, or even wife. I was just *me*, the real me, stripped of appearances, of southern gentility and pretension. I didn't have to wear make-up or panty hose. I didn't even have to smile. I was grateful for this simplicity.

A movement high on the bedroom wall . . . . I glanced up. A tiny pair of dark eyes scrutinized me from a slit between the logs. They were gone in an instant, only to reappear in another crevice. Looking. Curious, not frightened. The creature was a mouse, of course, a mouse with wonderfully large eyes and ears and a two-toned body, brownish-gray on top, white beneath. The game of peek-a-boo continued for another minute or so. When I got up for a closer look, it vamoosed.

Our late-morning arrival at the outpost meant no time for fishing before lunch. I went into the kitchen, prepared sandwiches, and opened a bag of chips. All the while I knew I was being watched. The same curious eyes peered at me from various angles: atop the fridge, above the dish cabinet, and from a food shelf. This latter position changed my attitude toward the cute little varmint.

"Steve, we've got mice!" Or at least a mouse. Cute or not, I didn't want it eating our staples.

Steve sauntered into the kitchen holding the brown paper bag.

"Bobby said we might have mice and gave me a bunch of mouse traps and mouse bait." He set the bag down on the counter and began investigating the contents. "He usually takes care of the problem before we get here, but this year, with all his duties at the lodge he didn't have a chance. He said to put the bait under the cabin and, inside, to set the traps with cheese or peanut butter at night."

"Good. Let's not forget to do that before we go to bed tonight."

After lunch we took the boat out. The sun was warm, the water was calm, and the poplars were again wearing my wedding colors. The fishing was so-so, but we caught a couple of walleyes for dinner, filleted them, and left the remains on the water-edge rock.

During the after-dinner cleanup, Steve put an arm around my neck and kissed my ear.

"There's something we forgot to do today," he said softly.

"Take care of the mouse business?"

"Not at all what I meant."

That was the end of the cleanup, and we didn't set out the bait or traps.

First night in the wilderness I sleep — a natural, clean, refreshing sleep, and I wake early. This year was no exception. Steve was awake. I rolled over the parallel mattress edges to his side of the bed and snuggled up. Seven days alone, just the two of us. No TV, no kids, no obligations. Just the pleasure of each other's company. I wondered if he felt the same way, if he appreciated this time together as much as I did. The job at Heyward took so much of his time. But most of all there was his book. Thank heavens that was drawing to a close. One more year and he would go up for tenure and promotion. After that life would be so much easier for him — for us both. Job security, no more pressure.

Steve turned on his side to face me. "Did you set up the coffee last night?"

"Uh . . . I don't think I had the opportunity."

"Well, then, you don't want to miss the opportunity again this morning. I'll wait right here."

"You lazy thing!" I did a reverse roll back to the other mattress, swung to a sitting position on the side of the bunk, stuck my feet into some mules, and slip-slided into the kitchenette.

First order of business was to clear the mouse pills off the countertop and stove. A brief inspection of the food shelves revealed an opening in the box of pancake mix and numerous droppings on the tops of cans.

Not a good way to start the day.

I opened a bag of Nabob coffee, inhaled the aroma, and reached into the flatware drawer for a spoon. My hand stopped in mid air, the drawer half open. The paper towel lining was in pieces, shredded — or chewed — to bits. I inched the drawer open fully. In a back corner there was something strange. It took me a few seconds to realize what I was looking at. A mother mouse had made a little nest out of the paper towel and had given birth to three baby mice. They were such tiny and helpless little things. Their eyes were not yet open. I leaned down to get a good look. I could see life pulsating beneath the paper-thin, almost invisible skin of the tiny bodies — all except one. One lay still, no sign of life. I was fascinated and repelled at the same time. I turned away from the mouse cradle. "Steve! We have a problem in the kitchen!" I yelled out.

While I stood staring into the drawer, Steve came padding in barefoot from the bedroom, wearing the T-shirt and sweat pants he'd slept in.

"What is it, Sweetheart?"

"Look!"

Steve leaned over the drawer then straightened up.

"I'll get rid of them."

"What do you mean?"

"Well, I mean we can't have mice breeding in the kitchen where all the food is."

"What are you gonna do?"

"I'm going to get dressed, take them out and drop them in the lake. The fish will recycle them."

"Oh, God! I hate to drown these innocent little babies. You're sure the fish will eat them?"

"I don't know, Hon. Probably so. Had you rather I just dump them outside? The mother might bring them back in."

"I guess you're right. The lake would be better."

Steve closed the drawer and finished making coffee. I had no appetite for breakfast.

We dressed in silence and methodically prepared for a morning on the lake, each to his and her own task. The good weather was holding out — calm water and warm sun. As I untied the boat, a pair of ducks flew low overhead, flapping madly against gravity and expressing themselves in hearty honking sounds.

Watching Steve pull the start cord on the motor, I noticed the empty can from last night's green peas on the bench beside him.

"What's the can for?" I projected over the sputtering of the cranking motor.

"It's the mice." His voice was solemn.

I rode facing backwards and staring at the pea can. The mother must have thought she was providing a safe place for her babies when she shredded the paper towel and gave birth in the back corner of that drawer. She had no way of knowing. Knowing the human reaction to house-invading creatures. I wondered if she would feel the pain of loss, if she would realize that we, *her* house-invading creatures, were responsible.

About fifty yards off shore Steve threw the motor into neutral and picked up the can.

"This is as good a place as any to dump them."

I repositioned myself to face the front of the boat.

"I can't watch, Steve. Just let me know when it's over."

My stomach felt queasy. *Good thing I didn't eat any breakfast or I'd be feeding the fish, too.*

"Okay, Sweetheart. The deed is done."

"I didn't hear a splash."

"Well, they didn't make one."

I closed my eyes and tears formed as I envisioned three blind mice sinking slowly. One was already dead. The others would drown. Their tiny bodies would probably not go down very deep but remain suspended until they were engulfed by some aquatic predator. A pike, most likely. Or a walleye, a duck, a turtle. They would never see the world they were born into. They would never see their mother.

I must not let this get to me. I must not let it spoil the day or any of our time at Poplar River. I wiped my wet cheeks on the sleeve of my flannel overshirt.

The sorrow of the mouse tragedy was gradually dispelled by the rays of the sun that warmed our hearts as they did the earth and the water. We did not keep any fish that day. Slipping them easily from our barbless hooks, we released every one and watched as they instinctively propelled themselves down to the illusory safety of deeper water.

The hearty swimmers of Canadian waters contrasted dramatically with the delicate goldfish depicted in Debussy's *Poisson d'or*, fish I imagined he had observed in the concrete basins and fountains of the Parisian *jardins publiques*. I wondered what he would have composed had he spent time on Poplar River.

As I thought about the Impressionist composer, a melodic theme began to play in my head. Where had I heard it before? Debussy? No, too romantic, with a distinctly familiar melody. I made a mental note to delve into that when I got back home.

Back "home" in the cabin the next morning, we had a rude awakening: mouse pills everywhere, especially in the unused bedroom. The food shelves had been raided again, the pancake mix contaminated, and the tops of boxes and cans well-decorated with poop pellets.

I picked up a roll of paper towels and got to work.

Well, this is sure reality. A far cry from my grandiose musical musings of yesterday afternoon. I enlisted Steve's help.

"I should have put out traps and bait last night," he confessed.

He located the brown bag again and set out open boxes of bait under the cabin and traps in several corners, two in the kitchenette.

The idea of mice dying a slow and painful death by poison bait didn't set well with me. At least the traps provided an immediate demise, no suffering no lingering. Still it was death all the same. I didn't really want to kill the mice, just get them out of the cabin. I decided I would have to devise a more humane tactic.

By the time we came in for lunch I had formulated a plan, a maneuver that would rid the cabin of all mice without doing them any harm: we would *corral* them and force them out the front door. During the afternoon fishing I mentally worked out the details of my grand scheme. I came in that evening feeling confident, even triumphant. I would clear the cabin of mice and save their minuscule lives.

As soon as dishes were done, I put my plan into action. Based on the number of droppings there, I deduced that the extra bedroom was their stronghold. I pulled the bedroom door to, leaving it open just a mouse width. Then I took the cartons used to transport our groceries and tore wide strips of cardboard. Proping them up with anything and everything I could find, I constructed a narrow corridor that led from the bedroom door to the front door: the gauntlet. The cardboard strips on one side, the interior wall on thc other. I took cheese, crackers, peanut butter, and cookies and laid them out on aluminum foil in the gauntlet.

"Karen, you're crazy. Do you think mice are like sheep? And you don't even have a border collie to help round them up!"

Steve's ridicule only egged me on. I stationed him at the front door, took the flashlight from our bedside, turned out the lanterns, and waited in the dark at the other end. It wasn't long before we could hear the scratching of tiny feet on tinfoil. I waited a few more moments, then snapped on the flashlight, jumped into the gauntlet, closed the mouse bedroom door, and shooed the panicked mice down the cardboard corridor toward the front door.

"Open it, Steve!"

He did, and the mice stampeded headlong onto the screened porch. About nine or ten of them. They were all out in a matter of seconds. Steve closed the steel door.

"Now they're all on the porch, KK. What next?"

"That's it for tonight," I said smugly.

"Don't you think they know how to get back in?"

"I'll worry about that tomorrow," I answered, playing Scarlett O'Hara. "You've got to admit that it was an ingenious plan that succeeded, at least temporarily."

"I'll admit I enjoyed seeing you and the mice running the gauntlet. Kind of a rodeo show."

I did feel proud of my project, but I knew full well Steve was right: they'd be back tomorrow. And they were. The battle between mouse and man — or woman — was not over yet.

* * *

The next two days were routine fishing days: out before eight, in for lunch and a nap, then back out until . . . well, that depended on the fishing action. We had brought in cans of beef stew, spaghetti, chicken and dumplings, and vegetables. The cans were mouse-proof, as was the beer, so preparing dinner was only a matter of turning the can opener and popping the top of a couple of LaBatts Blues. I had learned to "knock back" a beer or two. Both nights we were awakened by the snapping of mouse traps and the inevitable squeals which followed. I pulled a pillow over my head.

It was Bobby, of course, who solved the problem for us. During his mid-week visit we recounted our mice events while he changed propane tanks outside the kitchen.

"They're coming up through the shower drain. There should be a round metal plate somewhere in the washroom. Put it over the drain when the shower's not in use. That'll keep the majority of them out. Others will get caught in the traps. Some will eat the bait under the cabin and die. Sorry I didn't have a chance to take care of them before you got here. I should have told you about the drain plate. Anyway, I think it'll be all right now."

"They're really harmless, aren't they? Except for nibbling on some of our food." I still felt sorry for those bug-eyed, big-eared little critters.

"Actually they do carry a disease that humans can pick up, especially if you come into direct contact with their fecal matter — their so-called *pellets* or *pills*. That's why I like to rid my cabins of them before the guests arrive."

"A serious disease?" Steve asked.

"Serious enough. Some victims have died from it."

Oh, God! We're probably going to die of some horrible fever that doctors in Spring Hill know nothing about and will be unable to diagnose! I had to learn more.

"So these mice are not the same as those back home?"

"They're related, of course, but this is a different species: deer mice. They're cute, but it's best to keep 'em out of the cabins, away from the guests."

"That's what they're called — deer mice?" I wanted to get all the information so I could share it with Dr. Johnson before Steve and I succumbed to mouse fever, and so Meredith would know the cause of her parents' demise when she became an orphan.

"That's the common name for them. Just keep that plate down and you'll be rid of them for the rest of the week. You can concentrate on fishing. The walleyes are really starting to hit — that's what the guys over at Cinnamon outpost told me. You should start seeing some fast action. Try some colorful crankbait."

Bobby finished installing the full propane tank, ran the pump to refill the cabin's water tank, and checked our gasoline supply in the storage house. We followed him around like puppies.

"Can you stay for dinner? Please do," I urged him. "We're having cheese dogs wrapped in bacon."

"Really need to be back at the lodge by the time the boats get in for the day, just in case a guest or guide has a problem. But thanks. That actually sounds better than the prime rib the chef has planned for tonight."

"Yeah, sure!" Steve gave him a brotherly slap on the back.

As usual, we walked with Bobby down to the dock and stood there until the Cessna disappeared into the afternoon haze and the engine became inaudible. I always enjoyed Bobby's mid-week visits. He knew so much about the Canadian wilderness and about nature in general. But most of all, I loved being here with Steve, just the two of us, listening to the sound of the wind and the water.

* * *

"There must be something in the water up there in Canada, KK." Ellen dumped a packet of artificial sweetener into her cappuccino and swizzled it around with a red plastic stick. "This one must be due just about on Meredith's birthday."

"I hope so. Then I'll have to bake only one cake a year."

"You're so lucky. A home on the lake, one great kid already, another on the way, a good-looking husband who adores you. And I still haven't found Mr. Right, though God knows I've tried. It must be the librarian syndrome."

"Don't be silly! I've offered to set you up with one of Steve's colleagues at Heyward, or his cousin Bobby. You're either too picky or too stubborn."

"That's me." She gave me an ironic smile.

I glanced at my watch. "Oh! I've got to run. I have an appointment with Dr. Phillips for the ultrasound check. I'll call you later."

"I'll be at the Circulation Desk until ten tonight."

* * *

On the way home from Dr. Phillips' office I stopped by Mama's to pick up Meredith. While the child gathered up her books and toys, I shared the exciting news with my mother.

"He's certain it's twins?"

"He showed me on the screen. You know, Bobby's dad and Steve's dad were twin brothers."

"You'll have your work cut out for you, honey, and Steve as well. Two infants to take care of, plus Meredith. But don't you worry. You know Daddy and I will help all we can. How do you feel?"

"A little tired, but better than the first time. You can tell Daddy, Katherine, and Ted. I'll get Steve's reaction this evening. I think he'll be happy."

And he was. Thrilled. He lifted Meredith, sat her on his lap, and kissed her on the nose.

"You're going to have *two* baby sisters or brothers to play with. Or maybe one of each."

"I think I would like a brother and a sister."

"Me, too. That would be great, wouldn't it?"

So their conversation went. *Well, I'll see what I can do to accommodate the two of you!* Their enthusiasm warmed my heart.

* * *

October 20th. The pain started in mid-morning. The bleeding about noon. I called Dr. Phillips' office, then Mama.

"I'm coming to get you right now and take you to the emergency room. Lie down and try to stay calm 'till I get there."

I was scared. And dizzy. Nothing felt right.

"Oh, Lord God. Please help me!" I prayed out loud.

I unlocked the front door, wrapped myself in a blanket, and lay down on the sofa. The pain became more intense.

"I'll be all right once Mama gets here," I told myself. It had always been that way ever since I could remember. Whenever she walked into my sick room, I felt better. Her hand on my forehead would dispel a fever. A spoonful of soup slipped between my lips from her hands would calm a queasy stomach and bring on a little appetite.

"I wonder if Meredith feels that way about me?" I asked Mama as she helped me into the car, blanket and all.

"Don't try to talk, honey. Just close your eyes and take deep breaths. The hospital is only five minutes away. Dr. Phillips and Steve are on their way to meet us there."

I don't remember the exact sequence of events during the next twenty-four hours. I remember faces — Steve's, Dr. Phillips', Mama's, Daddy's, Ellen's. Various nurses came and went. I was hooked up to a bag full of liquid, to prevent dehydration, I supposed. I took pills — for what I don't know. But one thing I did know for sure: I had lost the twins.

I was in and out of consciousness for a while. When I finally regained my faculties, Mama was sitting on one side of the bed, Steve on the other.

"Mama?"

She took my hand. "Karen, honey, you're going to be fine. Just rest."

I turned my head toward Steve. "Hi," with a smile was all I could manage.

He stood up, leaned over and kissed me on the forehead. I saw the devastation in his eyes.

"You'll be okay. We'll be okay," I heard him whisper, as I floated back into a chemical dream world.

I was underwater. Murky water. In front of me, three mice were suspended. I reached out and grasped two of them, one in each hand. As I pulled them toward me, their eyelids opened, and they looked at me with large, curious eyes. I released them and watched them drift away. Then I grasped the third one and drew it to me. The eyelids did not open and I felt no pulse in the little body. I realized it was dead, and I gave way to grief.

* * *

"The miscarriage caused no permanent damage. You and Steve can have more children, if you wish. You're in excellent physical health."

Dr. Phillips sat at his desk, behind a stack of lab reports. He had had me tested from one end to the other and examined by a gynecologist, a hematologist, a clinical psychologist, and an I-don't-know-what-ologist. I was fine, as fine as any woman could be after the traumatic loss of unborn babies.

"There's something I need to tell you, Karen, something I haven't told your parents or your husband." He leaned forward in a gesture of confidentiality. "I wanted you to hear it directly from me: you lost your twins — twin boys. But there was a third fetus that had died several weeks before."

I took a deep breath.

"I knew that," I said, as I stood to go. I also knew the music that had played in my mind that day at Poplar, the day we drowned the mouse babies: a theme from Mahler's *Kindertotenlieder*, a song cycle on the death of children.

Chapter 10: The Year of the Mouse

Koh

I had been expecting the uprights ever since the warm season settled on us. The sound of the roaring bird confirmed their arrival.

"Never go into the uprights' nest during the great skylight period," one of my elders warned me repeatedly last warm season.

Despite this caution, I was eager to get a good look at these large creatures. I had never seen one close up. I waited until there was little or no activity in the huge nest. I slipped out from the burrow under their nest, scrambled up the water tube, and climbed one of the high log walls that stretched through the interior. There were numerous places where the grainy material between the logs had been worn or chewed away. I could sit in one of these spots and see into either side — where they eat and where they sleep.

In one of the sleeping areas, on a soft flat surface, an upright was lying. Face up. Eyes closed. For some reason I sensed it was a female. Her eyes opened, and she saw me. But she didn't jump up or make a loud squealing noise, like they say uprights often do. She just looked at me, softly. I ran from one opening to another for better views of her. I wasn't afraid of her until she stood in full upright position. Then I ran for cover.

The uprights are so big!

After a while my curiosity got the best of my better judgment. I came out of hiding and continued to watch her, always from a safe distance. I studied this upright. Unlike most of her species, she didn't seem to mind the presence of a squeaker. When she went into the food area, I followed. The enticing odors of the food she was handling made me realize how hungry I was. I jumped onto one of the planks where these tall creatures store their food. That was a mistake. As soon as she saw me there, she called out loudly to the other upright. In a panic, I headed straight for the water tube and slid down to the safety of our burrow.

I should have heeded my elder's admonition.

* * *

"Koh? The light cycle is ending. It's time to eat."

Nahj always called me to accompany him on his dark-cycle forays. Twink and Mohn were already awake, running and playing atop the logs above our nest.

I preferred to sleep with the young ones in a burrow under a pile of whitebark logs beneath the upright's enormous nest. Nahj slept in the old stump nest just outside.

"I'm going on up the water tube, Koh. The uprights are here, and they must have brought a supply of food that we can sample."

"Okay if I bring the little ones along?"

But Nahj was already up the tube and into the nest.

"Mohn! Twink! You're coming with us. There's food. Jump from the logs to the tube opening, dig your claws in, and move upward. Like this. Watch me."

As the oldest female in our squeaker clan, I considered it my duty to train the young ones to maneuver through tiny openings, to find and identify good food, and, most of all, to resist the snapping killers despite the appealing aroma of the cheese or nutty brown cream that usually sits on them.

Nahj seemed to have no fear of entering the uprights' nest. I always used extreme caution. Too many of our clan had lost their life spirits in the snapping killers. Still others had died from eating delectable morsels that proved deadly. Nevertheless, the uprights' food was a main source for us in the warm season.

At the top of the tube I waited for Twink and Mohn. Peering down, I could see them struggling to keep from falling back to the ground. Despite their youthful clumsiness, they both made it safely to the top.

"Now follow me to the food area. Stay close behind," I instructed, hoping they would remember all my lessons about the dangers inside.

Sticking close to the walls, I scurried through one of the sleeping areas and through the main section, straight to the food planks, Twink and Mohn still behind me.

"There's some really good powder in this box," Nahj said. His face was already covered in white.

"I chewed a hole in the box. Put your head in and taste it."

I did, and the coarse white powder tasted familiar.

"We've had this before, Nahj. It's safe. Let's get the young ones to try it."

Although Twink and Mohn were eager to eat the stolen food, their attention soon turned to climbing over the many novel objects on the wooden planks: hard cylindrical items of various sizes to explore, all sorts of boxes and bags to claw and nibble at.

I left Nahj, Twink, and Mohn enjoying themselves on the food planks. I had some exploring of my own to do. In one of the sliding cavities under the wide plank with a water trough in it, I found a soft, white material with hard silver objects lying on top of it. I shredded some of the white stuff.

It's perfect.

The cavity with the silver items would be perfect for the next batch of young ones: dark, hidden, and soft. And near the food. The new ones would be coming forth very soon. I knew from the movement in my belly, like parts loosening. At least that's the way it was with Twink and Mohn.

I was about to give birth for the second time. Finding this ideal birthing place made me very happy.

The dark cycles are short during the warm season. Before long the great light began to replace the darkness.

"We'd better get back down below," Nahj warned. "The uprights will start moving about soon."

"Go ahead with the young ones. I'll follow shortly." The movement in my belly was insistent.

"Be careful, Koh. You know how dangerous the uprights are."

"Don't worry. I won't be long."

I waited until Nahj, Twink, and Mohn had time to reach the water tube and get below. Then I made my way to the birthing place — not a whit too soon!

* * *

Three of them. Just like last time.

I cleared the birth debris and inspected the three new squeakers. Two had a life spirit pulsing within. One did not. Already I had lost one.

At least it was not eaten by a red bushytail, like Pon from the last batch, I consoled myself.

What's that noise?

A *swoosh-swish* sound was getting louder.

It's an upright coming this way!

I should have stayed with the little ones, but instinctively I hid in the darkness behind the sliding cavity. The upright came into the food area. I could hear a bag being opened. Then before I knew what was happening, the birthing cavity slid open.

My little ones!

Although I was safe in the dark space behind the sliding cavity, my fear was so great I couldn't move. The upright called out. I recognized the voice of the female. This time she called with more urgency than she did when she saw me on the food planks. The other one came quickly. Still I didn't move. The uprights spoke to each other, then slid the birthing cavity back under the plank, into the darkness. I waited.

It seemed as though the uprights were in the food area for such a long while. Finally the sound of their movements faded, and I climbed back into the cavity.

The little ones were undisturbed. The danger had passed, at least for now.

I must find a safer place for them as soon as possible. Perhaps I should take them to Nahj's burrow in the old stump. Whenever I wasn't sure what to do, I always turned to Nahj.

On the way to the stump nest to find him, I encountered Pohg and Min, the other females in our clan. They would both give birth soon, Min for the first time. Pohg had three young ones that were born shortly after Twink and Mohn. There were three or four other squeakers in our clan, but I didn't know much about them.

"I've heard that the uprights are here again and that they have brought a good supply of food," Pohg said. "As soon as they leave in the water-skimmer, we're going up to feast!"

"In the light cycle?" I asked with a tone of disapproval, but with a feeling of guilt over my earlier secret adventure inside the uprights' nest.

Min spoke up timidly. "I know it's risky, but I'm starving."

"Will you join us, Koh?" Pohg was trying to be polite, but I knew she resented my position as first female.

"I don't think so. Nahj and I have already been — during the dark cycle." I hoped she got my meaning. I wondered if Nahj was aware of their plans to break the rules handed down from our ancestors.

I found him in the stump nest nibbling on some seeds he had stored long ago before the white season began.

"Nahj, I've given birth to three little ones in a sliding cavity I prepared in the uprights' food area. Two of them are alive. I don't think the other one is." Nahj kept nibbling. But I knew he was listening.

"In any case, the uprights have discovered them, so we really should move them. I thought perhaps your stump nest, if you don't mind. I still have Twink and Mohn with me in the log nest." I explained, trying to conceal my alarm . . . and my guilt.

Nahj stopped nibbling. He was not pleased. "Why would you do such a thing? A birthing in the uprights' nest? That was not wise, Koh. I agree we should remove them to a safer place. My stump will be fine. I'll help you at the end of our next dark-cycle visit to the food planks. We'll take the new-born down below with us and bring them here, but you'll need to stay with them. I'll have to sleep with Twink and Mohn in the log nest. Honestly, Koh, I'm surprised at you for making such a mistake."

Not wanting to be the only one to displease Nahj, I thought of my conversation with the other two females.

"I just spoke with Pohg and Min. They were on their way to the food planks *now*, during the light cycle. They plan to go up the tube as soon as the uprights leave in the water-skimmer."

As I expected, Nahj was distressed to learn of this plan.

"I'll not allow them to do something so foolish. They'll go with us during the dark-cycle or not at all."

He hurried out of the stump to intercept the truants.

I should have followed my instincts and transported the newborn myself, right then and there. But I acquiesced to Nahj's idea. He always seemed to know when to do what. Yet I worried.

The light cycle was longer in the warm season, and this one seemed especially long. I went into the log nest and tried to sleep. Twink and Mohn had already settled down, eyes closed, and little feet tucked away underneath their brown and white bodies. They had eaten well, played hard, and sleep came easily for them. I tried to keep myself from thinking about the little ones in the darkness of the sliding cavity. I closed my eyes and distracted myself by imagining Nahj's confrontation with Pohg and Min. There would certainly be nose-to-nose contact that would make them understand just how foolhardy they were. Nahj's reprimand would probably save their lives. Since all that didn't matter a bit to me, I soon lost interest in those thoughts and started worrying about my little ones again.

If the uprights were going to hurt them — or even kill them — wouldn't they have done so when they discovered them? Maybe they are good uprights that mean us no harm. But why would our elders and our ancient instincts make us believe the opposite? Maybe because they are so big and make so much noise. Maybe because the snapping killers always appear when the uprights are here. Maybe because . . . .

Sleep finally came, and with it the dark cycle. I awoke from a horrible dream, my body pulsating wildly. I was in the water searching for my little ones. Then there they were, suspended in front of me, two of them looking at me with helpless eyes. But the third one had no sign of life. Eyes closed and quiet, it drifted away. Suddenly there was a great swirl in the water. A dark swimmer engulfed the two living ones.

It was Twink's squeaking that woke me up.

"It's time to go back up the water tube, Koh," she said, pressing her nose against mine. "And I'm hungry."

It took me a moment to register who and where I was. Then I remembered the urgency of the situation in the birthing place, and I was wide awake and ready to go. We had a short wait for Nahj, who had gone to get Pohg and Min. Then the four of us ascended the water tube, followed sheepishly by Min and Pohg with her three young ones.

By now everyone knew the way to the food planks. We all headed in that direction — through the unused sleeping area to the wonderful treasure trove of grains, powders, pastes, and all sorts of exotic treats.

SNAP!

The sound of a snapping killer made us all stop abruptly, practically skidding into each other.

Min! Her enlarged body jerked for a moment then lay still. She was gone — and the little ones within as well. I crept up to her.

Oh, Min, how altogether foolish you have been! I know that with the little ones in your belly you are hungry, but could you not have waited only a little bit longer to eat? We were almost there. Didn't you remember the elders warning about the nutty brown paste that lures us onto the snapping killers? Now we have lost not only you, but three or four little squeakers.

I turned away from the lifeless Min, thinking only of rescuing my own little ones. Faster and faster I ran toward the sliding cavity where I had left them. Through a tiny opening next to the wall I crawled into the dark space, then over the back of the sliding cavity into the birthing place.

Gone! They were gone!

I rushed from one corner of the cavity to the other. Then I searched other sliding cavities. I began running to and fro all over the food area.

I refuse to accept this loss. This can't be.

I ran here and there until others began to notice my frantic movements.

"Koh! Tell me what's wrong." Nahj pressed his nose against mine.

"They're gone, Nahj, the little ones are gone! I've looked everywhere. The uprights have taken them, I just know it."

"Well, at least you're still here. You can have more little ones."

"But you don't understand . . . ."

"I understand that we always suffer the consequences of our own foolishness. This time it was you — and Min. Next time you'll be wiser in selecting a birthing place."

Nahj was right, as usual. That's why he was the head of our clan. I resolved then and there to be more careful. I had learned to avoid the snapping killers and other enticements. I had learned how to hide myself under the leaves and bushes in the open areas and to move along the walls in the uprights' nest. I could distinguish good food from poisonous, and I could teach young ones to run and climb, and to listen and smell for danger.

"I will *never* trust the uprights again," I promised myself.

I was soon to learn the value of that promise.

* * *

During the next light cycle I took on the task of showing Twink and Mohn the edible greens and tiny live crawlers in the open. They needed to know about all our food sources, especially for those times when the water tube was blocked at the top. I called down into the log burrow:

"Twink! Mohn! Follow me . . . and do as I do." The young ones had eaten their fill of upright food and enjoyed a long nap in the log nest. Now they were wide awake and eager to find some diversion. Tumbling over one another, they hurried up to join me on top of the logs.

"We're going out into the open. Remember to stay under the bushes," I warned them. "There is a story about one of our ancestors who was taken up and devoured by a great whitehead. They can see you from way up in the sky, you know. So keep yourself under cover at all times." At these words, the two young squeakers exchanged fearful glances.

I took them to my favorite bush, and we began to nibble on its tender shoots. Mohn, the more courageous of the two, ventured around the plant to its more exposed side.

"Careful, Mohn. Stay hidden under the leaves. You're taking a risk." Twink crept up beside me, her little feet trembling.

"Is the great whitehead watching us now, Koh?"

"He may be. But he can't see you under here. Stay close to me and you'll be safe."

I guess I had said enough to frighten poor Twink. She was always so obedient. Mohn was different, almost defiant. Yet they must both learn to listen to the inner voice of our ancestors if they are to survive one or two warm-season-white-season cycles.

Swoosh! A flapping of wings.

"Mohn! Are you alright?" I squeaked.

No answer. I moved around the plant. Twink stuck to me like a wet leaf. I found Mohn at the base of the plant, his whole body shaking. I went closer and sniffed him. He seemed fine, just scared to death.

"W-w-was it the gr-great whitehead, k-k-Koh?" he stammered.

"No, but it was one of the broadwing flyers. You had a close call. I warned you to stay hidden. But never mind. You are foolish, like most of us squeakers. Now come, let's go back to the nest and wait for the dark cycle."

On the way back I started wondering.

Why didn't I see the flyer before he swooped? Why couldn't I hear his approach? I could have signaled Mohn.

I suppose it was in that moment I realized the limitations of my own kind.

We squeakers cannot see or hear like any of the flyers, or any of the bushytails, and certainly not like the longclaws or even the uprights. But we can squeeze through tiny apertures, we can find the best hiding places, we can eat the uprights' food, and we can train our young.

Those thoughts stirred in me a certain pride in being a squeaker. I was willing to die, if necessary, to help my clan survive. It was a good feeling that made me eager to attempt another raid on the uprights' food, and eager to bring more squeakers forth from my belly.

Just before reaching the nest we encountered Nahj, and with him the now-submissive Pohg. Nahj nosed up to me.

"Are the three of you going with us this dark cycle?"

"Of course!" my recently aquired pride blurted out. "I haven't yet had a chance to eat my fill of the white powder."

"Good. There's plenty of it. I think there will be quite a few from our clan coming along this time. Just be sure to remind Twink and Mohn — and yourself — about the snapping killers. Remember Min."

Nahj must now think I'm one of the foolish squeakers. But he'll see just how determined I've become.

"Take our young squeakers and go ahead up the tube. We're off to get Pohg's young ones. We'll be there shortly."

Nahj and Pohg moved on toward her nest in an old whitebark.

"I don't want to go into the upright's nest, Koh! Look — I'm still shaking."

"Now, Mohn, the danger from the flyer is past. You've got to recover your courage. Just listen to the inner voice of our ancestors, both of you, and remember all my instructions. There's no need to be afraid."

Mohn and Twink put their noses together and exchanged troubled glances, but they obeyed and followed as I led the way, trying my best to exude my renewed confidence.

When we reached the water tube, other squeakers had already started up. The tube was good and dry, so the ascent was easy. We gathered at the top of the tube opening in the uprights' nest and waited until Pohg, her young ones, and finally Nahj joined us.

With Nahj leading the brigade, we proceeded quietly and cautiously along our normal course through the unused sleeping area.

Something didn't seem quite right. There was only a small opening between the sleeping area and the large space we had to cross to access the food planks.

"Nahj!" I called from behind Pohg and her young ones, but he was too far ahead to hear me. Before I could call again I was stepping on some kind of crackling paper that made a scratching sound. It was spotted with cheese and the alluring nutty cream, like that used in the snapping killers. I was panic-stricken but didn't know what to do. All around me I could hear squeaker feet scratching on the paper and squeaker mouths eating the food.

"Mohn! Twink! Watch out! The nutty cream is . . ."

I didn't have a chance to complete the warning. At that moment the dark-cycle skylight appeared in the uprights' nest and a bright beam from it shone down on us. It moved along the surface we were running on.

How could it come down from the sky and into the uprights' nest? I wondered.

I had no time to consider the question, for the female upright started after us, and the entire clan began to rush forward following the beam of light. Everything was happening so fast. On one side of us there was some kind of barrier. On the other was the log wall I had climbed when the uprights' first arrived. I found myself running with the others, faster and faster.

The beam pointed the way to a large opening. Once we passed through it, the opening quickly closed behind the last squeaker. I wasn't sure where we were, but I could smell the whitebarks and longneedles. Although we were not completely out in the open yet, I knew we were safe. Nahj led us to a tiny hole through which we could drop one by one into the area beneath the nest.

All the squeakers were in a panic. I didn't even have to exert any effort. I was propelled forward by the general push to escape danger. I tumbled down below where the squeakers were falling pell-mell into a heap. There I was, wriggling on top of some squeakers I didn't even know. But at that moment we were all just trying to survive. There was general chaos. Some went running one way, some another, only to turn around and race in the opposite direction. Panic was in every eye.

"We're going to perish!" one squeaker cried.

"They're coming after us!" warned another.

"Quick! Take cover!"

I was jostled and knocked about but somehow managed to reach the log nest and slip down into the burrow. I found Mohn, Twink, and Nahj huddled together. Nahj stood up on his hind feet to greet me.

"Are you all right?" he asked, touching his nose to mine.

"I think so. I just haven't had time to understand what happened. There was so much confusion. But I'm unharmed. What about you and the young ones?"

"Twink was slightly injured when she fell below, but it's not bad. She'll be fine."

It took me some time to settle down after all the pandemonium. I tried to collect my thoughts, but all I could remember was the light that appeared so suddenly inside the uprights' nest.

It couldn't have been the dark-cycle skylight.

I closed my eyes to relive the moment.

No! It was in the female uprights' front paw. How could that be?

I remembered seeing lights in the uprights' nest during dark cycles while the skylight was outside.

The uprights have their own lights. But what was she doing with it? I just can't believe she meant us harm. She must have been . . . Yes! She must have been showing us the way to escape. That's it. She was trying to help us. After all, the light she held led us out and away from the food that was surely poisonous.

I hadn't forgotten the loss of my little ones, and I still didn't trust the uprights. I didn't even like them. But I was convinced that this one had tried to help us. She had shown us the way out with her light. We were all safe now.

The four of us nestled up together. Our pounding hearts resumed their normal rhythm and breathing became regular. In my inner vision I could still see the upright female lying in the sleeping area, watching me with the same curiosity with which I considered her. I could see her standing behind a stream of confused squeakers and projecting a beam of light to save us.

She saved us, I'm sure. I only hoped that someone would show her a way out if ever she were to be trapped in the darkness.

Chapter 11: The Year of the Bear

Karen

"What in the world are you looking for?"

Steve was ransacking the boxes of groceries that Bobby's friend at the Safeway in Winnipeg had so neatly packed.

"Something special — for us — that I asked Bobby to include." He went down on one knee and pulled the tape off another carton.

"What is it?"

"It was going to be a surprise — for us to celebrate."

"Celebrate what?" I began to put the helter-skelter groceries in some kind of order on the food shelves.

Steve stopped his search, propped a forearm on his horizontal thigh, and looked at me.

"Well, for one thing, we've just completed six years of marriage, and for another . . . ."

He stood up, sauntered over to me, put an arm around my shoulders, and announced the news he could no longer contain.

"The Ladies of the Lake are on their way to the publishers."

"You mean the manuscript has been accepted!" I gave him an excited hug.

"Not yet. But I feel pretty confident. Several colleagues looked over my work and gave me a thumbs-up. One said he thought I had a really good chance with a certain press. So off it went the day before we left."

"I'm so proud of you — but you should have told me! And what's the 'surprise' we're to celebrate with?"

"Champagne, of course. I asked Bobby to tuck a bottle in somewhere without letting you know about it. He's hidden it so well I can't find the damn thing."

The Perrier-Jouet turned up cushioned in Steve's clothing duffle. We let it chill in the freezer compartment of the refrigerator while we set up housekeeping and had lunch. Then we clinked mismatched water glasses from the dish cupboard and toasted each of our six years and each of Steve's literary Ladies.

"You know you can't drink and drive the boat, my dearly beloved," I said as I straddled his lap facing him, my hands clasped behind his neck.

"So I guess we'll have to think of something else to do this afternoon. Any ideas?"

I unbuttoned my flannel shirt under which I was braless. The shirt fell to the floor. And that's me — when I'm a woman in the wilderness.

* * *

The morning was cloudy with a misty rain. The wind was churning up white caps on the lake. Our celebration surprise had left me with a grand headache. Steve was sleeping it off, while I sipped black coffee on the screened porch thinking I should have used a little moderation.

The cold air felt refreshing at first, but now I was getting chilled.

Steve might enjoy a nice fire in the woodstove when he wakes up.

I slipped on a rain jacket, pulled up the hood, went down the steps and around the cabin. After a visit to the outhouse, I stopped at the woodpile. As I selected an armload of split wood, I noticed a strange odor. Not a pleasant one.

An animal. It's definitely an animal odor. And a large one at that. Has to be a moose or bear.

I stood perfectly still, senses heightened, and looked and listened. No sound other than the wind.

There! On the tree trunk.

I dropped the armload of wood and went to the edge of the cabin clearing to inspect the white bark of an aspen poplar. Waving gently with the movement of the wind were wisps of long black hair. Waist high.

Not a moose, and not small. He must have been roaming around while we slept.

Acting on an instinct of self-preservation, I grabbed up the wood and hurried to the safety of the cabin. When I reached the door to the interior, I remembered Bobby's early explanation to Steve about the necessity of a metal door rather than a wooden one. I slipped inside, put the wood down next to the heat stove, closed the metal cabin door firmly, and stood there shivering, not from the cold.

Steve must have heard me come in. He appeared at the bedroom door, hair rumpled, wearing only his sweat pants, and clutching the empty champagne bottle.

"Looking for this?" He held it up.

The sight and sound of him had a calming effect, and I managed to smile and answer in a somewhat collected manner.

"In another six years, maybe. Right now I think we have a bear problem."

"A *what* problem?"

"Seriously. I went outside to get some firewood, and I could smell a bear."

"You could *smell* it?"

"Well . . ., yes. And I found some black bear hair on a tree trunk."

"I feel like I had an encounter with a bear last night. At least, there was something kinda wild in the bed with me — as well as I can remember."

He set the bottle down on the central table, padded barefooted into the kitchen, poured himself some coffee, and padded back to the fire. I had it going pretty good by then and was wondering just how wild I had become last night.

Bobby had added an indoor couch in the cabin which we pulled up closer to the fire. We sat in silence for a while, mesmerized by the flames and the cracking sound of the burning wood.

Before long I wearied of inactivity.

"After lunch I'm going fishing, despite the wind, the rain, the cold, *and* the bear," I announced.

Steve drained his coffee cup. "Didn't take you long to get cabin fever, did it, KK?"

"It's fishing fever. I just have to get my line in the water. Besides, aren't you hungry for a fish dinner?"

"Right now I'm not hungry for anything, except maybe an Alka-Seltzer."

* * *

In the afternoon the skies lightened a bit, and the wind died down enough for us to get out on the lake. It rained a little — off and on — so we didn't venture too far from the cabin, but still we caught enough walleyes for a meal. Steve suggested that we not bother taking the fish skins and guts across the lake in the rain, so we tossed all the refuse into the shallow water in front of the cabin, next to the dock. I baked the fillets in aluminum foil, using a recipe Bobby told me the guides at Baldwin Lake used for shore lunch on rainy days: fresh tomatoes, onions, mushrooms, and canned applesauce.

"It's good," Steve commented, "but I still like 'em fried best."

"So do I. But it must be a lot healthier baked like this. I notice that there's none left."

Clean-up was easy. We discarded the used foil, washed two plates and two forks, put on heavy sweaters, and sat on the porch. The wind was calm. A bright white moon, shining through broken clouds, bathed the lake in silver luminescence. Steve talked a little about the graduate course he would like to create, naturally one based on the subject of his book.

"I would use it as the main textbook for the class."

I rambled on about the pieces I would like to program on my next recital.

Soon we were just sitting in the darkness, quietly listening to the sounds of nature — night birds, loons, ducks, the gentle lapping of the water, an occasional rustle of wind in the poplars.

Suddenly Steve jumped up, ran to the screen door, and looked out into the semi-darkness. He turned around and spoke in a half whisper.

"Something came crashing through the woods, headed this way!"

I scrambled to his side. "What is it? Can you see it?"

"He's gone back into the bush now. He must have seen me stand up."

We stood as still as statues, waiting, listening, looking.

Then I saw it. Outlined against the silver lake was the dark, unmistakable silhouette of a bear. Head down, he seemed to be scavenging at the edge of the lake, exactly where we had thrown the fish remains.

The scene was so imposing that I found myself more awed than afraid. From somewhere deep down inside me came an intuitive action. I called out to the creature.

"Get! . . . Go! Go! Get away from here!" I commanded him in a loud and authoritative voice. Immediately the bear obeyed. He turned around, loped alongside the lake, and disappeared into the darkness of the trees and underbrush.

Nevertheless, I continued the vigil. Steve went inside and returned with two stove pots.

"Here. Bang these together. I've heard that bears can be frightened off by loud noises and bright lights."

He left me banging away, while he lit all the butane lanterns in the cabin. We kept a noisy watch until well after midnight. There were no more signs of a bear present around the cabin. Steve convinced me that he was probably in the next province by now, I had scared him so badly. We decided to try to get some sleep.

"You really amazed me when you started yelling at the bear. You didn't seem at all afraid."

"I amazed myself, too. And, no, I wasn't afraid, especially after I saw him take off when I yelled. I think he's more afraid of us than we are of him."

"I sure hope so."

But our dealings with the bear were far from over.

* * *

Steve was the first one up the next morning, so I had *my* coffee served in bed for a change.

I sat up in the sleeping bag and took the cup of steaming brew from him.

"I could get used to this."

"I didn't get much sleep last night, did you?"

He did look a little droopy.

"Actually I did. In fact, I probably slept better than I ever have — no worries about a bear in the back of my mind. They're afraid of us and don't want any contact."

"I kept thinking I heard noises, like the bear coming back."

I took a sip of coffee. "It's strange, but now that I know bears are afraid of *me*, I don't have to be afraid of *them* anymore. After all, we were the ones to make a mistake. We cleaned the fish and left the remains in the lake out front. So who's to blame for the bear's intrusion?"

"But when I first heard him, he was coming toward the cabin. Why?"

"Hmmm. I don't know. We've been as careful as always with food. There has to be a reason. Something we're unaware of."

"Yea, well, just in case, I'm going to call Bobby on the radio phone and let him know the situation. He'll probably come and shoot the beast."

"That's a little drastic, don't you think? We can just go on making noise and lighting lanterns at night. That seems to keep it away."

"We'll see what Bobby says. For right now, get dressed, Sweetheart. Let's forget about the bear and go fishing. It's a beautiful day. We should take advantage of it."

I agreed whole-heartedly, relieved that the subject of bumping off the bear had been set aside. The weather was gorgeous, still a bit cool, but sunny and no wind. We decided to make a whole day of it: put food in the cooler and take it along in the boat and not return to the cabin for lunch. I packed ham sandwiches, a bag of potato chips, two cans of ginger ale, and a few chocolate cookies.

We spent the morning fishing around eagle-nest island, where I renewed acquaintance with my feathered friends. We couldn't determine whether there were eaglets or not, but the male and female were there, intrigued by our fishing efforts. We tied up on the island and sat in the boat to enjoy our lunch. I left part of a ham sandwich and a few chips on a rock for them to enjoy. They'd probably eat the ham, and gulls would get the rest.

That afternoon we did nothing but catch-and-release fishing. Canned spaghetti and meatballs were on the menu for dinner.

"Are you about ready to head home, KK?"

"Whenever you are." I began reeling in.

As Steve motored back through the channel toward the cabin, I became uneasy, apprehensive. I tried to ignore the feeling and concentrate on the beauty that surrounded me, but it kept growing stronger as we neared the cabin. My hands were visibly shaking as I tied the boat to the dock. I gathered my rods and picked up the cooler. Steve followed me with his rods and the tackle box. At the screened door I stopped.

"I smell it again, Steve." I spoke in a low voice.

"The bear?"

"I think so. It's the same odor I noticed yesterday morning, only stronger."

"Okay. Let's go in and call Bobby."

We sat everything down on the porch. Steve reached for the knob on the metal door, but before opening it, he turned around toward me.

"Stay out here on the porch until I check the cabin."

I nodded.

He stepped inside and closed the door quietly behind him.

I waited for what seemed like an eternity, my heart pounding in my ears. No sounds came from within. I guess that was a good sign. Then the door opened.

"It's all right. There's no bear in here now, but there has been, and he's pretty well eaten all our food. The kitchen's a mess."

With my back close to the doorjamb, I slithered into the cabin. At first glance everything looked normal, but the odor was sickening. Getting up my courage, I walked around the half-wall that separated the main room from the kitchenette. What I saw will remain permanently etched in my mind.

The refrigerator was on the floor, face up, with the door ripped off. There were broken jars, torn boxes and bags, and pots and pans everywhere. Food was smeared over the entire cooking area. The door to the wall cabinet that held the dishes had been pulled off and several of the plates and glasses shattered.

I felt nauseous, not so much from what I saw as from what I smelled — like the large mammal section of a zoo, only concentrated, overwhelming.

"He smashed through the back bedroom window, and I guess he went out the same way. The mattress on the bed under the window is all clawed up." Steve had made a thorough inspection of the cabin.

"He didn't go into our bedroom or the bathroom. Looks like he just wanted food."

Steve seemed to be thinking out loud. "We'd better call Bobby right now, and we'll have to do something about that open window right away. The bear may well come back through it. It's not safe for us to be in here."

"You're right. One thing I can say for sure: if he does come back, he won't find anything to eat."

Steve wasn't sure how to operate the radio phone, but after several attempts he reached an operator who said he would immediately relay the message to Baldwin Lake Lodge.

Within minutes Bobby called us.

"Probably a she-bear with hungry cubs. There's plywood under all the mattresses. Pull out one of those and nail it up over the window. I keep a few tools in the big storage box on the porch. You'll find a hammer and some heavy nails in there. That should be enough to deter her from re-entering. Besides, she'll not look for anymore food tonight. I'll fly in early tomorrow morning. I know it will be hard, but try to stay calm — and even get some sleep."

We tugged the plywood out from under the clawed mattress, then went to look for the hammer and nails in the storage box. When I raised the hinged lid, I made quite a startling discovery.

"So that's what was attracting the bear!" I knelt for a closer look.

The tool box was filled with snack food — open potato chips, open peanut butter, sticks of beef jerky, and candy bars, some unwrapped. There was even a carton of milk that had spoiled. I sat back on my heels in dismay.

"Maybe we couldn't smell this stuff, but I'm sure the bear could. And that's why he was coming toward the cabin last night. Wonder who left all this?"

"Obviously somebody was here before us this year."

"But we're always the first guests in. Bobby said so himself," I reminded Steve.

"I feel responsible for attracting the bear, Karen. I should have never suggested leaving the fish skins so close to the cabin."

"That was down by the lake, not here in the cabin. Whoever left the food in the toolbox is the culprit."

We cleared out the foodstuffs, located the hammer and nails, fixed the plywood over the window, and began working on the kitchen. There was very little food left, and it had been contaminated by the bear. It didn't matter, though, neither of us had any appetite for dinner. The only thing the bear hadn't consumed was the beer. And we sure needed that.

* * *

Bobby arrived about six a.m. The first thing he unloaded off the Cessna was a rifle.

"You remember how to fire one of these, Stevie?"

"It's been a few hundred years since Dad took us target practicing, but I think I can handle it." Bobby passed Steve the gun and a box of shells.

"If the bear shows up again, you'll have to shoot her. We can't have a spoiled bear coming into the camp. Aim for the head. That way you'll stop her cold — unless you miss. I've filled out a special hunting license for you. The government has pretty strict rules and regulations when it comes to killing wild animals."

I didn't say anything to either of the guys, but I wasn't going to let that mother bear be shot, not if I could help it. I'd make such a racket every night that she wouldn't dare come within a mile of the cabin. And we certainly wouldn't leave any more fish guts on this side of the lake.

Bobby then unloaded a large ice chest that contained food and drink from the lodge.

"It's mostly non-perishables — cans and boxes, but I did throw in a couple of ribeye steaks and some eggs. The ice in the chest should keep them cool enough for a couple of days. And there are blocks of ice from the lake in the ice shed, under all that pine straw. You can chip up some."

Steve helped him put up heavy boards across the outside of the broken window, carry out the old refrigerator, and get it into the plane.

I told Bobby about all the food we had found in the tool box.

"Who do you suppose left that stuff here?" I asked him.

"Must have been the guys I hired to fly in last week and fix up the place, hook up the butane, and get everything in working order. They were just careless, I guess. I'm sorry this had to happen while you're here, Karen. This is the first time I've ever had a bear to break in after the guests arrive. I hope it hasn't completely ruined your vacation."

"It's been a little unnerving, I'll admit — for both of us, and probably for you, too."

"Do you want to stay out the week? I can fly you back to Baldwin, if you'd rather."

"Of course not. We'll be fine. Thanks for replacing the food." I gave him a hug and watched the color rise to his cheeks.

After a few last-minute instructions to Steve about the use of the radio phone, Bobby and the Cessna took off and left us waving on the dock. We were alone again in the wilderness. Just Steve, me, and the bear. I wondered how brave I really was, and how good a marksman Steve was.

* * *

"A bear broke into your cabin? And ate all your food?"

Ellen hadn't touched her cappuccino during my account of the bear episode.

"It's hard for me to believe, too. But honestly, I wasn't too scared. She ran from me when I yelled, so I knew she didn't want to confront me.

She wasn't after me — just my food."

"*She*? How do you know it was a female?"

"That's what Bobby figured. A female with cubs somewhere."

"How did Steve react to all that?"

"He seemed pretty upset at first, but he was so heroic! He went into the cabin even though we thought the bear might be in there. Made me wait on the porch — he didn't have to twist my arm. I don't think he got much sleep the whole week. He kept the rifle propped by his side of the bed. Even since we've been home, he has had a lot of trouble sleeping. Finally Dr. Johnson gave him some knock-out pills."

The bear episode was much discussed in the family. Mama — and most of the ladies of the Spring Hill Woman's Club — thought we should stop going to Canada and start taking our vacations at one of the Carolina beaches.

"It would be so much more relaxing, and safe," Mama said.

And so boring, I thought but didn't say it. I learned long ago to listen to Mama and to give her advice serious consideration. She was usually right. But I never wanted to give up Poplar River. No one understood that except Bobby.

Everyone knew about the "bear business up there in the woods." It had been another hot topic of conversation in Spring Hill for several months now. People were quite concerned about my summertime safety. But I was more concerned about Steve.

He didn't seem to be himself anymore. Each week he became more morose. The mood swings he had demonstrated early in our marriage had reappeared, only worse. Nothing I did or didn't do made any difference. I didn't want Mama and Daddy worrying about that, too, so I didn't mention it to them.

By Thanksgiving he was in such a state that others began to notice. Katherine and Ted were the first to say anything to me about it. My sister pulled me aside after the traditional turkey dinner at Mama's and Daddy's.

"What's with Steve these days, KK? He's so quiet. Has nothing to say anymore. Is he ill?"

"I don't think so. Maybe it's just the pressure of his job. He's up for tenure this year, you know."

I wanted to talk to Steve about it before discussing it with anyone else. But Steve wouldn't talk.

"Don't worry about me," was all he'd say when I tried to get him to tell me what thc problem was.

We made it through the Christmas holidays okay. He even seemed to enjoy helping me decorate the tree. But that reprieve was short-lived.

By February I was really worried. All he did at home was play with Meredith, take his pills, and sleep. Of course he taught his classes but wasn't meeting with students as he usually did, nor was he attending conferences or researching at all. His book was finished, but helping students and presenting professional lectures were part of his responsibilities as a professor that he seemed to be neglecting. That wasn't at all like the Steve Marsten I knew.

I, on the other hand, was happily turning down more contracts for performance than I accepted. I had become very selective. No more music clubs or fund-raisers. I liked playing concertos with orchestras — good orchestras, not small-town high school ensembles. I was able to keep the perennial favorites well-honed: the Schumann, of course, the Rachmaninoff second, and the Beethoven fourth and fifth. They were always in demand. Besides, in order to honor my commitment to Heyward, I had to perform regularly as well as teach college piano majors three afternoons a week. I covered students' lessons for Lavinsky when he was away in performance, and he covered for me. Even with a couple of hours daily practicing, I still had time for Meredith and Steve. Occasionally I took time to cook a real family meal.

Spring break came a little later than usual — first week of April. Even so, the weather had not warmed up, and Steve cancelled our projected trip to Disneyworld. Meredith was devastated.

"Can't you just do this for your daughter? It means so much to her."

"I just want to stay home and rest."

"Are you really that tired? You don't seem to be working as hard as you used to. Maybe you should see Dr. Johnson again. Or another doctor." I had a psychiatrist in mind. I was getting a little put out with his behavior, especially the constant sleeping.

"Maybe you have some kind of chronic fatigue. A doctor could help."

"Well, I'm sorry, but I'm just tired. In fact, I'm going to take a nap before dinner, okay?"

"That's just fine. I'm making lasagna for tonight, and it takes a while. I hope you wake up when it's time to eat." I couldn't disguise the irritation in my voice.

Before turning to go upstairs, he came up to me, took me in his arms, and gave me a kiss — a warm, tender kiss.

"I love you, Sweetheart," he said, like the old Steve.

"I love you, too."

* * *

Two hours later — my lack of culinary skills not withstanding — the lasagna was a masterpiece. Meredith had been my sous-chef, fetching cans of tomatoes from the pantry and cheeses from the refrigerator.

"Now, Sugar, go wake up Daddy."

"Okay."

She skipped out of the kitchen and clamored up the steps. I set the table. In a few minutes Meredith came back into the kitchen holding an envelope.

"Daddy wouldn't wake up, Mama. So I went to my room to get the little fire truck that makes so much noise. I thought that would wake him up. And I found this, but it's not printed, it's the kind of writing I can't read yet."

She opened the envelope and pulled out a folded piece of paper.

"Let me see, Sweetie. Where did you find it?"

"Pooh Bear was holding it."

Dearest Karen, my only love,

I can never forgive myself for failing you and Meredith. Both of you deserve so much more. I have lost my sons, I have lost my job, I have failed in everything I have tried to do. I have no hope nor any self-respect left. And it is entirely my fault. KK, you are the successful one, I am only holding you back. No more. By the time you read this, I will be at peace, and you will be free.

All my love forever,
Steve

Chapter 12: The Year of the Bear

Malra

The birthing place I had prepared under some fallen longneedles pleased me. It was sheltered from the wind, and the needles, which were still green, provided a refreshing protective covering. The location was perfect: far enough away from the uprights' nest and close to a small flow of water. Edible greens abounded in the area, so I didn't have to go far from Brahn and Padda to feed myself. But the two younglings were drinking so much and growing so fast, my body couldn't produce sufficient milk to satisfy them.

During the last few dark cycles they kept crying, "More milk, Malra! More milk!" Their tiny squealing voices were compelling. I just had to eat more, and more often. I needed to go foraging for substantial food. But the cubs were not mature enough to come with me.

These younglings were not my first. I had brought forth new-born longclaws several times before. The first time, I lost one to a large bushytail, and from the next batch, one simply disappeared while I was out searching for food. I faced a dilemma: I needed to stay, and I needed to go.

For now, all was well. They were sleeping soundly, and I, too, wanted to rest. At the next light cycle I would decide what to do.

* * *

At first light, with the younglings sleeping, I emerged from the hollow and sniffed the air in all directions.

Something nutty. I smell something nutty.

I stood on my hind feet and sniffed again, trying to judge its location. The aroma was definitely coming from the direction of the uprights' nest.

There had been no activity in the nest in the last few light-dark cycles, so I felt pretty safe as I loped along the path.

Once in the clearing around the uprights' log nest I rubbed against some whitebarks to mark the area as mine. Kohn, the longclaw who had sired all my younglings, sometimes roamed this far. I wanted him to know that I claimed this part of our territory, along with the uprights. It contained a profusion of berry bushes that would be filled with delicious blue fruit the cubs and I could enjoy later in the warm season. I knew it was dangerous to feed this close to the uprights' nest, but I could never resist the berries.

As I neared the structure, my nose indicated that there was a variety of interesting food in the more open part of the uprights' nest, the part facing the water. Just as I began circling the big nest looking for an easy way in, the distant but unmistakable sound of the roaring bird caught my attention.

The uprights are coming.

I hurried away from the nest area, ran into the bush and back along the path to the hollow.

"Malra! Milk!"

They must have heard me approaching, and, of course, they were hungry.

"Come on, younglings, let me teach you how to find white and black crawlers under rocks and moss." A lesson they needed to learn, and a diversion from my near-empty milk sacks.

I showed them how to use their front claws to turn over the rocks and scoop out the white crawlers. They learned how to claw up moss to find the black ones. Before long they were enjoying the discovery of a hidden food source, tearing up moss and flipping one rock after another.

"This is fun, Malra, but I still want milk." Brahn told me in no uncertain terms.

"You'll have milk soon. I promise you both."

I knew that I could go to the uprights' nest for food. They always bring edibles with them in the roaring bird, I can smell them. And I frequently detect the aroma of freshly killed swimmers and the burned flesh of unknown animals coming from their nest. But I've always been hesitant to scavenge inside their nest — I was too afraid of the uprights. Especially the ones who, with their firesticks, have been known to take away the life spirit of longclaws and great antlered ones. Those that used the water-skimmers were not so frightening. But I could never be sure. I feared them all and normally stayed away from their small territory, except to nibble on the blue fruit. The uprights were very unpredictable. Yet the nutty flavor I noticed earlier was strongly attracting me.

While I watched the younglings flipping rocks, I lay down and made plans to enter the uprights' nest.

They're usually quiet during dark cycles, probably sleeping. In the next dark cycle I'll try again to find the nutty food. I know it will help make milk for Brahn and Padda. Nuts are always good and filling. But none are available this early in the warm season. Just thinking about nuts made my mouth water. Yes, as soon as the dark cycle comes again, I'll look for nuts in the uprights' nest.

The younglings had filled their bellies with crawlers. Now flipping stones and tossing moss had become playtime for them. After that, they amused themselves with several vigorous mock fights. The food and energetic play assured an immediate and deep slumber.

The great light faded and hid itself below the horizon. With the younglings sound asleep in the hollow, I set out once again on the path. The dark-cycle skylight was especially bright, lighting up the sky, the water, and the uprights' angular nest. There was no sound or light coming from inside the nest, but food aromas were everywhere. It was the nutty-flavored food I craved. Its odor grew stronger as I approached the front of the nest. It was definitely coming from the front — where the uprights go in and out with their long sticks and strings, to and from the water-skimmer and the roaring bird.

The nutty aroma was causing my mouth juices to flow uncontrollably. I could almost taste it, whatever it was.

About halfway into the clearing in front of the nest, one of the uprights stood up and came toward me. It must have been guarding the nutty food.

It may be coming after me with a firestick!

I ran back into the woods where I hoped the upright couldn't see me. I had to stay alive. The younglings could not yet survive without me.

Safe in the darkness of the trees and bushes, I listened for the sound of the firestick. But there was none. Only the voices of the uprights speaking in low, soft tones.

I wonder if they smelled me, or heard me, or saw me? Since they are guarding the nutty food, I can't get to it. But I am so hungry. I must eat.

I sniffed the air and picked up the scent of dead swimmers coming from the water's edge. I went toward it. Before I knew it, my snout was in the water, and I was swallowing golden swimmer skins. That wasn't what I wanted, not what I came looking for, but I didn't care. It was food, and I needed food.

The sound of an upright shouting caused me again to take cover. Although I had not eaten enough, I had risked enough. I wanted more swimmer skins, and I hungered for the nutty food, but I followed my deep care-giver instincts back to the cubs.

* * *

At early light the younglings, half awake, began nuzzling my belly, seeking the milk sacks. While they were drinking what little there was, I listened for sounds from the uprights' nest.

As soon as I heard the noise of the water-skimmer I knew they were leaving the nest for a while, and it would be safe for me to enter.

"Brahn, you and Padda must stay at the hollow. You can play around outside and search for crawlers, but under no circumstances are you to wander away. I'm going foraging, but I'll be back soon, and there will be more milk."

I stood on all fours, crawled out of the hollow and onto the path. After a few steps I turned to look back. Two little longclaw faces were watching me, wide-eyed and innocent, from the opening to the hollow. The sight of them filled me with the joy of being a female longtoothed longclaw. I was determined to care and provide for these younglings until it was time for them to start their separate lives.

Staying under the cover of bushes and trees, I moved up and around to the back of the uprights' nest. I stood very still for a while and listened, just to be sure there were no sounds in the nest. I spotted some squeakers scurrying around underneath the nest and remembered how, not so many warm seasons back, I would have caught an antlered youngling if he had not slipped under the nest. His horns were barely beginning to show. He would have been so tender and tasty! The thought of him made me step through the clearing to the back of the nest.

By chance there may be another one hiding under there.

Lowering my shoulders to peer under the nest, I sniffed long and hard but couldn't smell any creature other than the squeakers who had all hidden when I stuck my head in. But I could smell food — the uprights' food. Then I remembered why I had come. Not for squeakers or a young antlered one, but for upright food, the nutty food.

There were two openings in the back of the nest, one low enough for me to look inside, if I stood on my hind feet. I found it covered with something hard, but I could still see through it. Digging my claws into the logs around the opening I pushed my head through, shattering the hard, clear covering with a loud crashing sound.

What if the uprights should hear that?

But it was too late. I was inside standing on a soft flat surface raised slightly above the bottom layer of the nest. The odor of uprights was strong. I jumped off the softness to the hard layer below it. I raised my head and sniffed. I recognized the aroma of smoked flesh and followed it into the food area. There were containers of various shapes. I bit into them one by one and found exotic flavors that were unknown to me. Some of the containers held greens, some yellow kernels. Some contained powders, some flesh. I delighted in them all!

But where is that smoked flesh I smelled at first? And there is animal fat somewhere. Where are these especially good aromas coming from?

I sniffed a large white box that stood almost as tall as I am when on my hind feet.

There! That's where the good stuff is.

I swatted my paws at the object until it fell over and opened up. And there they were, fatty strips of smoked flesh and bars of yellow, rich fat. I devoured them both, along with unhatched shells and all the other food I found inside the white box. I ate and ate and ate. I still hadn't found the nutty food, but I wasn't hungry any more.

I'll come back in another light cycle to get it.

I left the food area and, standing on the soft surface, hoisted myself out the same opening I had entered.

Now Brahn and Padda will have milk.

I felt content as I loped back along the path toward the hollow and my younglings.

* * *

Late in the next light cycle I took the young longclaws to a place where flowing water rippled over rocks and logs.

"You'll learn to catch some swimmers here," I told them. As usual, they thought of it more as a game rather than work to feed themselves. I showed them how to put their claws under the water between two rocks and trap the swimmers that were passing through.

"And if there are no swimmers, the bark from these soft, wet branches lying in the water can be stripped off and eaten."

I wasn't sure Brahn and Padda were absorbing the lesson, for they were busy chasing each other over the wet rocks, slipping, sliding, and falling in. Besides, they had spent the morning drinking milk and were probably not very keen on working for food. Furthermore, during the lesson they were distracted by the sound of the roaring bird.

"What's that, Malra?"

I tried to define it, not really knowing myself what that bird-like monster was.

"It's a great flyer that brings the uprights to their nest." That feeble explanation seemed to satisfy their curiosity, and the frolicking commenced anew.

On the way back to the hollow I stopped, stood up, and sniffed. It was a familiar odor — a longclaw. Kohn. The odor was getting stronger, so I knew he was coming this way.

"Brahn! Padda! Come here. Stay with me now. Kohn is coming."

Kohn was the largest longclaw I had ever seen. Many warm seasons ago, when I first wandered away from my birthing area and came into his territory, he terrified me, standing erect and making powerful snorting sounds. I ran to the nearest white bark and climbed up, hoping to get away from him. He circled beneath me, snarling and blowing. I just knew he would climb up after me and hurt me, maybe take my life spirit away. Instead, he made strange sounds I had never heard before, alluring sounds.

"Come down," he said. "I won't harm you. Just come down to me."

He was very persuasive, and deep inside I felt the urge to be with him. I backed down the whitebark. Once I was on the ground, he made low, growling sounds that attracted me even more. He circled me several times then stood up against my rear part.

"This must be the ritual dance my ancestors have whispered about in my inward ear." Then I realized he was putting younglings into my belly.

Even though we had repeated the dance many times since then, I still feared him. He was strong. He could destroy flattail nests and devour the young. And paddlers, and long-eared hoppers. He never seemed to be without food.

He was close now. I could see his enormous, dark body lumbering down the path ahead. As soon as he came into full view, I snorted and blew several warnings, then turned and ran to the safety of a thick-trunked longneedle. I stood up and with my front paws held my underside against the trunk. Brahn and Padda did the same, retreating a little farther behind me.

Kohn stood up and snorted. Then he continued toward me.

He is not signaling the dance. He is behaving as though he wants to tell me something.

I let go of the tree, resumed a four-footed stance, and waited for him to approach me. The younglings held fast to the trunk of their longneedle. They had never seen Kohn or any longclaw other than me. I knew they were scared.

He came closer and closer. Suddenly, without thinking, I rushed at him, blowing as hard as I could. Then I stopped short, turned and retreated slowly, clacking my jaws. I was worried he might harm the younglings, though he never had before. I charged again and he met me. We both stood and nipped warnings at each other's faces and necks. But we inflicted no injuries.

Convinced that he meant us no harm, I settled down to hear what he had to communicate.

"Listen, Malra, the roaring bird has returned . . ."

"Yes, I know. I heard it."

"I think the upright in the bird brought a firestick."

"I thought these were the ones with sticks and strings, not the ones with firesticks. They usually get here much later, just before the white season begins."

"I was drinking from the streamlet in the flattail pond area, when the roaring bird landed on the water and came to the log perch. One upright climbed down out of the bird and gave what looked like a firestick to the male upright who's been staying in the nest. They may be looking for an antlered one, but it could be a longclaw they're after. Have you been near the nest?"

I turned my head, pretending to look for the younglings. How could I explain to Kohn why I had gone against the inner voice of our ancestors when I invaded the uprights's nest and ate their food. Kohn would never understand the need of a life-giver for food, not for herself, but for the younglings.

"I . . . went looking for berries near the nest, as I do every warm season — with never any confrontation."

"Berries? It's much too early in the warm season for berries. What were you thinking? You should be more careful, Malra. When uprights go after a longclaw, they will use their firesticks on any or all of us. You are endangering not only yourself, but all longclaws in the area — the younglings and me as well. I advise you to stay away from any uprights, even the ones with sticks and strings. Food is abundant in our territory, and you know how to find it. Don't be enticed by aromas from the uprights' nest. Don't take unnecessary risks. Heed my admonition, Malra. And teach it well to every one of your younglings."

With that, the great Kohn swung his head from side to side, took one look at the younglings, turned and strode away with a mighty gait.

He is the greatest of the longclaws, I thought, as I watched him go. *What strength, what wisdom, what magnificence he embodies. I only hope Brahn will be like him someday.*

I felt confused about my foray into the uprights' nest. Had I really done it for the younglings, or was it my own desire for the nutty food? I resolved then and there never to intrude again, even if I desperately needed milk for younglings, even if there were no other solution. I certainly wouldn't want them to take away the great Kohn's life spirit because of me.

* * *

The next few cycles were uneventful. The uprights made horrendous noises in and around their nest just before each dark cycle, and during the light cycles they came and went in their water-skimmer.

I occasionally stood up and sniffed in their direction, hoping to catch a whiff of the nutty food that had so attracted me. But food odors from the nest were faint and, for the most part, unappealing. At least, that's the way I felt about them now.

Each cycle I could see Brahn and Padda maturing. Less play, more serious food-searching. The hollow was barely able to contain the three of us now, for I, too, was increasing in size as more of the forest food became available. Thus we were more often than not away from the birthing hollow. Little by little I forgot about the nutty food and my gorging in the uprights' nest.

I was determined not to neglect the task Kohn had imposed on me. I had already begun teaching the younglings about the uprights and the danger of their firesticks.

"Come along, now. I have something to show you."

The two young longclaws were always ready for an adventure, so they were eager to follow me down a new path — the path to the uprights' nest. As we came near, I could hear the front opening of the nest banging. At the edge of the clearing I stopped, keeping the three of us well out of sight. "Be completely still and quiet," I signaled the younglings.

We watched the male and female go up and down the hill carrying bundles and piling them on the flatlog perch. Before long, the low sound of the roaring bird could be heard above the breath of the wind in the whitebarks. As the noise became louder, and the big bird circled above, the younglings' eyes widened with fear.

"Yes, you should be afraid. These are the uprights that come in the roaring bird. They have sticks and strings with which they can take the swimmers out of the water. What's more, they have firesticks that can take away the life spirit of any of the forest animals. And this clearing is their territory. You must never set foot in it. Do you understand?

Brahn and Padda backed a few steps farther into the bush, their little jaws clacking for the first time.

I knew they had understood.

During our walk back along the path through the woods, the roaring bird soared up off the water, taking these uprights away. But it would doubtless be back soon, bringing more of their clan to occupy the nest and skim the water.

The younglings, back in familiar surroundings, ran ahead. The sound of the great bird faded, but in my inner ear I heard again the voice of the upright who shouted at me and the low tones of both uprights speaking to each other. Yes, I went against ancient instincts when I invaded their nest and ate their food. Nevertheless, I had the distinct feeling that my intrusion into their nest was more than the foray of a reckless and hungry longclaw. It was the harbinger of a much greater disturbance yet to come into their lives.

Chapter 13: The Year of the Loon

Karen

"You want to sit all alone in the cabin for a week?"

"Yes."

"I don't think that's such a good idea, Karen."

"Please, Bobby. It's not only what I want, it's what I *need*. I have to sort through all of this. I want to relive the memories. With no distractions. By myself. At Poplar River."

"The only way I would let you do that is if I were to fly in whenever I could to check on you and talk with you on the radio phone every single day I didn't fly in."

"You can't do that, Bobby, running the lodge and all. I couldn't ask you to do that for me."

"Let me worry about the lodge. Will you agree to those conditions?"

"If you insist. But it's not necessary."

"I *do* insist. Would you prefer to send me a food order or grocery shop yourself?"

"Go ahead and order anything for me. I won't eat much."

"I'll see to it, and I'll meet you at the Winnipeg airport next Saturday. I'm going to fly you up to Poplar in the Cessna, and I won't take 'no' for an answer."

I held the phone for a long time after Bobby hung up. It had been well over a year since Meredith unknowingly found Steve's suicide note. Sixty weeks, to be exact — sixty weeks that seemed like one long, dark night of the soul.

I knew Mama would be totally opposed to the idea of my going to Poplar River alone, but Daddy could somehow convince her it would be all right.

With Ellen's help, Meredith and I had moved in with Mama and Daddy, into the comfort of my old room and Mama's cooking. I just couldn't stay in our house. Eventually I would go back — maybe. I did love that house, especially the tiled screened porch overlooking the lake and the extra-large living room where I had spent so many hours at the Steinway grand. But what did it mean without Steve? It was *our* house, *our* life, *our* future, *our* love. What was I without all that now? A pianist? A mother? A daughter? A teacher? Did I have a future? Did I even *want* a future? Why did God allow this to happen?

My head was full of questions, and my heart was full of sorrow. That's why I decided to go to Poplar River. Maybe there in the solitude of the wilderness, where I am really me, I just might find some answers, some solace, and perhaps even a little hope.

Daddy drove me to the Columbia airport. Mama came along, of course, giving me all sorts of last-minute advice.

"Please tell Bobby to call us regularly during the week. I'll be worried to death about you, Honey, 'til you get back home."

"I'll be fine, Mama."

I had only one carry-on, no other luggage — no rod or reel case, no duffle bag, no tackle box. We were always so loaded down. The two sleeping bags took up one large duffle. And there were clothes, towels, waterproof rain suits, a filet knife, the fish-finder, and dozens of other items we deemed necessary.

Never again, I thought, as I passed through Security. I knew I was taking the flights to Minneapolis and Winnipeg for the last time. Although going through the familiar routine alone added to my sadness, strangely enough the finality of it seemed to ease the pain.

While I was buckling the belt of my window seat, a middle-aged woman sat down in the aisle seat next to me.

"Are you from South Carolina?" she asked.

"Born and raised in a little town not far from Columbia."

"This was my first trip to the Carolinas. My daughter's husband took a job in Myrtle Beach managing a big golf course, and they invited me down for a visit. I don't play golf, but the beach is really beautiful, and the water's so warm! I hated to leave, but since they're newlyweds, I didn't want to overstay my welcome. So I'm on my way back to Saint Paul. Are you visiting the Twin Cities?"

I wasn't in the mood for a chatty conversation. Besides, the image of the woman's daughter and husband was unsettling.

"No, I'm just changing planes there."

Offering no further information about my travel plans, I settled back and closed my eyes. Steve would always sleep on the plane. I never could. I was just too excited about going to the wilderness and re-connecting with nature and her creatures.

Maybe this time I could sleep, too. And I did.

There wasn't much of a layover in the Minneapolis airport, so within a short time I was in Winnipeg. Before leaving the secure area, I stopped in the airport bookshop. They still carried copies of Wilkin's flora and fauna book. As I stood there looking over the familiar pages, remembering my animal friends, I was attracted to the tape playing on the store's PA system. It was not music, but a haunting, melodious sound I had heard many times in the wilderness.

"What do you have playing right now?" I asked the fellow behind the counter.

"Oh, that's uh . . ." He picked up the tape case. *Calls of the Common Loon*. We have it for sale on tape or CD."

I purchased a CD, tucked it into my carry-on, and went to meet Bobby in the passenger pick-up zone outside the main door. He took my bag and opened the door of Fred Eaton's van for me. His familiar smile reassured me.

My laconic mood prevailed. Despite Bobby's efforts there was no conversation beyond the necessary. At North Falls I asked to ride in the back seat of the Cessna. Just like always. We reached Poplar River.

* * *

"As you requested, I have a sleeping bag for you, Madam."

Bobby unloaded the sleeping bag and the groceries from the Cessna while I scanned the shoreline looking for any sign of wildlife. Nothing yet. But I could sense they were there, watching us.

"Grab a bag and your carry-on, and let's get you into the cabin, comfy and cozy."

With both of us carrying bag and baggage, one trip was all that was needed.

"I do have a case of beer in the plane, if you like, Karen. There's also a bottle of scotch."

"No thanks, Bobby. I want a clear head the whole week. My doctor gave me some tranquilizers in case I needed them, but I know I won't take any."

Bobby helped me put away the groceries, roll the sleeping bag out on one of the beds in the front bedroom, and brought in a load of split logs.

"Don't want you getting chilled," he said, as he stacked the wood beside the iron stove. "Do you remember how the phone works?"

"I think so. At least I know how to answer it."

"In any case, I made sure there are written instructions on the note pad by the phone."

He came to me, put his hands on my upper arms, and looked squarely at me.

"Karen, you must call me *immediately*, if there is any problem whatsoever. Do you promise?"

"I promise you."

While he verified the proper functioning of the kitchen appliances, I set my toiletries on the washroom counter, then went into the bedroom, slipped on a lightweight cardigan sweater, and took a comb out of my purse.

"Will you stay for lunch, or do you have to get back to the lodge right away?" I called out from the bedroom.

"How can I refuse?"

I turned around to find him leaning against the bedroom door jamb, watching me comb my hair.

"I've heard the sandwiches around here are delicious, made from scratch." He grinned his old endearing grin. I returned a smile. He had been so thoughtful and good to me and Meredith over the past year. Susan and Phil never would have made it without him. It seemed as though we all depended on his strength. Yet Steve was like a brother to him. Bobby must have suffered just as much as the rest of us. Maybe even more. The two of them had been so close since infancy. At times in the past I had felt jealous of that closeness.

We made ham sandwiches together in the kitchenette and ate them at the big table in the main room. After lunch I put on a pot of coffee while Bobby called to learn the latest weather conditions between Poplar and the lodge. I took the pot and two cups out to the porch. Bobby joined me after completing his call.

"Forecast for this evening is okay, but tomorrow doesn't look good. There's a storm system moving through. I may not be able to get in."

"Don't you dare take any chances for my sake. You stay safe. Now it's my turn to make *you* promise *me*."

We sipped on hot, black coffee in silence for a while, listening to the wind whistling through the screen panels.

"You must know a bit about solitude, Bobby. You're constantly with people at the lodge, but during the long, Canadian winters you're alone in Winnipeg, aren't you? Forgive me! I shouldn't be so nosy."

"It's all right, Karen. I'm really not home alone that much. A good part of the winter I'm in Iowa City with Susan and Phil — occasionally in Spring Hill — and I travel around the U.S. and Canada to sport shows to peddle my wares, so to speak. It's the best way to advertise the lodge and outposts to fishermen and hunters. I get a lot of my business that way. And there's a pile of paperwork involved in running the operation between seasons, especially the lodge. I have to replace any guides that quit, or the cook, or the waitress, have the Otter and the Cessna serviced, and so on. And the guides and I are up there even before ice-out."

"It's a year-round business, then."

"It is."

I took a couple of sips of coffee.

"Now my next question may really be too personal, so feel free not to answer. Steve said you've had lots of girlfriends. Do you have one now?"

"I was going out with a young lady when Steve . . . passed away, but I broke it off then. It . . . wasn't anything serious."

"I've often wondered why you haven't married. Never found the right one?"

Bobby set his coffee cup down and looked out over the lake. For a minute or so he said nothing.

"Do you believe in love at first sight, Karen?"

"Well, I'm sure it happens."

"It happened to me years ago," he said, still staring at the water.

"And why didn't . . ."

"She married someone else."

"Oh. I'm so sorry, Bobby. You deserve the best. Where is she now?"

"She's . . . still around."

"Do you ever see her?"

"On occasion."

"That must be very difficult for you."

Bobby was obviously growing uncomfortable discussing his lost love, so I changed the subject.

"Look! Isn't that a loon out there . . . with its black head and black-and-white neck band?"

"You're right. It's what's known as a Common Loon," Bobby said, relief evident in his voice. "There's been a pair in the cabin area for years, ever since I've owned it."

"The same pair?"

"I believe so. People have always said that loons mate for life, but modern science has tried to disprove that myth."

"So they do 'change partners' then?"

"Not exactly. If there's a reason — like a failed nest, or the death of a mate . . . oh, I'm sorry, Karen."

"It's okay. Go ahead, tell me more."

"Sometimes a very aggressive male intruder will run off the established male and take over the female. But I think that's really rare."

"I bought a CD of loon calls in the Winnipeg airport. It was playing in the bookstore, and I recognized the sounds. I knew I had heard them before."

"Listen closely in the evening and you'll hear them right here, live, not recorded."

A heavy gust of wind rippled across the water and shook the poplars so forcibly their leaves rattled and hissed like a swarm of angry serpents.

Bobby stood. "I'd better get going. Looks like that storm front is moving in faster than expected."

He extended his hand to help me up, an obvious invitation to accompany him to the dock.

Just before shoving off, he slipped an arm around my shoulders.

"The rifle and shells are in one corner of the front bedroom. Close yourself in with it at night, and don't hesitate to use it."

"You mean the bear might come back?"

"No one has seen any evidence of it since the break in two years ago. But just to be safe . . ."

"I'll bang pots and pans every evening before going to bed."

"Might help." He grinned and gave my shoulders a squeeze before dropping his arm and stepping onto the pontoon. In his characteristic manner he pushed off, climbed into the pilot's seat, and cranked the engine.

I lost sight of him taxiing down river, but soon I heard the sound of full throttle. I loved to watch him take off against the wind. There was nothing like speeding over the water, spray walling up on each side, and then the lift off.

When the sound of the plane became inaudible, I lowered my gaze to the surface of the lake and saw a black head, with a black-and-white necklace, and a red eye looking at me.

"Well, hello there! Are you going to be my friend this week?"

The head rolled forward into the water, and the loon disappeared, only to pop up about ten yards down the shoreline.

"So you like to play the same game as my beaver buddy!"

Like the beaver, the loon seemed to be checking me out.

"Where's your partner? Off hunting food while you play with me?"

Head under again. Up again. I studied the black and white body.

His bill is much more pointed than a duck's. Must have something to do with what loons eat. I wonder what they do eat?

Suddenly he raised his breast off the water, puffed it out, and started running across the surface. Then his wings began flapping furiously as he continued to run faster and faster on top of the water until he was airborne. He made a high, shrill sound like crazy laughter as he took off across the lake.

"Don't leave! I'm sorry I frightened you off. Please come back." But he was already out of sight.

Before going back to the cabin, I glanced toward the beaver lodge.

I wonder if the beaver who saved me is still living there?

On the porch I stopped at the metal door and evoked the memory of my first grand entrance: Steve scooping me up, carrying me over the threshold, tripping, and sending us both sprawling. And another memory of reaching the door, soaking wet and freezing:

"Oh, KK! I almost lost you! Thank God you're okay!"

And finally the memory of standing trembling at the door while Steve went to confront whatever bear might be inside:

"It's all right. There no bear in here now, but there has been, and he's pretty well eaten all our food."

I went inside and closed the door behind me. How many times we had gone out of this same door to pick up rods and tackle box and carried them down to the boat to start a day of fishing. Or to find kindling. Or to go to the outhouse. Or just to sit on the porch. How many times we had come in the same door, always laughing, always exhilarated, regardless of our fishing luck.

Eight years of memories were being unleashed.

This is why I'm here.

The afternoon lingered, and so did ghosts from the past, until finally I started to get hungry. *I guess that's a good sign. First time I've had any appetite since . . . then.*

I opened a can of spaghetti and a bag of cookies, heated up the coffee left over from lunch with Bobby, threw a jacket on over the cardigan, and took my cup onto the porch. How many times I had come out onto the porch with a cup of coffee in my hand! Sitting on the couch I continued to open the floodgates of the past. This time the memories came in reverse order, the more recent ones first:

Lifting the lid of the tool box to find it full of open peanut butter jars and bags of chips, and other junk food.

Steve, standing up in the semi-darkness of a moonlit night:

"Something came crashing through the woods, headed this way!"

The gauntlet that ushered a hoard of frightened mice onto the porch.

"Steve, what is that light in the sky that keeps getting brighter?" "The Aurora Borealis, the Northern Lights."

Bobby handing me his can of beer. My first one ever.

I loved this porch.

* * *

Ever since the initial shock of Steve's death, I had been unable to cry. No tears. There were too many questions for which there were no answers. Why did he feel he failed us? What did he mean, he'd lost his job? How could he think he was holding me back?

After this period of confusion came the anger: How could he leave us

— without once talking about his feelings? How could he do this to me — to us?

I got some answers the day I looked through the boxes that Roger Kaufmann, one of Steve's colleagues at Heyward, brought to the house. He had been kind enough to save me the agony of cleaning out Steve's office at the college. The first item I put my hands on was a letter from the dean of Arts and Sciences informing Steve that the committee had denied his request for tenure. *Why hadn't anyone told me? That's what he meant — he really had lost his job!* The dean commended his effective and innovative teaching and praised his high student evaluations, but he cited the lack of publications as the basis for this negative decision. He offered Steve a terminal year at Heyward, while strongly encouraging him to apply at once for a position elsewhere.

Then there were the usual files on each of the courses he had taught, files for the various committees he had served on, and so forth. One file in particular caught my attention: *Ladies of the Lake: publishers.* Along with a list of publishing houses were five letters, five letters of rejection, short and sweet. There were three more similar letters in a stack of opened but unanswered mail. The book had been rejected eight times. After the first two swift refusals, Steve had in desperation broken the rules and made multiple simultaneous submissions.

But there was a fourth unopened letter, dated a few days after Steve's death.

Dear Professor Marsten:

We are pleased to inform you that your book-length submission, Ladies of the Lake, has been approved for publication. We are returning the manuscript to you under separate cover. Our editors have made a few suggested changes for you to take under consideration.

We anticipate going to press this spring in order to make the book widely available for adoption as a textbook the next fall.

Congratulations on your fine work.

Aaron Moskowitz, Editor-in-chief
Littleton Press

I responded immediately, explaining the situation and expressing my hope that my letter was not too late. I gave the editors permission to make all suggested amendments. Shortly before leaving for Canada, I received the long-awaited package from Littleton Press containing twelve copies of their latest release, Steven Marsten's *Ladies of the Lake: Women Writers of the Romantic Period in England.*

* * *

"Oh, Steve! If only you had waited a little longer! You gave up too soon — you gave up everything for no reason."

I spoke aloud, hoping that he was here with me in our honeymoon cabin in spirit, hoping that he could hear me. I *had* to believe that. I fell silent, completely silent and still, waiting, listening, looking for any sign of his presence.

A loud, mournful wail pierced the air. Then another one, resonating around the lake. The loon. How perfectly that sound conveyed the depth of my sorrow, my loss, my helplessness. I opened my heart to the doleful melody, allowing the threnody of the loon to engulf my soul. I could discern a single black head protruding from a black-and-white feathered body sitting on the water in front of the cabin. Only one, not a pair anymore. Then I realized that the two of us were expressing our profound grief — the loon with vocalizations and I with tears which at last flowed freely and profusely.

* * *

The storm system moved in during the night. I awoke to bolts of lightning, rolling thunderclaps, and the sound of rain beating against the cabin windows. I thought of times during past storms that I had snuggled up in Steve's arms and pulled our double sleeping bag over my head. Now I was alone. One bag, one bunk bed. I got up, put on my sweater, and went to the bedroom window. In the semi-darkness of the Canadian summer night I could see the poplars bending and twisting against the wind like recalcitrant children. I thought of Steve's parents.

They must have endured many sleepless, grief-filled nights. Steve, their only child, gone so young.

I hadn't told them about the letter from Littleton. I wanted to spare them the extra pain of knowing that he died for nothing. Now they would have to know. The book was out. I had put off the inevitable. How could I tell them?

I'll ask Bobby. He'll know the best way to do it.

My thoughts then shifted to Bobby. As a baby he lost his parents, he lost his one true love, now he'd lost a friend closer than a brother.

How does he deal with all of that? He seems so focused, so in control, so able to accept adversity and go on.

Looking out at the river I found the answer to my question:

He has the wilderness. Nature. He understands its ways and his own connection to it, and he respects it. He lives in it and soars over it. That's the secret of his survival and strength. And that's exactly why I'm here. I'm like a hothouse plant in South Carolina, even though it's a part of me I love. Here I am natural. Here I am in the world as it was created, untouched. I can embrace the course of life, including change . . . and death.

I felt enlivened by the storm, as though God, displaying his power through his creation, was trying to communicate these ideas to me, and by so doing, to renew my spirit and restore my soul.

Yes, I will accept. Yes, I will live.

And this was only my first night alone at Poplar River.

* * *

Although the morning was still cloudy and a little windy, the weather cleared enough for the plane to get in late the next afternoon.

"I brought you a rod and reel and a small tackle box so you could fish off the dock if you felt like it."

"Oh, I do, Bobby! Thanks. In fact, what if I were to take the boat out to catch a few black devils and golden angels?"

"No way! You're a grown woman and a good fisherman, but we don't fish alone on the water in the wilderness."

"I was afraid you'd say something like that."

"I'll tell you what. The next time I fly in, I'll make sure I have enough time to take you out on the lake. Maybe even up to the falls. I think that's where the action is right now."

"And we can have a walleye dinner?"

"I'm gonna count on it."

"For now, at least come up to the cabin and I'll make us some tea."

Bobby left the fishing equipment on the dock and followed as I sprinted up the hill. When we reached the cabin, I rushed to the kitchenette, filled a pot with water, and set it on the stove.

"Wow! You seem awfully energetic today — and much improved in spirit."

"I am. It's the loon who's helping me sort things out. Uh . . . does that sound crazy?"

"Of course not. Loons are good at that. They've helped me many times before."

I thought about my meditation on Bobby's spiritual stamina during last night's storm.

"There's only one of them now. I'm sure that he or she has lost a mate."

"It's possible. Come to think of it, I haven't seen the pair of them myself for some time."

We had our tea party, I assured Bobby that everything was fine, and before I knew it, he was back in the clouds. I wished he could have stayed longer. I had so much to tell him and to ask him. I completely forgot to mention the book and ask his advice on how to tell Susan and Phil about it.

Oh, well. Next time he comes.

Washing the cups I remembered another tea party, a raspberry tea party with Tom. I put the cups back into the dish cabinet — the one whose door had been torn off by the bear. It had been replaced.

Bobby and I talked everyday by phone. I never ran out of things to share with him, in fact, I had become positively chatty. The solitude, I suppose. From the lodge he was in regular communication with Mama and Daddy, as he had promised. After he had answered all Mama's questions about my safety, she told him all was fine down south, so I had nothing to worry about except taking care of myself. And that was sort of the way I was beginning to feel. I enjoyed catching a few fish off the dock, but I really looked forward to Bobby's return, when he would take me up to the falls for some great fishing.

I spent every evening listening and learning from the loon. I watched it poke its head under the water as though looking around, for food I guessed. I saw it dive, then come up some distance away. I heard the shrill tremolos, hooting sounds, and a kind of yodel. But what helped me — healed me — was the evening song, the wailing, the mourning. It was the song of the loon's spirit . . . and mine.

It wasn't until Friday, the last day, that Bobby was able to get away for any length of time. We fished at the falls for a while, catching and releasing all but a few walleyes, which he filleted on the shore near the falls. Dinner was divine. Bobby made fish kabobs with cubes of fish, mushrooms, onions, peppers, and bacon and grilled them on an open fire. Meanwhile, I prepared mashed potatoes with real butter and opened a can of peas, the first I'd been able to open since the mouse episode.

While we sat feasting at the table in the main room, Bobby regaled me with stories about some of his guests at the lodge — four American guys that come up the same week every year. One of them, Allen, always sat up in the prow of the boat and smoked one cigar after another while he fished.

"But he catches big, trophy fish."

"Maybe the secret is the cigar. Maybe I should try it." I was half serious.

"Another one, a dentist named Joe, had to sew up a lady's leg with needle and dental floss for thread. She'd fallen in the boat and cut herself pretty bad. She drank a big glass of Crown Royal before the 'operation' . . . and two more afterwards. Went around telling everybody Joe was a hero.

And George, a lawyer, also a member of what I call 'the quartet' — I thought you'd appreciate the term — he's allergic to fish. So he brings a big roll of salami and makes himself sandwiches for shore lunch, while the other three happily gobble up his catch of walleye. He always wears a bandana around his neck.

Last but not least is Stanley, a gray-headed, pony-tailed grandfather. He's up there in years, but except for the gray hair, you'd never know it. He's out there in any kind of weather all day and back out in the evening. Catches lots of fish. Sometimes outfishes the whole camp."

It felt so good to laugh again, to sense my interest in life reawakening.

"Thank you, Bobby!"

"For what?"

"For this week. For making me laugh. For always being so good to me. For teaching me about life in the wilderness. For every year and the extraordinary experiences I've had here."

I put my fork down and took a deep breath.

"You know, Bobby, I've had a lot of time to think about things this week, and there's something I have to ask you."

"Go ahead."

"The time that you fell in love at first sight, how long ago was that?"

"A little over eight years ago."

"And do you still love that woman?"

"More than ever."

"Tell me who she is, Bobby. I have to know."

"I think you already know."

Chapter 14: The Year of the Loon

Zon

Ducking my head underwater, I searched the depths on one side and the other. It was the season for the newly-hatched golden swimmers. They were so tender and easy to eat — my favorite food. But so far I hadn't been able to find any. I was in the area where they were abundant last warm season, but they weren't here now.

In spite of my natural inclination to stay in deeper water, I decided to hunt closer to shore. I paddled toward the water edge and searched again. Still none. When I popped my head up, I heard a loud whir above me.

The roaring bird. The first of the uprights are coming to occupy their nest.

The uprights themselves didn't alarm me. It was their water-skimmers that I disliked. More then disliked. One of them had taken away the life spirit of a very young water-dancer from among our first born. Katyra was devastated. For the rest of the warm season she wailed the mourning song throughout every light and dark cycle, sometimes even in her sleep. She made no other sound. She would dive for enough food to feed the remaining young one but ate almost nothing herself. I thought I would lose her then. Perhaps it would have been better if I had. The pain of loss would not have been as intense nor lasted as long.

We had so many warm seasons together here, and cold seasons in the region far to the south, at the earth's end, beside the vast, curling water. In fact, that's where I first saw her. She was young, flying in late with the other young water-dancers. Her feathers, then a brownish-gray, became the most brilliant black and white I had ever seen. Her movements were elegant, even her take-offs and landings were graceful, certainly compared to most of us black-and-white water-dancers.

The moment I caught a glimpse of her perfect neckband and alluring throat patch, I knew she was the female I wanted to pursue as my life-friend. So I did. She followed me here, and we danced together, swimming, dipping our bills, and diving in all directions. I watched her preen for me and curve her dark head backwards, rubbing it against her plumage. Then we synchronized our motions and continued our ritual. Suddenly she swam away from me. I followed at a distance and watched her roll over onto a clump of wet, marshy grass at the water edge. I paddled to her as fast as I could while she waited for the coupling.

We built our nest near that coupling site. Even though it was her first time to have a nest, she knew exactly what to do. She insisted on elevating it slightly so that sudden high-water swells would not wash the shells or nestlings out.

"My life-givers told me that it happens to the nests of many water-dancers. Yet few have learned to prepare for it."

"We will always elevate our nests, then," I said as I piled on some twigs.

"Not too much, Zon. After all, we have to get in and out of it ourselves. Besides, we don't want to make the nest too easy for ringtails, bushytails, or odor-sprayers to find. Best to keep it hidden."

She constantly amazed me with her instinctive ability to do anything. Once, when I made a deep dive, my wings became entangled in one of the uprights' strings that was loose in the water. She used her bill to tear and pull at the tough line until I could swim free of it.

Where could she have gone? Why hasn't she come back?

Many light and dark cycles had passed since I awoke one first light to find her gone. The nest was prepared — slightly elevated — and she was due to place the shells in it anytime.

Why did she go? What can I do other than call to her over and over again?

Two uprights emerged from the roaring bird and carried bundles up the hill into the nest. For a while all was quiet, and I returned to fishing and remembering. I wanted to remember everything we did together through the many warm and cold seasons. I wanted to hear her calls with my inward ear, to see her clearly with my inward vision. More than this, I wanted to find her, though I had no idea where she could possibly be.

I spent the rest of the light cycle half-heartedly looking for food, diving after small swimmers and eating a few. I realized that a large part of the pleasure of eating was swimming and diving with Katyra. Sometimes she would dive for a young golden one, pierce it with her bill, swim back up and offer it to me. The taste of it was always sweeter, and I delighted in it.

As I floated on the water surface, I felt the wind blow stronger against my feathers. I heard the roaring bird again and watched it rise into a darkening sky. Only one upright remained standing on the flatlog landing — a female.

She saw me, opened her beakless mouth, and spoke to me. I ducked under. Coming up a short distance away, I took a longer look at her. She spoke again. I ducked under again.

I'm too close. I'd better give her a warning and move away. Fly to another part of the water. Look for Katyra.

This time when I surfaced I filled myself with as much air as I could take in. The front of my body stood up on the water.

Now I look like an upright!

I paddle and flapped hard until I lifted off the water.

"I don't want to be disturbed! I want to be left alone! Stay away!" I cried in a high, shaking voice.

I didn't fly far, landing in the bay just over the little peninsula that jutted out in front of the uprights' nest. I wasn't afraid of this upright, and I didn't believe she would hurt me or any of the forest dwellers, but I wanted nothing to keep Katyra from returning. Ever since the water-skimmer incident she could not tolerate the uprights. She relocated our nest to this area around the peninsula, farther away from them.

The nest. As soon as I thought of it, I wanted to see it.

Maybe she put her shells in it, and she's sitting on them now!

I knew this bit of hope was in vain, for we always shared the covering of the shells. It felt so good each time I took her place over them. The perfect little green speckled shells held her warmth, and I could feel it rise through my under feathers whenever I settled on them. So many times. Season after season.

Never again.

The remnants of the nest were still there — slightly elevated. I swam up to it and stuck my bill over the rim. A black feather lay woven into the strands of water plants.

"Katyra!"

A cry rose in my throat. A long, loud wail that echoed around the shore.

"Where are you? Where are you? Where are you?"

Over and over I repeated the call, as I have at every fading light and well into the dark cycle. As always, I tell myself, *She will hear it and answer this time.*

But after the echos died, there was only silence. Yet I had the distinct feeling that I was not the only one calling out.

Could it be Katyra?

No, it wasn't a water-dancer crying. I listened again, this time with my inward ear.

It's the upright. Like me, she is calling to her life-friend. Like me, she is remembering.

A storm was moving in. The wind was rising, and the sky covering thickened. My wailing continued, transforming itself from a desperate call to an involuntary lament.

She is lost to me forever. Lost forever. Lost forever.

The distant rumblings became more threatening, as the flashes in the sky grew brighter. The whitebarks and longneedles bent and swayed as though wrestling with some great, invisible longclaw. The wind lifted my feathers, and water swells slapped against me, spattering droplets into my eyes. I stopped paddling and allowed the gusts to push me to shore. I slipped out of the water and tucked my head under a wing. The sky water pelted my feathers and rolled off in drops that formed tiny streams flowing back into the lake.

Something stirred inside me. An uplifting impulse that came to me from the sound of the wind, the smell of the sky water, the feel of the storm.

Even if I am alone, I will survive. I will dive and swim and fish and eat. I will call out each time the great light turns into bands of color and fades into the darkness. I can release Katyra while holding fast the memory of her.

I pulled my head from its position under the wing, lifted it high, and listened. From somewhere, above the sounds of the storm, I heard a soft, cooing voice.

"I am here, Zon. I will always be with you. Try hard and you will feel my neck rub against yours. Listen as you are listening now, and you will hear my voice calling to you over the waters, whispering to you in the rustle of whitebark leaves, and singing to you in the sound of the sky water as it splashes on the surface of the river. Listen and remember."

I *did* remember. The next few light cycles were spent recalling our regular routines, the unexpected events, our work, and our play together. And Katyra loved to play, especially the chase, underwater and on the surface, or a combination of the two. She was a fast swimmer. With a toss of her head she would challenge me to catch her. Holding her wings tight against her body, she would dive long, straight dives to the bottom. Before I could reach her, she would swim away, cutting sharply one way and then another. A brief rise to the surface for air, then back down and off again. I rarely caught up with her and usually found myself floating exhausted on top of the water, turning around and around with my feet, watching to see where she would surface. When she did, she would throw her head back, and then shake it from side to side, letting me know she had won. She always won.

She also loved to take the young nestlings for a ride on her back. Positioning herself next to the "slightly elevated" nest, she would let one or both of the downy chicks climb on. She glided along serenely, keeping her back straight, even when dipping her head.

"Down there! Young golden ones!"

That meant she wanted me to dive after them and bring some up for the nestlings — and for her. Of course, I fished my best on those occasions when I could present her and the young ones with a meal. My success as a provider was normally followed by extensive neck and bill rubbings.

* * *

The female upright came down to the flatlog landing, picked up a stick-and-string, and hurled the string into the water. I was curious. So, keeping a safe distance, I watched. After a while, she pulled a black swimmer out, and then threw it back into the water. She did this several times. There seemed to be something at the bottom of the string that attracted the swimmers and made them take it into their mouths. I don't think it hurt the swimmers, and she didn't eat them. It was all so strange to me. I could understand the ways of the flattails, the paddlers, the longclaws, the large and small bushytails, and all of the flyers. But the behavior of the uprights was beyond my comprehension. Yet I knew one thing for certain: this particular upright had lost a life-friend for whom she has grieved. Now she — and I — would go on living.

The roaring bird landed again during the next light cycle but didn't stay long. After a few more light-dark cycles passed, the upright in the roaring bird returned to the nest. He and the female got into the water-skimmer and headed upriver with their sticks and strings. I welcomed the solitude and the chance to fish around the flatlog landing where the female upright had caught some black swimmers.

Young ones are probably in the area — most likely under the flat logs.

The larger black ones were feeding on the smaller ones. I was hungry, too. Since last skybright I had eaten one small green bent-legged jumper. I wanted a tender young swimmer.

I floated up under the flatlog landing and dipped my head to search. When I raised up, I saw something on the lake that startled me. There in the deeper water was a black-and-white water-dancer.

Katyra?

I paddled out from beneath the flatlogs to get a better look.

A male. Young, but fully grown. He should not be in my territory. I need to make him understand that.

I paddled to within a short distance of the interloper. Then in a shrill voice I warned him.

"You are trespassing on my territory! You must leave at once!"

To my surprise he answered back.

"You're old and have no life-friend. Why should you control one of the best fishing areas on the river? I'm young, and my female needs a fine nesting place with plenty of food. It is *you* who must leave!"

His challenge stirred me to action, as in old times. I puffed up my chest, flapped furiously, and ran across the surface toward him, clearly enunciating a territorial defense cry.

He responded in kind, puffing and flapping as he rushed to meet me. Facing one another, we flapped and yelled. I warned, and he defied. His movements were quick and his young bill much sharper than mine. It had been many seasons since I fended off an intruder, but I had not forgotten how to prevail.

He began to jab at my neck and my head, but I regulated my air intake to raise or lower my chest and confuse his aim. I let him jab and flap and scream while I concentrated my efforts on avoiding his beak and waiting for his youthful fervor to tire him. It did, very quickly. When he least expected it, I stabbed him at the base of the neck. Stunned, he stopped screaming. The dark red life-stream began to seep through his shiny black and white feathers. He let the air out of his chest and settled on the water. I remained in the upright position.

"What is your name, young water-dancer?"

"Torago," he answered, head drooping.

"You have been defeated, Torago, but you fought well. Now go. I have not seriously wounded you. Continue your search. You will surely find a territory for you and your female friend. Leave me in peace."

Torago could only paddle away slowly. When he reached the open water, he went under for what seemed like a long time.

The stab wound must have been worse than I thought.

I waited. Then a banded black head came up at some distance down river. I was relieved to see him surface, and even more relieved to see that he was headed the other way. I knew he would recover his strength quickly and fly back to the waiting female who would help cure his torn flesh and wounded self-esteem. I hoped he had learned a lesson of self-control.

I gave up the idea of fishing for the time being and settled down in deep water, not far from the nesting site, where I could calm myself with recollections of Katyra.

She would have been pleased with my defeat of young Torago.

* * *

Victory over the transgressing water-dancer had given me renewed appreciation for the territory that I had defended, the territory that Katyra and I had enjoyed for so many warm seasons. I made up my mind to explore all of it, even the remote areas.

I'll discover new things, perhaps find new foods and make new friends.

"Just make sure you stay clear of water-skimmers," I told myself, voicing what Katyra would have said.

At skybright I ate well and set out on the journey. I swam west through the channel to the island of the great whiteheads. The male was perched atop a tall whitebark. I could see Cherra below on the nest.

"No water-dancer chicks for you to prey on this season, Trosk!"

He made no response except to turn his white head, fix his long-vision on me, and watch as I passed his island. I continued the excursion through my domain.

The next expanse of water to the west was not an area we used, for the fishing was not as good here. There was little structure underwater for the fish to hide in, and the weed beds near the shore were too shallow. However, it did serve as a buffer zone between us and the territory of another pair of water-dancers. We seldom encountered them, since they kept to the west of their waters, and we kept to the east of ours.

Paddling slowly but steadily I circled the boundary area and turned back eastward along the northern shoreline. I dived under, swam back through the channel, and surfaced near the water-edge rock. Two young longclaws, one behind the other, were scampering down a path that sloped toward the rock. I recognized Brahn and Padda.

"I'm afraid the gray-and-white flyers have left nothing for you longclaws."

Of course they paid no heed to my message and investigated the situation for themselves.

Paddling into deeper water midstream, I continued eastward into one of my favorite fishing bays. A long, rocky peninsula protected it from the wind, and many swimmers spawned here. I dived under and found myself amid a cluster of small black ones. I clamped one in my beak, swallowed it and surfaced. Then I floated while the meal settled and my feet rested.

There was heavy movement in the trees and shrubs. A magnificent antlered one stepped out onto the rocky promontory of the peninsula. Judging from his horns he looked fully grown but youthful.

What a superb koda!

He stood, head erect, smelling and listening. His eyes were alert, his muscles taut. He glanced at me briefly before lowering his head to consume some fresh greens growing up through the rocks.

He has grown a fine rack of horns. A proud and hardy koda, he will surely sire many cuvas.

I had seen him develop from a cuva. As a tova, he had once asked

Katyra if she would be his noda. He certainly didn't need anyone now.

I turned back toward the bay of the uprights' nest, the bay where I had almost succumbed to my sorrow. From out of a bush, a squeaker darted to safety under the log nest. *Koh's clan. They are still numerous, still thriving on the uprights' food, no doubt.*

The uprights had pulled the water-skimmer up onto the bank.

She will be leaving in the next light cycle, I surmised.

There was activity as usual at the beavers' nest. Pruu and Ghinn were repairing the seasonal damage to their home. I liked flattails. They were hard workers, and they were harmless. That's one reason Katyra chose their pond as our first nesting site. And this was where I preferred to stay. Swimmers were plentiful, and there was deep water only a short way out, directly in front of the uprights' nest. What more could I want?

I was content with the survey of my territory. Rather than discover new things, I had found old familiar forest creatures, and that gave me much satisfaction.

The great skylight was dissolving into bands of color. It was time to call. So I called.

"I am Zon, a male water-dancer alone in the wilderness. I am Zon, a male water-dancer alone in the wilderness . . . in the wilderness . . . the wilderness."

I listened as the river carried my call away with it.

I wailed again."I am Zon, a male water-dancer alone in the wilderness . . . in the wilderness . . . the wilderness."

I heard the echo of my call die away into the silence of the fading light.

Then, an answer from somewhere distant on the river.

"I am Matta, a female water-dancer alone in the wilderness. I am Matta, a female water-dancer alone in the wilderness.

"Where are you? . . . Where are you . . .are you . . . are you?"

Chapter 15: The Year of the Full Moon

Karen

Bobby had become a regular visitor at the Kingsley home in Spring Hill, South Carolina. Meredith and I moved back into the house by the lake. The child was adjusting fairly well to the loss of her father, especially now that "Uncle Bobby" was giving her time and attention, not to mention gifts from Canada — a stuffed Canada goose toy, a flag with a large red maple leaf, a hockey stick, a pair of ice skates, and other equally useful items for an eight-year old living in the southeastern heat belt. She loved them. It had become apparent to family and friends that Bobby was a hopeful suitor, the prevailing one, since I had nipped all others in the bud.

Ellen usually brought up the subject of Bobby at our Coffee Bean parleys.

"And you wanted to introduce *me* to him!"

"I'm sorry, I guess I did. But everything is so different now that Steve is gone. Oh, Ellen, I don't really know what's going on. Please forgive me if I led you astray. I couldn't foresee the future."

"Nor could any of us, KK. But there's nothing to apologize for. I've met someone, and we're pretty serious."

"Oh, my god! You didn't tell me."

"It's somewhat mundane compared to your exotic existence."

"Don't be silly. Who is he? Where did you meet him?"

"He's one of the professors at Heyward — a friend of Steve's. That's why I couldn't tell you until now . . . now that you seem to be going on with your life."

"I'm so happy for you. You've waited a long time. You deserve every happiness. I only hope I'm part of the wedding plans — the organist, maybe?"

"How about the matron of honor?"

"Oh, Ellen, you're the best friend a person could have. I *am* honored."

She reached over the little table and took my hand.

"And you deserve every happiness, too. Bobby is phenomenal. I should be terribly jealous and angry, but I'm just glad to see you alive again." She gave my hand a squeeze before letting go.

There was a period of silence as we both tried to fathom the turn of events in our lives.

"You didn't tell me his name, Ellen."

"Roger Kaufman."

"Oh, I know him. He cleaned out Steve's office and brought his things to me. He's a good guy."

"Yeah, he is."

"When's the wedding?"

"We're thinking of late May or early June, when classes are out and his grades have been turned in."

The words stung. Just what Steve and I had done. I glanced down at my now-cold cappuccino to hide the hurt and saw the ringless finger of my left hand.

"What about you and Bobby?" Ellen asked.

"What do you mean 'What about you and Bobby'?"

"I mean what are *your* plans?"

"We don't have any plans. He just comes to visit . . ."

"Yeah . . .like several days a month. . . . is he a good lover?"

"Ellen! We haven't gone beyond holding hands. Well . . . he did sorta kiss me goodnight on the porch one night after dinner with Mama and Daddy."

"And how was that?"

"Electrifying!"

At that reply we both broke into laughter over the silly school-girl direction our conversation had taken.

The truth was my parents had given Bobby an open invitation to stay with them anytime. They loved having him. He would do all kinds of handyman work around the house and yard — Daddy had never been too good at that sort of thing. Bobby enjoyed Mama's southern cooking and praised her lavishly for it. As a result, at every visit Mama showed off her culinary skills by putting on a big family dinner for her devotees. Other than Bobby, Meredith, and myself, she included Katherine and Ted, and later Ellen and Roger. It was food, family, friends, and fun.

Mama and I always did the dishes afterwards. She washed the good china and silverware, I dried them. It was our special time together. One evening she spoke her mind. "That boy can't take his eyes off you, honey. What are you gonna do about him? Do you love him?"

"I don't know what I feel. He's like my soul mate, Mama. I miss him a lot between visits — more and more. He wants me to spend a week at the lodge this June. There's a little cabin for one person he said he'd reserve for me."

"I think you ought to go. Give him a chance."

I laid the dishcloth down on the countertop.

"I just can't stop remembering my life with Steve. I can't help it."

"It's okay to remember it — everything about it. They're your memories forever. Never give them up. But you need to keep building memories, too . . . with somebody else . . . while you're still young."

"Sometimes I feel so old, Mama."

"Nonsense. Now go on, talk to Bobby. Tell him you'll come up to the lodge. He's going back to Winnipeg tomorrow and may not get down here again before his new season starts up."

I took Mama's advice. In the living room Daddy sat in the big recliner with Meredith ensconced in his lap, her legs now dragging the floor. I interrupted his reading of her favorite Walt Disney book.

"Where is everybody?"

"Katherine and Ted just left. Bobby's on the front porch."

He turned his attention back to *Tinkerbell.*

I'm beginning to believe they've all ganged up on me. I pulled on an old cardigan sweater out of the coat closet, fluffed my hair with my fingers, and opened the front door.

The cool air of an early March evening felt good after the heat of the kitchen. Bobby was sitting on the top step.

"You're going back to Winnipeg tomorrow?" That was the best conversation opener I could think of.

"After a stop in Iowa City to check on Susan and Phil."

I took a seat beside him and doubled my sweater across my chest to protect myself from the chill of the air and to cover the pounding of my heart.

"I'd like to accept your offer to stay at the lodge this year . . . but I don't want to get in the way of your work."

Bobby gave a soft chuckle. "How could you ever 'get in the way'? Besides, I'll put you to work." There was an adorable shyness about the smile he gave me.

"That would be great. I like to feel useful. I think you've seen how well I dry dishes."

He reached over, took my hand, and interlaced his fingers with mine. The streetlights of Oakmont Avenue illuminated his face, enhancing the brilliance of his intense blue-gray eyes. Deep within me longings were being revived. I felt guilty about that.

"I'd better take Meredith home. I'm sure she's fast asleep in Daddy's lap by now. Will you help me get her into the car?"

I extended my hand to push back a lock of loose black curls from

Bobby's face. As I did, my fingers grazed his lips. This was the "kiss" I told Ellen about, and yes, it was electrifying.

* * *

Bad weather delayed the Big Bear flight from Winnipeg to Baldwin Lake Lodge. We didn't take off until almost ten a.m. The groups of fishermen accepted the situation rather philosophically. In the waiting room they kidded around, drank coffee and soft drinks, read magazines and newspapers, and managed to entertain themselves until the flight was called. Once we took off, they chatted for a while, ate their muffins, and then slept. I was the only female on board other than the flight attendant, and we were the only two on board to stay awake — except for the pilot and copilot, I presumed.

The commercial plane flew above the cloud cover at about thirty thousand feet, so I couldn't enjoy the changing patterns on the ground below. But I did have a good novel to read, and before I knew it, we were landing at Baldwin Lake. No ice, I was relieved to see, as we dropped below the clouds and began our approach to the hard-surface runway.

Bobby personally greeted the lodge guests one by one as they deplaned. I had sat in the back and was the last person to get off the Big Bear.

"I thought for a minute you had changed your mind."

Bobby took my carry-on and escorted me to a small cabin at the end of the row of guest cottages where my fishing gear and huge duffle sat waiting. It was surprisingly well-arranged. There was a sitting room with a sofa, table, chair, microwave oven, and a view of the lake. A full bath with shower opened off a tiny bedroom with a single bed and nightstand that served as a chest of drawers.

"I think you'll be comfortable here. There's a separate heat control for each room. If you need anything — anything at all — anytime — you know where my office is and where I sleep."

The idea of going into his quarters in the main building for whatever reason sent a jolt through my nervous system.

What in the world is going on with me? I felt like a stranger in my own skin.

"Lunch will be served at noon, so you have a little time to freshen up. If you're dressed for fishing, I have Cedrick — our best guide — ready to take you out on Baldwin afterwards."

The mention of fishing helped me to relax a little, and I began to feel somewhat in control. I could at least decide which rod and which reel to use, and what to wear. The guide would know where to find the fish.

"Okay, that sounds great. Tell, uh . . . Cedrick I'd love to go out this afternoon."

With his hand on the knob and the door half open, Bobby turned back around.

"I'm glad you're here, Karen. And I'm glad you're going fishing today. I'll see you for dinner."

There was nothing special in the words he spoke, but there was everything special in the expression in his eyes.

Dear God. The man has been in love with me for almost ten years.

I had to sit down and think all this out. I could be totally wrong about this. After all, I came to this conclusion by piecing together things that people said to me over the years.

Steve told me he thought Bobby had a crush on me. Mama said he couldn't take his eyes off of me. Ellen said he was . . . what was her word? . . . 'phenominal'. Was he referring to me when he said 'You already know' after I asked him who was the woman he loved at first sight? He traveled long distances to show up unexpectedly at some of my concerts. And I was always thrilled when he did. I've been able to communicate to him thoughts that no one else would understand. It's Bobby who gave me the Canadian wilderness, my most treasured possession. He can answer all my questions about nature. I feel totally myself around him. I don't have to worry about his moods or his perception of me. I don't have to wear make-up, or fuss over my hair, or be concerned about how well I do anything. I know that to him it's always more than okay. Why am I so self-conscious around him now?

It was all too much for me to comprehend in one sitting. I needed air.

I changed into jeans, T-shirt, pullover sweater, slipped on a windbreaker and donned a fishing cap, then walked down to the dock where the guides were preparing their boats to take guests out for an afternoon of fishing.

"Which one of you is Cedrick?" I asked the guide in the nearest boat.

"He's down there about three from the end — the old guy."

That appellation brought on a round of laughs from the guides. I walked farther out the dock.

Third from the end.

A short, stocky but well-built man with a pleasant face was tidying his boat.

"Cedrick?" I asked.

Yes, ma'am."

"I'm Karen. Bobby said you're taking me fishing this afternoon."

"Yes, ma'am." He lowered his eyes.

He was shy — and totally adorable. Like Bobby.

"He always gets the pretty girls!" a young guide with a beard said loud enough for the others to hear.

Cedrick smiled, and his round face reddened.

"I'll be back after lunch with all my gear," I told him.

"Just put it on the stoop of your cabin, and I'll take care of bringing it down to the boat for you."

"Why, thank you, Cedrick. I'll do that right now."

I felt light-hearted for the first time in a long time. I think I actually felt happy, but I still wasn't sure of anything.

* * *

Bobby was watching for me when I came into the dining room.

"Here's your table, Karen. By the window. I hope you like the homemade soup and roast beef sandwich." He checked out my attire. "Looks like you're ready to go get 'em!"

"Ready and raring to go!"

"I'll try to stop by the dock before you and Cedrick head out."

"And maybe give me some last-minute advice?"

"I don't think you need any from me. Cedrick knows these waters better than anybody. If you want good advice, get it from him, and you'll catch a trophy."

He patted my shoulder then went around the dining room stopping at each table to welcome the guests personally and to answer any questions. I was amazed at the natural ease with which Bobby greeted each one. He was in his element. And I was in mine.

* * *

Bobby's words were prophetic. I used the lure Cedrick recommended, cast where he told me to, and on the second cast hooked into a forty-four inch northern pike. It took at least fifteen minutes to land him. He made several sudden dives under the boat, then swam out and around a few times, creating swirls and circles on the surface of the water.

"Let 'im go. Keep the line tight. Easy now. Start reeling, slowly." Cedrick coached me all the way. We had him at the side of the boat three or four times, but just as Cedrick tried to net him, he would take a dive or make a run for it, almost taking me with him — rod, reel, and all. What a triumph when Cedrick pulled the net into the boat with the enormous fish in it.

"He's huge, Cedrick!" I was out of breath and shaking from head to toe, literally. "I've never seen a fish that big."

Cedrick calmly removed the hook from the big guy's mouth. "We get a lot of 'em around here. You wanna hold 'im for a picture?"

"Oh, no! I didn't bring a camera with me."

"I got a digital right here." He pulled a little Nikkon out of the boat storage box, showed me how to hold the fish properly, and snapped the picture that would soon become a sensation in Spring Hill, duplicate copies made and passed around among grizzled old catfish and bass fishermen.

"Dern thing's bigger 'n' any fish I ever caught."

"Yea. And that's that piano-playin' Kingsley girl that's a-holdin' it."

"You reckon she caught it herself?"

"They say she did."

"Well I'll be!"

At least, that's how I imagined the conversations ran.

* * *

Joyous is the only word to describe the way I felt when I entered the dining room that evening. Bobby's smile was broader than I'd ever seen it. He was behind the bar helping the waitress fix drinks for the guests.

"Your drink is on the house, miss," he said as he poured me a Crown Royal on the rocks.

I really didn't need any alcohol — I was already in high spirits. Being the only female guest at the lodge and having all those experienced fishermen congratulating me on my trophy was about as much exhilaration as I could stand in one week. But there was much more in store.

The next morning I awoke to sounds of wind and rain blowing against the cabin. Pulling the blanket up over my ears, I curled into a fetal position.

No fishing today.

Before I could drift back into dreamland, there was a soft knock on the door.

Who in the world? I reached for my robe and glanced at my watch.

At six a.m.?

I opened the door to a woman wearing a hooded rain jacket, dark strands of wet hair sticking to her face. She was holding what looked like a thermal pitcher.

"Your coffee," she smiled, slipped in, pushed her hood back, and set the pitcher down on the microwave, next to a cup and packages of creamer and sugar.

"Why, thank you! This is very nice. Did Bobby send you?"

"We deliver coffee or tea to all the guests every morning at six. You must be Karen, Mr. Marsten's special guest.

"Yes, I guess I am."

"I'm Cedrick's wife. He told me about your trophy pike yesterday. Congratulations."

"Thank you. I couldn't have caught it without your husband's help."

She pulled her hood back up. "I suspect they'll be baking the walleyes for shore lunch today."

"They're going to fish today — in the pouring rain?"

"Oh, yes. The guides will take the guests out in any weather, as long as it's safe. Do you have a rain suit?"

"I think I brought one."

"You'll need it this morning for sure. Breakfast is at seven, and the boats leave at eight." She slipped out quietly into the rain.

No lazy morning in bed for me.

I opened my duffle and pulled out a fresh T-shirt, a heavy wool sweater, and rain gear: rubberized bibbed waders, hooded jacket, and clompy waterproof boots.

This is certainly not my most alluring outfit.

With that thought, I decided to wait until the last minute to put on the waders.

Breakfast was hearty. There was everything: juices, oatmeal, muffins, toast, eggs any style, bacon, sausage, and, of course, blueberry pancakes. Bobby was in the office fielding questions from the guests, the guides, the cook, and the waitress, first one and then another. Despite the weather, the fishermen were raring to get out there, and the atmosphere was highly charged with big-fish expectations. They had me and my second-cast trophy to thank for that.

While eating pancakes and drinking coffee, I looked around at the lodge guests: a father and his teenage son, a table of ten loud and hefty guys wearing matching fishing-club jackets, two parties of three fishermen talking in low voices, and in one corner a table of four middle-aged men. One of them sported a bandana around his neck, another had a curly gray pony tail.

George and Stanley, I told myself. The other two were obviously Allen and Joe. I think I knew which was which. I could picture Joe sewing up a woman's leg while she belted whiskey and Allen puffing on a cigar while hauling in a trophy.

After my last bite of pancakes, I rose and clomped in my waterproof boots to their table, straight to the man with the bandana.

"You must be George."

"I am."

"And you're Joe, the dentist."

"That's right."

"Well, if I need surgery, I know who to call on."

That brought chuckles from all four.

"I'm Bobby's friend Karen."

"Everybody knows who you are," Allen said. He had a winning smile.

Stanley, acting the gentleman, stood and asked if I would like to sit down.

"Thanks, but I have to put on my rain suit and do a dozen things before the boats take off. Good luck out there today. Bobby says you guys are the best."

I hoped I would have a chance to speak to Bobby before I left the main building. The office had cleared out, but Bobby was on the phone. He gave me a wink and a wave.

I clomped back to the cabin.

* * *

We motored through back waters until we came to a place Cedrick called Otter Creek. I lost count of the number of walleye I caught there. Cedrick certainly knew where to find them and how to position the boat so I could catch them, one after another. Within minutes we had more than enough for lunch.

"You must be hungry. You're keeping so many. I can eat only one, or two at the most."

"Better to have too many than not enough." There was always a mischievous twinkle in his eyes.

In spite of my words about my modest eating habits, I was starving when Cedrick pulled into our shore lunch spot. It was a picturesque site within view of rushing rapids that sent a chilly wind downstream to nip our cheeks and whet our appetites — as if we needed it. The rain had stopped, and patches of blue Canadian sky could be seen here and there.

"Those are the West Rapids." Cedrick pointed upstream. "Lot of fish in this part of the lake."

"Lot of fish everywhere," was my comment.

"We see quite a few bear in this area. One came in here last year during shore lunch. We had to grab our plates and run to the boat."

"Thanks a lot, Cedrick, for sharing that bit of news." I started watching the woods instead of the water.

The lunch clearing was supplied with cut logs, a huge iron skillet, an oversized spatula, a fire pit, and a picnic table with two benches. I found the ladies room behind a clump of bushes where I became an easy target for any itinerant bear. Then I sat down on one of the benches to watch my amazing guide take on the role of master chef. Cedrick wasted no time getting the wood split, the fire going, the oil hot, the fish filleted, and the potatoes cut. The breeze kept the fire blazing, while the cold air enhanced the aroma of burning wood and frying fish.

"Can I help?" As if I knew what to do.

"Just relax. There are soft drinks and beer in the cooler. Help yourself."

I was about to pop open a soda, when I heard the sound of an approaching motor boat.

"Someone's coming, Cedrick."

"It's a little surprise," he grinned.

The boat pulled up next to ours, and its driver stepped out onto the shore.

"Bobby!" I rose to greet him.

"Hi! I see you caught lunch for us."

"Why didn't you tell me? Cedrick knew, didn't he?"

"I have a little spare time today, so I thought we could have lunch together, but I didn't want to take you off the lake. Here. I have something special for you." He stepped back into the boat, picked up a small cooler, and set it down in front of me. Inside I found a half bottle of white wine and a real wine goblet.

"Only one glass?"

"Cedrick and I are driving. It's all yours!"

Bobby opened the wine and poured. "Not many Baldwin guests get *this* kind of service."

I sampled the wine, and Bobby opened my soda for himself. Cedrick set a pan of fried potatoes, mushrooms, and onions on the table so Bobby and I could "munch before lunch" while the fish cooked up nice and crispy.

"They are predicting really nice weather for Friday, all day. I thought you might like to fly down to Poplar River for a change of scene. There are some repairs I need to take care of before a group comes in next week."

"I'd love that." For me, a trip to Manitoba would not be complete without some time at Poplar. Of course Bobby understood that, without my saying a word.

* * *

The next few days flew by. Every evening in the dining room guests shared stories of the day's adventures. The love of the sport turned every guest into a fishing buddy. George, Stanley, Allen, and Joe all landed trophies. I listened attentively to the detailed account of each catch. And they listened to my fish tales. There were numerous wildlife sightings and strange events to report. During the day Cedrick kept me busy pulling in fish after fish practically without reprieve. No more trophies, but lots of big walleyes, northerns, and lake trout. The latter was a novel experience for me. Whether reeling them up slowly and carefully from way down deep or hooking them in fast-moving water, a new dimension was added to my fishing repertoire.

I fished and I ate. Dinners at the lodge were copious — mouth-watering ribs, steaks, gourmet Cornish game hens, chicken, and pork chops — with delectable accompaniments and desserts. All that on top of Cedrick's fantastic shore lunches.

By Saturday morning I had to lie down on the bed and let out all my breath in order to zip up my jeans.

Bobby's going to think I'm fat!

So I passed on breakfast, settling for a small glass of orange juice. I had arranged to meet Bobby before eight at the float plane dock. When I arrived, Bobby and an assistant were loading the plane. I recognized a familiar face.

"Tom!" I dropped my carry-on bag and gave him a hug. "I never expected to see you here."

"I help my friend Bobby out now and then here at the lodge — in exchange for transportation to my summer place."

"I have never thanked you for the wonderful gift you sent me. But I did have faith in your promise to see me again."

"So you could read the Anishinaabe language?"

"I've been trying to learn."

Tom smiled and picked up my bag.

"Milady's chariot awaits." Bobby steadied me as I climbed up into the passenger seat. It seemed so strange to occupy the front seat. Steve's seat. The years of being crammed into the back seat with duffle bags, groceries, rods, and reels, viewing Manitoba through the lens of a video camera were gone forever. My throat tightened. Tears formed.

I don't want Bobby to see me cry.

He hopped in, door still ajar. Tom shoved us off. Before he put on the headphones, Bobby turned toward me, his eyes dazzling. He reached over and squeezed my hand.

"Ready for Poplar?"

I could manage only an affirmative nod, so conflicting were the emotions coursing through me, not to mention the hormones. I wanted to throw my arms around his neck and kiss him wildly, and at the same time I wanted to crawl into the back seat and have Steve magically appear in the front. But I knew only one of the two was possible. I did neither. Thank goodness the noise of the engine and Bobby's headphones made conversation impossible. I needed time to regain composure.

*　*　*

Bobby went ahead onto the porch. Halfway up the steps I noticed above the screened door a wooden board engraved with the words "Karen's Kabin."

"Bobby, what's this?"

He came back to the door and opened it for me. "I named the outpost cabins. Thought you might like to have KK preserved somewhere."

"You are always full of surprises. Thank you."

Out of the storage box on the porch Bobby took a hammer, a package of nails, and a wire cutter. "Let's do the repairs first, then we can have the afternoon free to fish or do whatever we want."

"Business before pleasure, right?" *Why are my comments so dumb?*

"Sometimes it should be the other way around, don't you think?" Bobby handed me the hammer and nails.

He had brought new screening and a fresh cylinder of propane for the stove and refrigerator. And we went to work — at least he worked. I handed him the tools when he wanted them, yelled "okay" when the stove would light and when the water pump had filled the water storage tank to overflowing. I did help him turn the boats upright, move them down into the water, and attach the motors.

"A party of six is coming in tomorrow. They'll need all three of these boats."

While I watched him work I tried to recall the day I first met Bobby, Susan, and Phil. It was in March, just before our June wedding. Spring was late that year. In Iowa City there were vestiges of snow everywhere and ice on the river. The rambling two-story white frame house looked like something from *House and Garden*. Susan and Phil both met us at the door. Bobby was coming down the stairs of the central hall when we walked in.

There was the usual polite conversation, questions about our trip up from South Carolina, about my family, my education. Something was said about Bobby with the dark curls having inherited from the Italian side — his mother's, and the golden boy Steve being more Norwegian. I wasn't used to distinguishing nationalities. In the South we were just Americans. I remember that Bobby was quiet but, like Mama said, couldn't take his eyes off me. I assumed he was just checking out his cousin's fiancée. Could this have been the love-at-first-sight moment?

Bobby oiled the motors and attached life jackets to the seatbacks. He was a hard worker. But what really amazed me that day was the way he could haul the heavy gas tank around, manipulating the large propane cylinder out of the plane and up the hill.

"That Bobby's as strong as an ox," was Daddy's judgment when, during the construction of a new fence around Mama's vegetable garden, Bobby carried a load of two-by-fours from the garage to the backyard.

When all the chores were done, it was lunch time. The lodge cook had prepared us a boxed lunch of roast beef sandwiches and homemade chocolate chip cookies. In the same small cooler that Bobby had brought with him to shore lunch were two cans of Coca-Cola. We sat down at the big table — the same table where Steve had sketched out his plan for *Ladies of the Lake*.

Bobby finished his sandwich in a hurry and took a swig of Coke.

"I have a business proposition for you, Karen."

"A business proposition? You're serious?"

"Very. You yourself said there was a lot of work involved in managing the lodge. I think you've seen it first hand now. I need a partner to help me run the place — just in the summer. I know you have an active career as a pianist, and I wouldn't want this to hamper that at all. But if you would consider spending May through August at Baldwin helping out with the guests, the correspondence, the bookkeeping, the phone . . . things like that, I would offer you a third of the profits."

"You know I have to practice all year, Bobby, even in the summer."

"I've thought of that. I'd fly in an electronic keyboard — or a real piano, even if I had to take it apart and put it back together piece by piece. And I would make sure you had enough free time to practice . . . and to fish."

"Do you actually mean this?"

"Of course I do. I know you love it up here as much as I do."

"To tell the truth, it would be a dream come true for *me*, but what about Meredith?"

"Well . . . ," he said with a sheepish look, "she's the real reason for the offer. She would be the darling of the camp and discover the appeal of the wilderness early in life. I've already promised to teach her how to drive a boat and fly a plane."

"And you would do it, too, wouldn't you!"

"You know I would."

"Is there a place for us to stay at the camp?"

"I think I could find something . . . or I'd build one myself, if necessary. So you will consider the offer?"

"I already have, and I accept." I was acting on impulse, or was I just obeying my heart and not listening to my head?

"All right, then." Bobby stood up. "We'll work out all the details later. Right now, *partner*, let's go fishing."

I swallowed the last bite of my sandwich. Bobby grabbed my hand

and pulled me along as he hurried down to the dock, picked up fishing gear, and stepped into one of the boats.

As we motored away from the cabin, I found myself once again dealing with conflicting emotions. I was ecstatic at the prospect of spending four months a year in the Canadian wilderness but disappointed that Bobby's proposition was all business.

He's probably met someone. Maybe even had another love-at-first-sight experience. He just feels sorry for me now.

I was fishing half-heartedly and catching nothing. Bobby shut the motor off and let the boat drift.

"Look, Karen. See how the rocky shoreline and its reflection in the water form symmetrical patterns that resemble First Nation art, especially the bead work."

I swiveled to face him.

"I didn't think anyone else in the world had ever noticed that." I said, searching his eyes, trying to understand.

How can he look at me the way he does so often, yet think of me only as a business partner? I began to feel foolish.

How could everyone have been so wrong about his sentiments toward me?

The seeds of love for him had been planted somewhere along the way and had lay dormant until, nourished by his kindness and watered by my tears of grief for Steve, they had taken root and grown by leaps and bounds at each of his visits — in spite of my feelings of guilt and betrayal. In an ironic reversal of fate, now I was the one who would see him every summer and watch him share his life with someone else.

I swiveled to face the prow of the boat. A lump formed in my throat.

"Hey, partner. I have something for you here that may tell you a little more about your employment and quarters at the lodge."

I heard him open the mini tackle box he always carried with him, the same one he had left on the dock for me when I stayed alone at Poplar. Over my shoulder I saw him take out a tiny white envelope. I swiveled back around.

"Here. Open it." He handed the little envelope to me.

There was something hard inside.

Another fishing lure? A key? I wondered.

I opened the flap of the envelope and slid the object into my hand.

A thin platinum band lightly filigreed and edged with delicately hammered gold lay in my palm. It took me a few seconds to grasp the full meaning of it. I looked up at him.

"It's the most beautiful ring I've ever seen!"

Bobby's words came slowly. "It was . . . my mother's. . . . She was a pianist, too. Gave recitals . . . once played with the Des Moines Symphony."

"Bobby — you never told me. She must have been an accomplished musician."

"That's what they say. My father chose a simple ring that he knew wouldn't hinder her during performances. Susan has saved it for me all these years."

He took the ring from my palm.

"Will you accept this partnership, too?"

"Yes, Bobby. With all my heart."

He slipped the ring on my finger.

"It's a perfect fit," he said. "And you know, you won't have to change your name again." He took both my hands in his, and looked deep into my eyes.

We could each sense the pain, the years of longing, and the grief in our souls being healed by nature's great balm — a gift to all her creatures: the irrepressible instinct to survive, to live, and to love.

"You know, Bobby, you've never kissed me."

"Oh, yes I have. A million times — in my mind, and in my dreams." He gave a little laugh. "And not just kisses." I smiled at his true confession.

Life with Bobby is not going to be dull.

The sun had dropped low on the horizon. Bands of pink, purple, and orange formed in the west.

"This place is so beautiful — and so very special."

"It's yours now, forever."

He brought my left hand — with the ring — to his lips.

We sat for a few more minutes, watching nature celebrate our joy in glorious color across the sky.

"We need to get back to the lodge, Karen. There's a full moon tonight, and I'd like to spend a romantic evening with my fiancée, perhaps even give her a real kiss or two."

"By all means. Your place or mine?"

"Both."

Life with Bobby is definitely not going to be dull.

We motored back and pulled the boat partway up onto the shore alongside the other two, ready to go for tomorrow's fishermen. While Bobby reloaded the fishing gear and prepared the plane for departure, I lingered on the dock listening to the wind and water whisper echoes of the past into my inward ear:

A thing of beauty is a joy forever . . . Its loveliness increases; it will never pass into nothingness, but still will keep a bower quiet for us, and a sleep full of sweet dreams.

Then loving arms released a golden one into the timeless waters of Poplar River.

OTHER GREAT FICTION FROM THOMASMAX PUBLISHING

WRITTEN ON A ROCK
By Martha Phillips, $14.95

Dee Dupree loves her new home in Elberton, Georgia, where she's just secured a job teaching history. Sharing an apartment with her best friend, Emmy, and starting a romance with Emmy's brother, it seems that everything is almost perfect in Dee's life. But Elberton has brought out weird feelings in Dee, and when she buys a pair of eyeglasses at an estate sale -- glasses that belonged to a girl who disappeared more than four decades ago – the strange sensations lossom into nightmares. But they're more than bad dreams . . . they're horrible visions that provoke Dee to investigate the missing girl's past. And now she is reluctantly drawn into a murder that took place more than 20 years ago . . . before Dee was born. Winner of the 2007 ThomasMax "You Are Published" Contest.

THE RESEMBLANCE
By Randall Arnold, $14.95

Jim Grayson is the last of a rich, prestigious line. He lives in Delphi mansion in rural Georgia near a town named for his family with an old black brother-and-sister couple, the only family he has known since his grandfather died. Jim loves the forest, and he knows every inch of his vast acreage. He also loves reading and updating his family journals, books kept for generations that document everything from love to angels to deer hunting. When he falls in love with Mary from Atlanta, his world is turned upside down when his solitary life meets her city ways. Mary's son, also named Jim, has had a problem with alcohol since the death of his own father. Could a city woman find happiness with the man of her dreams far away from her urban pleasures? And somewhere in that simple country life of Delphi, could there be hope for addicted son? Winner of the 2006 ThomasMax "You Are Published" Contest.

FICTION FOR YOUNGER READERS FROM THOMASMAX PUBLISHING

PRINCIPAL MURDER
By Kathleen McKenzie, $ 9.95

What would you do if your parents were suspected of murder? For Jennifer McManes, it's simple: find the guilty party. But as she and her best friend Tam dig deeper into the mysterious death of their school's principal, things don't look quite so simple. And if they're not careful, they may discover more than they bargained for! Winner of the 2008 ThomasMax "You Are Published" Award. For Young Adult readers, 12 and up.

INCREDIBOY: BE CAREFUL WHAT YOU WISH
By Lee Clevenger, $12.95

To Christian Savage, age 11, life is a cruel joke. To escape life's cruelties, he resorts to daydreams, and in his favorite fantasy he's a superhero he calls IncrediBoy. His life changes when he finds two rings lost by Yoqe, an evil man-eating alien. Through the power of the rings, he becomes IncrediBoy in real life. But Christian learns that being a superhero isn't all it's cracked up to be. And Christian doesn't know it, but Yoqe is on his way back to Earth to reclaim his rings. Can Christian's incredipowers defeat Yoqe? Or will Christian be the alien's next meal? Or could it be that Christian has an un-incredible ace up his sleeve for his showdown with Yoqe? For ages 9 and up.

All ThomasMax books are available wherever books are sold or through most internet sellers such as Amazon.com. If your favorite bookstore doesn't have the book that you want, ask the store to order it for you.

www.ingramcontent.com/pod-product-compliance
Lightning Source LLC
LaVergne TN
LVHW090943080826
845145LV00003B/868

* 9 7 8 0 9 8 2 2 1 8 9 7 6 *